SPECIAL MESSAGE TO READERS

This book is published under the auspices of

THE ULVERSCROFT FOUNDATION

(registered charity No. 264873 UK)

Established in 1972 to provide funds for research, diagnosis and treatment of eye diseases. Examples of contributions made are: —

A Children's Assessment Unit at Moorfield's Hospital, London.

•

Twin operating theatres at the Western Ophthalmic Hospital, London.

•

A Chair of Ophthalmology at the Royal Australian College of Ophthalmologists.

•

The Ulverscroft Children's Eye Unit at the Great Ormond Street Hospital For Sick Children, London.

You can help further the work of the Foundation by making a donation or leaving a legacy. Every contribution, no matter how small, is received with gratitude. Please write for details to:

THE ULVERSCROFT FOUNDATION,
The Green, Bradgate Road, Anstey,
Leicester LE7 7FU, England.
Telephone: (0116) 236 4325

In Australia write to:
THE ULVERSCROFT FOUNDATION,
c/o The Royal Australian and New Zealand College of Ophthalmologists,
94-98 Chalmers Street, Surry Hills,
N.S.W. 2010, Australia

Five interesting things about Janet Gover:

1. I grew up in a small Queensland town which I believe is the only place in the world with a memorial dedicated to an insect.

2. While working as a television journalist in Brisbane, I once rode my horse to work and tethered it on the helicopter landing pad.

3. People ask me why I left Australia's sunny shores for England. The reason is about five foot ten inches tall, with green eyes and he plays guitar.

4. Despite working at Pinewood movie studios during the making of four James Bond films, I have never seen Pierce Brosnan or Daniel Craig.

5. While shooting a television report about the demise of an exclusive men's club, I was filmed playing on the billiard table — which almost gave one member a fit. Women were not even permitted in the room — far less allowed to play. The club was closed the next day and the building was torn down. I guess that says it all.

THE FARMER NEEDS A WIFE

Helen Woodley is editor of Australia's top magazine. When she starts a new weekly column profiling the country's lovelorn farmers, she has no idea how successful it will be. But soon readers are queueing up to date the featured agriculturists. People like: The Artistic Farmer Greg — he'd rather be doing something creative; The Confused Farmer Peter, who expects a nanny for his twins, not a pretty girl wanting romance! And there's The Unsuspecting Farmer Matt, who has no idea his photo's been published . . . yet. Then finally, there's Leigh, the beautiful winegrower, who deserves a new chance at romance . . .

JANET GOVER

THE FARMER NEEDS A WIFE

Complete and Unabridged

ULVERSCROFT
Leicester

First published in Great Britain in 2009 by
Little Black Dress
An imprint of Headline Publishing Group
London

First Large Print Edition
published 2010
by arrangement with
Headline Publishing Group
An Hachette Livre UK Company
London

British Library CIP Data

Gover, Janet.
The farmer needs a wife.
1. Farmers- -Australia- -Fiction.
2. Australian periodicals- -Fiction.
3. Love stories . 4. Large type books.
I. Title
823.9′2–dc22

ISBN 978–1–44480–020–3

Published by
F. A. Thorpe (Publishing)
Anstey, Leicestershire

Set by Words & Graphics Ltd.
Anstey, Leicestershire
Printed and bound in Great Britain by
T. J. International Ltd., Padstow, Cornwall

This book is printed on acid-free paper

This is for Dad — who taught me to love books,
And for John — who believed in this one.

Acknowledgements

I would like to thank Scott, David, Gill and Joe for answering many, many questions about sugarcane, wine, cattle and farming in general. Thanks also to Rachel for pointing me in the right direction. I have been given great advice and unwavering support by the members of the Romantic Novelists' Association, in particular the London and South-East chapter. Thanks ladies and gents. For enthusiasm above and beyond the call of friendship — thanks Michelle. And last, but by no means least, thanks to my editor Catherine Cobain and the team at Little Black Dress for making it come true.

1

The newspaper-seller watched the blonde woman walk out through the gleaming glass doors of her apartment block. Without looking at his watch, he knew it was eight o'clock. She always came through those doors on the dot of eight. As usual, the white Mercedes was waiting for her at the side of the road. He knew that today she would hand her heavy briefcase to the driver, but not get inside the car. Today was the second Tuesday of the month.

The woman turned away from her driver and walked across the road towards him. She was good looking. Well groomed, but not too made up. Hair in a neat bob. She was a bit too thin for his taste, but elegant in those expensive tailored outfits she wore each working day. She had good legs, too, the paper-seller thought for the umpteenth time. And she knew how to walk in high heels. A lot of women never really mastered that. She looked to be in her mid-thirties, but he would put money on her being very close to forty. She was one of those women who spent a lot of money to look younger than they really were.

When she reached his stand, the woman stopped in front of the magazines. Her long fingers flicked quickly down the rack, counting. On the second Tuesday of the month, she counted how many copies he carried of every magazine. Then she bought one. Always the same one.

'Good morning,' he said as she handed over the money. 'Nice day.'

'Yes. Very nice.' She smiled back with remote courtesy.

The paper-seller had no idea why he always thought her smile was sad. The woman seemed to have everything. An apartment in a building with great views of Sydney Harbour. She must have a good job — the Mercedes was evidence of that. She certainly wasn't poor.

'You know, that magazine is changing,' he volunteered as he gave her her change.

'Really?'

'Yes. It's becoming a weekly.'

The woman turned the magazine over in her hands, studying the cover. He never understood why, out of all the magazines on his stand, she always chose that one. *Australian Life* was not exactly a high-class glossy. It was colourful and brassy, but to his mind a little trashy. Not at all like her. She was all class.

'Do you think people will buy it as a weekly?' she asked.

'I don't know,' he answered. 'I hope so. More money in my pocket if they do.'

She smiled and nodded goodbye as she turned towards the train station. The paper-seller watched her go. For a year she had been coming to his stand. She was always friendly enough; exchanged some small talk about the weather or one of the newspaper headlines. Asked how his sales were going. Never anything personal. In fact, he didn't even know her name, and he would have been very surprised if she knew his. She kept her distance. And not just from him. He saw a lot from his position near the entrance to the station. One thing he had never seen was the woman enter or leave her home with another person, male or female. Underneath that well-presented exterior she must be lonely, the paper-seller thought as he turned to his next customer.

* * *

Helen kept the magazine rolled in her hand as she walked through the barrier and on to the platform. Milson's Point station was the last stop before the train crossed Sydney Harbour. It was crowded with commuters heading across the big bridge with its famous iron arch to their city jobs. They were mostly young, middle class and upwardly mobile. They were her demographic.

She walked the length of the platform, but for once she ignored the glorious arc of brilliant blue sky, dramatically accented by the arc of the bridge. April was doing its best to impress, before the winter set in. Helen's attention, however, was totally focused on the hands of her fellow travellers. Carefully she noted which magazines had been purchased for on-train reading. She took particular notice of two girls sharing a copy of the same magazine that she herself held. Their heads were bent in conversation over some item on the page. That was good. She saw a couple of other publications, but that was to be expected. All in all, about the result she saw every time she took this journey. If her gamble paid off, the next time she stood on this platform it would be different.

When she took her seat in the carriage, Helen watched another young woman reading *Australian Life*. She was engrossed in one particular page. At last Helen opened her own copy of the magazine. She quickly flicked forward two pages. She knew exactly what had captured the other reader's attention.

THE FARMER NEEDS A WIFE

The headline was in bold black letters, but it was the accompanying photograph that caught the eye. The young man leaning against the wooden fence was utterly gorgeous. His eyes were blue, his sandy hair flecked with gold. His open-necked check shirt displayed a glimpse of muscular chest, tanned a deep honey colour. He was holding an Akubra hat, and smiling. He was every woman's fantasy in blue jeans and riding boots.

> Imagine your very own Man from Snowy River. He's half Hugh Jackman, mixed with a little Keith Urban and a dash of Eric Bana. The great Australian bushman is out there, and he needs a wife.
>
> What woman hasn't dreamed of getting close to nature with a man as strong as the very earth itself?
>
> *Australian Life* believes in true love and happy-ever-afters — and we have taken on the challenge of finding the perfect mate for the man on the land.
>
> Right now, we are looking to hear from farmers. Tell us about the woman of your dreams. What is she like? What can you offer her? And what would your life together be like?

Girls — you won't have to wait long for your men. From this issue, *Australian Life* will be published weekly. This time next week, we'll have the first of our farmers for you.

Looking for romance? So are we. Let's find it together.

Signed: Helen Woodley, Editor

Helen looked at her name. It was quite possibly the only thing on the page that was real. The 'farmer' of the photo was in fact a male model, whose streaked blond hair and golden tan were the product of a city salon rather than the outback sun. She didn't know if the model had ever sat on a horse, but she doubted it. And he certainly wasn't looking for a wife. She had been present at the photo shoot, and the model had been very keen to get back to the comforts of the city, and his boyfriend.

It was all a fantasy. That was her job — creating fantasies. She was very good at it.

The train pulled into Wynyard station. Helen stood up and stepped out onto the platform. She kept looking at the magazines in the female commuters' hands as she made her way to street level. From here, it was a short walk to work.

Helen's office was on the twenty-third

floor. It had a large glass and chrome desk, as befitted her status, and picture windows with a spectacular view of Sydney Harbour. It also had a huge anteroom with desks to accommodate her editorial team. A large table dominated the centre of the room. It was cluttered with paper and photographs, odd bits of fabric and bottles of cosmetics. Her people were gathered around it, already intent on their work.

'Good morning, Helen.'

Her assistant's greeting was immediately echoed by the rest of the team.

'Good morning,' Helen replied to the room in general and continued into her office. Her assistant followed her, as he did every morning, notebook in hand. Helen desperately wanted to tell him to wait, that today she needed a few minutes to herself. A few minutes of peace. But today of all days she couldn't show any weakness. Not even in front of her own staff.

Richard Gordon was a new graduate from journalism school when she hired him as her assistant a year ago. He was twenty-three years old, well dressed and handsome, bright and ambitious. He always arrived at work before she did, and would stay until she left, unless she told him to go. Helen knew that he looked on her as his stepping stone to bigger and better things. That didn't bother her. Quite the opposite. He reminded Helen of herself when she was his age. She trusted him as much as she trusted anyone, which wasn't a great deal. She wanted to ask him if there had been any response yet. It was far too early, of course. The magazine had literally hit the streets in the early hours of that morning. But surely in these days of e-mail, there could already be a response. Had even a single farmer e-mailed to say he wanted a wife? Her whole career was on the line. If she failed, she would be looking for a new job, and there were not a lot of openings for failed magazine editors.

'Contact the printers,' she told Richard, who had followed her into her office. 'Check that everything will be right for next week.'

'I spoke to them yesterday,' Richard replied. 'They'll be ready. They need the final farmer page layout by close of business Thursday.'

Thursday! That was just two days away. She had two days to find fifteen presentable farmers and get their faces and stories on to the printed page. If she didn't, she would be a laughing stock in the industry. Helen didn't acknowledge the sudden twist of panic in her gut.

'That's fine. I expect we'll be getting our

first e-mails shortly.' Her voice echoed a confidence she didn't feel. 'I'll want a short-list on my desk by Thursday lunchtime.'

'Yes, Helen.'

'And I want a close eye kept on the sales figures. We may need a second print run.' Maybe saying it out loud would make it come true.

'Okay.'

'Now, what else have I got today?'

'A radio interview this morning. You can do that by phone. Then over to Channel Ten for *The Talk Show* interview. That will be live, so you'll be finished by lunchtime. The GM has invited you to lunch.'

Much as she wanted to cancel it, Helen knew that lunch with the powerful general manager of the television network was almost as important as the interview. She took her place behind the desk.

'The proofs of your newspaper profile will be here this afternoon,' Richard continued. 'I'll bring them in as soon as they get here.'

Helen nodded. She was nervous about that profile, but no one was ever going to know. 'Anything else?'

'Nothing urgent.'

'All right. Thanks, Richard.'

Richard recognised the dismissal and withdrew, closing the office door behind him.

Helen swivelled the large leather chair to face the big window and its glorious view. Although her eyes were looking at one of the most famous sights in the world, her mind was elsewhere, calculating sales figures and printing costs. She would have to decide tomorrow if there would be another run of the current issue. After that, the printers would be working towards the next.

A year ago, *Australian Life* had been languishing in the market, barely paying its way. The huge media conglomerate that owned it had faced two options — fix it or close it. Helen had been working as the deputy editor of a more successful rival at the time. She had quit her job and presented herself at the offices of *Australian Life* with a bold plan to turn the ailing monthly into a weekly. It had taken a month to convince them. A month of waking each morning and wondering if she had made a ghastly mistake. A month of wondering if she should ask her old boss to take her back. But she had held out, and at last the owners of *Australian Life* had agreed to her plan.

That had been a year ago: the hardest year of Helen's life, as she had battled to bring her vision to reality. She was changing more than the magazine's publishing schedule. She had designed a whole new look and feel for

Australian Life — targeting an audience that had previously belonged to her competitors. She had worked seven long days each week, meeting advertisers and printers, planning campaigns, studying costs and returns. The next few weeks would see her succeed or fail.

In all those long months, none of her staff had seen the slightest doubt in Helen's manner. Her outward confidence had never faltered, not for one second. The doubts had been reserved for the long nights when she was too tense to sleep. Only when she was alone was she able to acknowledge her fears. If she was wrong, *Australian Life* would never recover. If the magazine closed, the failure was hers alone, and the whole publishing industry would know. Her career would never recover. If she lost that, she had nothing else.

The whole farmer campaign had been her idea — a hook with which to launch the new-look weekly. She needed it to work. She turned back to her desk. There was surprisingly little for her to do. The next three magazines were already laid out — except for the farmer pages. She had cleared her calendar for these few days, leaving herself free to do the publicity rounds that were such a vital part of the launch.

As if in response to her thoughts, the phone on her desk rang softly.

She picked it up. 'Richard?'

'The radio station wants to check the lines and levels,' he said. 'The interview will start in about three or four minutes.'

She hated these interviews. It was fine while the questions dealt with the magazine. But inevitably the interviewer would raise the one subject she didn't want to discuss. It didn't matter how many times the questions were asked, they never got any easier to answer.

Helen took a slow deep breath. 'Put them through,' she said as she carefully donned her professional mask.

'Ms Woodley?' a voice said in her ear.

'Yes, this is Helen Woodley.' Helen spoke clearly and not too quickly.

'I'll be putting you through in a moment. I just wanted to make sure you don't have your radio playing near the phone, as that will cause us problems.'

'No. I don't have the radio playing.' Helen was a veteran of many such interviews, and knew how they worked.

'That's fine. We are in a commercial break at the moment. I'm putting you through.'

A few moments later, the DJ's cheerful voice sounded in her ear. 'Welcome back to the breakfast show — and welcome also to Helen Woodley, editor of *Australian Life* magazine, which today launches a brand-new look. Welcome, Helen.'

'Good morning, Tyrone,' Helen replied in her best broadcast voice. 'It's always a pleasure to talk to you.'

'So, Helen, you've become a matchmaker?'

'I don't know that I'd put it quite like that.' Helen kept her tone light as she tried to steer the interview in the direction she wanted. '*Australian Life* has always reached out to all sectors of the country. Now that the magazine is becoming a weekly, there are new opportunities for us, as the publishers, to make a difference in our readers' lives.'

The words were part of the campaign devised by the company's publicity department to accompany the new-look magazine. Even to Helen's ears they sounded false and shallow. But her job was to toe the company line.

'Your headline says 'The Farmer Needs a Wife' — and you're inviting people to write in. That sounds like matchmaking to me.' The DJ wasn't going to be deflected by clever publicity lines.

'We're giving people in different parts of the country a rare chance to reach out to each other,' Helen said.

'Please tell our listeners how it works.'

'Well, at the moment we are looking to hear

from farmers. Write or e-mail telling us about the woman of your dreams. We'll publish as many as we can. Then our female readers can write back to the farmer they would like to meet.'

'And you'll select a wife for each farmer?'

'Oh, no. I'm not the one to make that decision.' Helen tried to keep her tone light. She didn't want her personal bitterness to intrude. 'Every letter will be passed on to the farmer it's addressed to. Then it's up to the farmers and the letter-writers themselves to decide if they want to take it any further.'

'And tell me, Helen, are you hoping to find yourself a farmer?'

Helen took a long, slow breath. She had expected this, but that didn't make it any less intrusive. 'No, Tyrone, I'm not.'

'But Helen, you're a single woman. One of the most eligible bachelorettes around.'

'Every woman who sees a farmer in *Australian Life* can be assured that he will get her letter,' Helen said, ignoring the personal comment.

'And how many farmers have you got?' the DJ asked.

'I honestly don't know,' Helen responded. 'The magazine only came out today. But you can be certain that there will be farmers' details in the next issue, which will be out just one week from today.'

When the interview ended a few moments later, Helen hung up feeling reasonably satisfied. The questions hadn't got as personal as she'd feared, and she had managed to promote the magazine, which was the reason for the interview.

She glanced down at her unusually empty desk. There was little now for her to do but wait. Her reputation was at stake.

There must be some lonely farmers out there . . .

* * *

The slamming of the fly-screen door at the back of the house was immediately followed by the thudding of elastic-sided riding boots on a wooden floor.

'Don't get up, sis. I've got it under control.'

Jenny relaxed back into the canvas sling of the squatter's chair, her hand going automatically to the growing bulge at her waist. She was only five months' pregnant, but was already feeling awkward.

'Do you want a cuppa?' The voice was softer as its owner walked on to the shady veranda where Jenny was resting.

She looked up at her brother. Just under two metres tall, and built to match, Peter

Nichols was a big man. His skin was tanned, with lines to mark thirty-five years of life in the outback sun. He looked strong and capable, because he was. He could wrestle a half-grown bull to the ground, fly a plane or dredge a watercourse from the parched earth. He was also a useful hand in the kitchen.

'Tea would be great,' Jenny said. 'Thanks.'

Before long he was back, with Jenny's tea in one hand and a huge glass of cold water for himself in the other. He leaned against the veranda rail as he drank.

'Are Chris and Sara still in class?'

Jenny nodded. Living in the outback did not mean kids were excused school. It just meant that their classroom was in their own home. When she and Peter were young, they had used a high-frequency radio to attend the School of the Air, listening to lessons from a teacher hundreds of kilometres away. Peter's eight-year-old twins now had the internet as well as a radio, but the regime was the same. Each day they spent at least an hour working with their teacher and a couple of hours more doing homework, which Jenny supervised.

Of course, when they were a little older, they would be better served by attending a boarding school. But Peter wasn't ready to talk about that.

As a girl, Jenny had hero-worshipped her

tall, handsome brother. He could ride and shoot better than she could. He was stronger and faster. When she was too small to put a halter over her horse's head, he had done it for her. Like any good hero, he was constantly rescuing her when she got into scrapes. He had got her down off the top of the water tank when the ladder broke, and helped her find the thoroughbred stallion she had accidentally released from its yard. He had even blacked the eye of a certain city boy who had become overly friendly. Later, he had been best man at her wedding.

And she had been bridesmaid at his.

Even now, Jenny felt deep sorrow as she pictured Karen and Peter standing side by side taking their vows. 'Until death us do part.' If the words still rang in Jenny's ears, how much louder must they sound to her brother? He was given just two short years of marriage — followed by grief that seemed endless. The only joy in his life since his wife's death came from his children. He wasn't yet ready to let them go to boarding school, and that was a problem, because Jenny wouldn't be around much longer to look after them.

Jenny still found it hard to believe that she and Ken were about to become parents. Ken had come to River Downs Station as an eighteen-year-old jackaroo, employed by her father. Raised on Queensland's beaches, he had been determined to make a place for himself in the harsh outback. And he had. Ten years later, he was as skilled a property manager as someone born to the life. Somewhere along the way, he had also fallen in love with the boss's daughter. They had married with her father's blessing a few months before the old man and his wife retired to the east coast. Now Ken and Jenny were also moving east. Ken had been offered a job managing a property in Queensland. He was keen to take on the challenge, and Jenny liked the idea of being closer to her parents when the baby was born. A few weeks from now, she and Ken would be gone from here.

She didn't have much time to sort out her brother's life.

Peter had asked her to find a nanny for the twins. She had tried, placing ads in several newspapers both locally and in Darwin. She had even advertised across the border in Queensland. Not one applicant had seemed even slightly suitable. They were all too young or too old. None had ever been in the outback before, and she doubted they would stay long. Maybe she was being too picky.

'There were a few letters on the plane,' Peter said, almost as if his thoughts had followed the same path as hers. 'There might be a nanny there.'

'I hope so,' Jenny replied. 'We are rapidly running out of time.'

'We're going to miss you. I don't suppose I can convince you to leave Ken and stay with us?' Peter grinned to emphasise the joke.

'Sorry.'

'Well, we'll just have to learn to manage without you.'

Peter disappeared into the house for a few seconds, returning with the mail parcel. The mail plane only called once a week, so the bundle also contained a collection of newspapers and magazines. Peter left it on the table beside Jenny's chair.

'Thanks for doing this,' he said.

'It's the least I can do, since I'm abandoning you.'

'Ken still in the machinery shed?' he asked as he placed his dusty Akubra hat on top of his brown hair.

'I think so.' Her husband was spending the day on general repairs and maintenance of the motorbikes that were used for daily transport around the property.

'Okay. See you later, sis.' Peter went down the wooden stairs two at a time.

Jenny watched him walk across the brown earth towards the cluster of outbuildings. The weathered timber sheds with their metal roofs and cool dark interiors had been her playground; the wooden rails of the cattle yards were her swings and roundabouts. She closed her eyes, and gave herself up to the peace of the almost silent house she had grown up in. Her ears caught the gentle tick-tick of the metal roof expanding in the afternoon sun. The faint cawing of crows in the home paddocks was as much a part of her life as the feel of the red-brown earth beneath her feet. Two thousand square kilometres of near desert wasn't everyone's idea of paradise, but she loved it and she was going to miss it.

Jenny reached for the pile of letters and magazines on the table next to her. The mail plane would also have brought the household supplies she had ordered by phone yesterday. Without looking, she knew Peter would have left the box on the kitchen bench. That could wait. The kids would have finished class soon, so she had only a short time to read her mail, including any letters from potential nannies. Although the children didn't really need a nanny, they needed a mother. And what her brother needed was a wife . . .

Jenny stared at the magazine cover.

A wife!

Quickly she flicked over the pages. This was

perfect. It was exactly what she needed. Her brother had rescued her often enough; now it was her turn. She took the magazine with her as she walked through to the large airy study that served as classroom for the kids and office for their father.

'How's the homework?' she asked the twins.

'We're done, Aunt Jenny.' Sara was a serious and truthful little girl, the image of her mother.

'Can we go down to help Dad now?' Chris asked.

'No,' Jenny said quickly. 'Your dad and uncle are too busy to have the two of you underfoot.'

The answer gave rise to looks of acute disappointment.

'However,' Jenny continued, 'if you were to pack away the groceries, and then stay out of my hair for the next half an hour, we could walk down to the machinery shed later.'

'All right!' In a flurry of brown limbs, the twins hugged their aunt and vanished.

They hadn't turned the computer off. Quickly Jenny typed in the *Australian Life* web address. She scanned the pages as they appeared in front of her. The magazine wanted a photo. Jenny had taken some only recently to send to her parents. She called up a blank document, ready to compose the letter. She would have to be careful. Peter would kill her if he knew what she was doing. Of course, he'd get over it when she found him a wife. For now, she'd simply tell him she was looking for a nanny.

* * *

Greg Anderson stared down at his hands, which lay clasped in his lap. Already they were showing the signs of the past few weeks of hard work. There were a few small cuts on skin which was dark red-brown from exposure to the sun. His hands were starting to look like farmer's hands. Like his father's hands. That was wrong. He was only twenty-three. And he was not a farmer. At least, he hadn't planned to be. But a lot had changed in the last few minutes.

'... come to terms with it.' The voice dragged him back to the here and now.

'I'm sorry,' Greg said. 'What did you say?'

'I've told your father,' the doctor repeated in his best professional manner, 'but it's obviously a difficult thing for him to accept.'

Difficult was something of an understatement. His father had no time for weakness in others, and would never admit to it in himself.

'How long?'

'With this condition, it's hard to say,' the doctor answered. 'Perhaps years. But I have to be blunt. This form of cardiomyopathy has no cure. All we can do is try to ease the symptoms.'

'When can he go home?'

'Greg . . . ' The doctor hesitated. 'I think I had better explain. You may be able to take him home for short periods. It'll be good for him. But they will only be visits. He will need constant monitoring and round-the-clock care.'

'Then he'll be stuck in hospital for the rest of his life?'

'There is a good long-term care facility here in Townsville, and I'm sure we can place Robert there.'

Care facility? That was for old men. Greg was struggling to take in the knowledge that his father would never work the farm again.

'I know Robert is expecting to see you today,' the doctor continued calmly. 'Why don't you go and talk to him? We can meet again in a few days when you have had a chance to think.'

Greg picked up the briefcase he had brought, and left the office in a daze. He walked slowly down the long hallway, his eyes turning neither left nor right. He ignored the cheerful prints on the walls, and the practical tiled floor. He tried not to hear the low sounds from the rooms on either side; tried not to smell the disinfectant that couldn't disguise the odour of illness and decay. He stopped at the second door from the end. It was open. Greg steeled himself and walked into the room.

The man on the bed appeared to be asleep. His eyes were closed, and his mouth hung slightly open; the bedcover rose and fell with his slow, deep breathing. He had once been a big man, tall and muscular, but illness had robbed him of that. His face was sunken and much older than his fifty years. His fingers seemed unnaturally long and terribly fragile where his hand lay on his chest, no longer giving the impression of great strength.

As Greg stepped into the room, the man on the bed opened his eyes. There was no sign of confusion or concern in their steely grey glance.

'You're late.'

'Sorry, Dad.' Greg's response was automatic, learned as a child.

'Did you bring the papers?'

'Yes.' Greg pulled a chair towards the bed, but not too close. Sitting down, he took the briefcase on to his knees but didn't open it. 'Dad, I've just been talking to the doctor. He told me that we should start thinking about the future.'

'I am thinking about the future. That's why I need to see those papers.' Robert held out one demanding hand. 'If I don't tell you what to do, the farm will be ruined by the time I get out of this place.'

'That's what the doctor wanted to talk to me about.' Greg tried again. 'He says your condition is — '

'I don't want to hear it!' Robert's voice was too weak to be called a shout, but it carried the same presumption of obedience that it always had. 'Doctors! Vultures, I say. I'm not spending the rest of my life in this place. I'm getting out of here. Be better off without all their poking and prodding anyway. Now, I don't want to hear any more about that. Did you get that water pump repaired? What was the final cost?'

The old man held out his hand again. It was trembling. Greg didn't know if that was due to illness or anger. Reluctantly he opened the briefcase and handed over the paperwork he'd brought.

The old man just grunted and started reading.

Greg stared out the window. One more harvest. That was all it was supposed to be. One more harvest.

It hadn't been easy being Robert Anderson's son. Greg had tried. He did everything his father asked and more. When he was at school, his holidays were spent at the sugar mill. While his friends were chasing girls and partying, he was driving a tractor or harvesting cane. But whatever he did, it was never good enough. Greg sometimes wondered if Robert had been a different man when he was young. When his wife was with him.

Robert had always assumed his son would follow him on the farm. Greg had always known that he wouldn't. He had dreamed of a different future, and planned his escape. Over and over again. The time had never seemed right. He had no skills, other than those needed to be a cane-farmer. He had an adequate education, but no higher qualifications. He had a handsome face and an easy way with people, but you couldn't base your life on that. He had one small talent, but that had never seemed enough. Until a few months ago. The talent that resided in Greg's hands and heart had opened a door, and he was eager to step through it.

Then his father fell ill. At first it seemed like a bad case of flu, and Robert had ignored it. Then it became something else. Greg didn't like his father. He doubted that he even loved him. But he couldn't just walk away. One more harvest, he told himself. He would stay just a few months, until his father was well again.

Greg reached into the pocket of his jeans, for the object that was always there. His fingers closed around the lump of polished metal, his fingertips seeking out the lines and curves that he had wrought on the gleaming surface. His first professional quality piece of silversmithing. His good-luck charm. He closed his fist around the metal so tightly that it hurt. It wasn't going to be just one more harvest.

'What's this?'

Greg forced his attention back to the room. His father was holding out the accounts book, pointing to an entry with one trembling finger. Greg had been expecting this.

'I bought a computer.'

'A computer! We don't need a computer!' The old man was shaking now with anger.

'Yes, we do.' Greg forced his voice to remain calm. 'You should have got one years ago. I'm using it for business accounts, letters and so forth.' It wasn't exactly a lie. He would use it for farm accounts. But it did have another purpose.

'Can't you write letters by hand? I did it for years.'

He could, but he wasn't going to admit it. 'I'm getting internet services installed this week,' he added, determined to get this over with.

'Internct! Rubbish.' Robert Anderson's body might have weakened, but he was still a man of strong opinion. 'Our family has run that farm for generations without the internet.'

Grcg could continue to run the farm without the internet, but that wasn't the point. If he was to be trapped on the farm, the internet could be his link to a different world. He might be able to start a website. Sell his jewellery. It would be his escape.

'It's only thirty-five dollars a month, Dad. And it's a tax deduction. There's no need for you to worry about it.'

'I see what you're trying to do. You want to cut me out, don't you? Just because I'm stuck in this place. When I get out, things will change . . . '

Thirty minutes later, Greg left. He got behind the wheel of the dusty farm utility, started the engine and headed homewards. Within a few minutes he had left the town behind. The long straight line of the road stretched ahead of him, like the years he was going to face, chained to a house that had never felt like a home and to a bitter and sick man. Without a conscious thought, he finally turned off the main road on to the gravel farm road, pausing briefly to collect a bundle of envelopes from the rusty old oil drum that served as the Anderson farm mailbox.

A bright flash of lightning woke him from the daze he had been in since he left the hospital. There was a storm coming. The lightning also drew his attention to a plastic-covered parcel lying on the ground. Greg reached for it as the first drops of rain started to splatter on his windscreen. It was a magazine, addressed to his neighbour's wife. Obviously it had been dropped by mistake. Greg would simply put it in the oil drum for the mailman to collect the next day. Before he could, his eye caught the headline and he paused.

THE FARMER NEEDS A WIFE

He almost laughed out loud. Then he tossed the magazine on to the seat beside him. If he was going to be a farmer after all, he might as well order a farmer's wife.

* * *

Leigh Kenyon grunted with effort as she braced one foot against the fence post.

Carefully she leaned her whole weight against the pull of the wire. Twisting her hands, she locked the wire around the post a second time. Quickly reversing the long-handled fencing pliers, she took a twist on the wire. Then she released her pent-up breath, eased off the tension and tested the wire with her hand. It was locked around the post, taut as a guitar string. She caught the wire in the pliers oncc again and added two more twists. Satisfied, she stepped back, pulled off her leather gloves and her baseball cap and used the back of her hand to wipe away the sweat that was running down her face.

High summer had passed and it wasn't that hot, but mending the trellises that supported her vines was hard work. Leigh slipped the pliers into the back pocket of her dusty blue jeans as she walked back to her truck. The water bottle was sitting on the ground in the shade near the back of the vehicle. She unscrewed the top and lifted it to take a long draught of the cool liquid. She poured a little over her head, and ran her fingers roughly through her short dark hair, then leaned back against the vehicle and ran her eye down along the trellis.

That's not too bad, she thought.

The wire was once more taut. The vines had already been pruned after the harvest, but when the new growth came in the spring, the trellis would be there to support it.

'Just three more to go,' Leigh said out loud, with some satisfaction. Once the repairs were complete, she could start building more trellis lines, opening a new block ready for planting in the spring. It would be the first new planting since she had walked on to the small winery three years before. She slowly turned her head to run her eyes over the neat blocks, down to the cluster of buildings.

She wasn't doing too badly. Just twenty-nine years of age, and the owner of a winery in the Hunter Valley. The name Leigh Kenyon was now listed among the growers in Australia's premier wine region.

'Take that and shove it, Jack Thorne,' she whispered, then laughed out loud, telling herself that it didn't hurt any more. It really didn't.

Leigh didn't wear a wristwatch when she was working. She didn't need to. A glance at the sun told her she still had some daylight left. Enough time to start working on the next run. She took a final swig from the water bottle, then bent to drag the roll of fencing wire across to the next post.

An hour later, she was struggling with the same roll of wire. The sun was low and her working day was almost over. All she had left to do was load her tools into the back of her truck and she could head for the house and a welcome shower. She had dragged the roll of fencing wire to the back of the truck, and just had to lift it a couple of feet on to the tailgate. A simple thing, but not so easy to do. The wire was just that bit too heavy for her at the end of the day when she was tired.

There were times when being alone really sucked.

Almost as if it had been called by her words, Leigh heard the sound of an engine on the dirt track that ran beside her property.

'No. Please, not him.' But it couldn't be anyone else.

She heard the engine stop. Without turning around, she knew her neighbour would be striding towards her with that self-assurance that she found so irritating. And why did he always appear when she was covered with sweat? Just once she would like to meet him with her hair combed and maybe wearing some make-up.

'Leigh. I was passing. Do you need some help?'

Why did he always sound so patronising? Leigh fixed a smile on her face and turned around.

'Hello, Simon.'

It wasn't fair that such an annoying person

should look like that. Simon Bradford should have been a movie star or a model. He was a head taller than Leigh. A lifetime of outdoor work had made his body muscular and hard. His skin was tanned a healthy brown and the sun had also touched his wavy hair with gold. He had blue eyes to die for, and when he smiled, as he did now, he revealed a set of perfect white teeth. He was as clever and successful as he was good looking. He was enough to set any girl's pulse racing.

He was also number two on Leigh's most hated men list, second only to Jack Thorne, her ex-fiancé.

'Let me get that.' He reached down and took a hold of the heavy roll of wire. With the greatest of ease, he swung it into the back of the truck, where it landed with a loud crash. 'There you go.'

'Thanks,' Leigh muttered, trying to be gracious. She was also fighting the urge to tidy her short hair, or hide her sweaty hands with their chipped and dirty nails.

'No problem.' Simon started collecting the tools Leigh had dropped to the ground while she struggled with the wire roll.

'Leave them,' she told him. 'I can do that.'

'It's nothing.' The fencing bar and pliers followed the wire into the truck. Simon turned his whole attention to Leigh. 'I just want to help. I'm always here if you need me. You know that.'

Leigh knew no such thing. 'I'm fine. Really. I will call if I need you.' Like hell she would.

'Good.'

He just stood looking down at her, making her feel small and inadequate. She *was* small, of course, but she was actually highly capable and very confident of her own abilities. Except when she was around Simon Bradford. Something about him turned her into a gibbering idiot.

Leigh knew that what he really wanted was her land. Her tiny winery sat almost smack in the middle of Simon's vast holdings. The previous owner had refused to sell it to him, not wanting his pride and joy to be swallowed up by a vast corporate machine. Instead, he'd sold to an eager young couple about to embark on a life together.

When Jack left, it didn't take long for Simon to come knocking on Leigh's door, offering to relieve her of the burden.

Not in this life — or the next.

But harsh reality had forced her to make one compromise. Until she was able to make and market her own wine, she had to sell her harvest. Simon's big winery was close and needed more grapes than he could grow. She sold him hers because it was a financial necessity, but she didn't like it. It also meant she had to be friendly to the man and hide her contempt beneath a cheerful exterior. Next year, she should be able to make her own wine, and would take great pleasure in refusing Simon's offer for her fruit. She desperately hoped that when she did, her success would annoy Simon as much as everything about him annoyed her.

'Have you got your tickets for the Winegrowers' Dinner yet?' he asked.

Leigh hadn't. She wasn't planning to go. The annual dinner was *the* social event of the season. All the winegrowers attended. Three years ago, Leigh and Jack had gone together and she had enjoyed mixing with other growers. The next two years she had gone alone, and hated every sympathetic smile she had received from men and women alike. Simon had been there, of course, looking resplendent in a tailor-made dinner suit, some beautiful young thing draped over his arm.

'No. Not yet.' She wasn't about to say she wasn't going.

'Don't wait too long,' Simon advised. 'They are selling fast. You don't want to miss out.'

Yes, I do, Leigh thought.

'If you don't have a date,' Simon

continued, oblivious to her growing tension, 'I might be able to help. I've already invited someone, but I know one or two — '

'There's no need,' Leigh interrupted, wondering if it was time to promote him to number one on her hate list. 'I have a date, thank you.' She smiled at him as she seethed inside.

'Oh, good. I look forward to meeting him. Perhaps we can have a dance?' Simon added lightly.

The thought almost made Leigh choke.

Simon ran an expert eye down the fence line she was building. 'This is a good bit of land. The vines will do well here.'

My vines, she wanted to say. They'll never be yours, so don't even bother making another offer. Instead she said, 'I think so too.'

Her voice must have given some hint of her thoughts. Simon cast a sideways glance at her, a slight frown creasing his brow. Then, with a nod, he turned away to walk back to his car. Leigh did not watch him go. She checked that all her fencing tools were back in her truck, and then got behind the wheel and started her engine.

Her anger faded quickly as she drove off her own land, down the road towards the small shop at the crossroads. What had she been thinking, lying like that? She didn't have a date for the dinner. She hadn't had a date since Jack left, and wasn't likely to either. Keeping the small vineyard going took all of her time and energy. She couldn't remember the last time she had gone out to dinner. Her irregular phone calls to her parents in Sydney were about the closest she came to a social life.

Inside the shop, Leigh collected her bread and milk. She was selecting her usual wine-related magazines from the rack when her eye fell on the cover of *Australian Life*. She saw the headline and didn't pause to think. She picked the magazine up and paid for it with the others. She did think about it as she drove home and walked into her kitchen. Then she found a pen and pad, and started writing, before her courage failed her.

Dear Editor,

My name is Leigh. I am a woman, and I am a farmer too . . .

* * *

'Here's the short-list, Helen.' Richard dropped a folder filled with letters and photos on to Helen's desk.

'How many have we had?' Helen asked.

'Up to this morning, just over three hundred, including e-mails,' her assistant enthused.

Helen closed her eyes for a moment, relief flooding through her.

'That's a great response in just three days,' Richard continued. 'There should be a similar number again as the snail mail comes in from the more remote places. And this is just the first week.'

'That's all good news.' Helen smiled at him. 'Based on those figures, I think we can easily sustain farmers for three weeks. I'll have this week's list ready in about an hour.'

'I'll tell layout that it's coming,' Richard said as he left.

Helen allowed herself a few quiet moments of satisfaction. It looked like her idea was working. Thank God!

She opened the folder and glanced at the top sheet. It was a list of names, ages and locations. Her team had already selected the most promising letters. Thirty names chosen from three hundred. That was just one in ten. The others were simply not handsome enough, or perhaps their letters were dull. Some would have been out of contention because of poor-quality photographs. The magazine needed farmers who were saleable. Helen frowned. She didn't like the way that sounded. Still, it was only in her head. The rejected farmers would receive a polite letter explaining the overwhelming response and the lack of space to include everyone. The thirty farmers in her folder were the lucky ones. Half of them would feature in the next issue of *Australian Life*. It was her job to pick them.

Helen spread the files out across the glass top of her desk, with the photos clearly visible. Without reading a single word about the candidates, she rejected three simply because she didn't like the photos. That left twenty-seven.

She wanted to include the widest possible range of ages, types of farm and locations in the magazine. With that in mind, she cut another three applicants, then settled down to read the rest carefully.

An hour later, she was almost done. The rejects were back in the short-list folder. They would get a second chance next week. Fourteen applications lay in a pile by her left hand. The final two sat side by side in front of her, while she weighed them up. One was a New South Wales cattleman; the other a canegrower from Townsville.

She reviewed the cattleman's letter. It was articulate and interesting, and the accompanying photo was good. But she already had one cattleman. A quick look through the pile of accepted farmers located that particular letter. It was great. Thirty-five years old. A widower with two small children living in the back of nowhere in the Northern Territory. Even the station name was romantic: River Downs — two thousand square kilometres of Australian outback. This one was a winner.

The canefarmer was very young. In the photograph he looked handsome. Dark hair, blue eyes. Nice broad shoulders. Helen wondered why someone like that needed her magazine to find a wife. Still, that wasn't her problem. Her job was selling magazines, and if the canefarmer would help, then he would have the final place. He listed making jewellery as one of his hobbies. That would attract some interest.

'All right, Greg Anderson, twenty-three years old, of Townsville,' she said as she added the file to the accepted pile. 'You're in.'

That made fifteen.

Helen spread the photos out across her desk for one last review. She was very pleased with the selection. Something for everyone was the magazine's promise — and that was what she had chosen. Young and old, they farmed everything from sheep to tomatoes. One even farmed ostriches. He hadn't been particularly handsome, nor was his letter very articulate. But an ostrich farmer was an attention-getter.

As was the woman.

Helen picked up the file, and studied the face that stared back at her. She was young and quite pretty, was this . . . Helen checked the file . . . Leigh Kenyon. A winegrower in the Hunter Valley. Helen wondered briefly if life was as difficult for a single woman winegrower as it was for a single woman editor of a national magazine. Not that it mattered. The important thing was that having a female farmer would increase the appeal of the campaign.

Helen gathered up both sets of files and walked into the main office.

'Keep these,' she instructed Richard as she handed him the rejects. 'We can review them when we see what new applicants we get for next week.'

She walked to the big layout desk. Pushing aside the clutter to make room, she laid the photos out one by one, listening closely to the reactions of her team. If these farmers got her team talking, they'd do the same to her readers. The excited buzz as the photos were passed around the table told her everything she needed to know. She stood back a little and allowed her staff to do the job they were paid for.

A loud knock at the open door announced the arrival of her boss.

'Helen!' Jim Sommerton was a short, round man with a big voice.

'Jim.' She moved to intercept the chief executive before he could involve himself in the work that was taking place. Jim was a man with a great head for running a media empire, but a lousy head for designing a magazine.

'It's looking good,' he boomed. 'The sales figures. The second printing. That's the right stuff!'

'Thank you,' Helen said. 'I expect next week will do even better.'

'I hope so.' Jim was obviously keeping a close eye on what she was doing. 'I want to see the mail room overflowing with lonely-hearts letters.'

Helen nodded. Jim was a bit hard to take in large doses. He had originally opposed her idea. Now she expected he'd try to take some of the credit.

'Now don't you go giving away all those brawny men.' He nudged her roughly in the side with one elbow and winked. 'You might want to keep one for yourself.'

Helen forced a laugh, but it faded as soon as Jim walked out. He hadn't made her feel like laughing. With just a few words and a leer, he had made the whole farmer campaign seem slightly sleazy and left a bitter taste in her mouth.

'It's ready, Helen.' The layout artist called her back to the big table.

Helen looked over the pages.

'Get it to the printer,' she said.

2

Donna Boyd stepped out on to the tiny balcony and draped her damp bikini over a metal clothes hanger. She pulled the towel from her head and ran her fingers through her wet, wavy auburn hair. She was wearing shorts and a cropped top and, stretching her arms wide, she revelled in the caress of the fresh air against bronzed skin still glowing from her early-morning swim. She closed her eyes and took a long, slow breath of the salt-tinged air of paradise. With her eyes closed, she could still see the white-capped waves rolling gently on to the golden beach while the gulls rode the air currents above the shoreline. When she opened her eyes, the beach was still there, but it was a small patch of crowded sand, barely visible between the high-rise glass and concrete towers that lined the shore. Her ninth-floor flat boasted beach glimpses, rather than beach views. That was still a big improvement on the grey tarmac and brick walls on show outside the window of her tiny flat in London.

It wasn't quite the tropical paradise she had dreamed about, but it was close enough.

Donna leaned against the balcony rail, enjoying the bite of the sun on her skin. How she loved that warmth. At this time of year, London would still be grey and wet, the bleak days hiding even the smallest sign of spring. There were times when she still didn't quite believe she was here. Surfers Paradise. The name had called to her across half a world, and she had answered. The plane fare had used up most of her savings, but that didn't matter. She had stepped off the flight from London just two days after her twenty-fifth birthday, ready to welcome adventure with open arms.

Perhaps adventure was too strong a word, but she hadn't done badly during the past eight months.

The first thing she had learned was that Australians seemed to really like the English — except perhaps for their sporting teams. Her accent and upbringing had helped her land a great job at a travel agency. She had no idea why anyone would want to exchange sunny Queensland for rainy old London, but if that was what they wanted, she had the local knowledge to help them. England was, she told them, a great place for a holiday. She just didn't want to live there any more. Donna enjoyed her job. It wasn't as fulfilling as her teaching job in London, but there were compensations. It paid the bills, and a few weeks ago she had scored a cheap weekend in Sydney, to look at the harbour bridge and the opera house.

Her job had also been her introduction to her flatmates. Cathy Manning was another travel consultant. She and Donna had hit it off from day one, and within a week Cathy had invited Donna to move into the flat she shared with her twin sister Anna. The arrangement worked well. The girls soon became firm friends, and shared expenses meant Donna was saving some money. Australia was a big country, and she wanted to see more of it before her visa ran out and she had to board a plane home.

She had fulfilled so many dreams. She had the tan. She swam in the blue Pacific Ocean most mornings. She had even made love to a handsome blond lifesaver on a beach in the moonlight. Which wasn't all it was cracked up to be. The sand got everywhere!

She loved it all: the country and the people. But she couldn't help thinking she was missing something. She didn't know what it was, but she hoped she would find out soon.

'Donna! Are you here?' Cathy always sounded enthusiastic about everything, but her voice seemed even more excited than usual.

'Hi, Cathy.' Donna walked into the living room, where her friend had just arrived back from the local store with fresh croissants for their breakfast.

'Donna, I've found it.'

'Found what?'

'The answer to your problem.'

'What problem might that be?' Donna asked.

Cathy flung herself on to the couch and started digging inside a plastic shopping bag that seemed far too big for breakfast for two. 'You want to stay here, don't you? After your visa expires?'

'Of course I do.' Donna dropped into an armchair opposite her friend. 'I love it here. But I'm not eligible for resident's status. You know that.'

'You would be if you were married!' Cathy announced.

'That's true. But — '

'Ta da!' With a dramatic flourish, Cathy thrust an open magazine at Donna. 'The answer to all your problems!'

THE FARMER NEEDS A WIFE, the headline declared. Donna ran her eyes over the first few lines, then looked up at Cathy's expectant face. 'You are kidding?' she said.

'It's the perfect solution,' Cathy insisted.

'No, it's not!' Donna wasn't going to let

this continue. 'I am not going to be a mail-order bride for some outback farmer.'

'They're not all from the outback,' Cathy pointed out. 'There's a very cute one who grows vegctables in the Brisbane Valley.'

'No.'

'It's close to the coast. You'd be able to come and stay with us on weekends.'

'With or without this mythical husband?' Donna chuckled. 'I have to leave for work soon. Let's have breakfast.'

'You'd be a dead cert to catch a good one.' Cathy carried the shopping bag into the kitchen behind her. 'You're pretty. Great figure. Blue eyes. As for your hair — it's gorgeous! Everyone loves your accent. You're smart, too.'

'I'm not interested.' Donna flicked the power on the electric kettle and reached for the coffee mugs.

'You could send that great photo of you in your bikini on the beach. That would be sure to get an answer.'

'I wouldn't send that one. It would give the wrong impression, and anyway,' Donna hurried on, 'I'm not interested.'

'You should be.'

'How many times do I have to say no? Do you want honey or jam on your croissant?'

'Stop changing the subject.' Cathy laid the

open magazine on the table where they would be eating breakfast. 'How about a canefarmer from Townsville?'

Donna laughed. 'No!' Cathy could talk her into almost anything. But not this time.

In the end, Donna took the magazine to work with her. It seemed the easy way out. Cathy had the day off, and Donna promised she would read all about the farmers when she had a spare moment. She promptly forgot all about it as she lost herself in planning trips to her homeland for excited Australians.

As was her habit each working day, she strolled the two blocks from the office to the beach, to eat her lunch watching the waves and the tourists. The sound of the surf washing onto the beach was a soothing release from the hectic pace at work. She sat down on a low stone wall, took off her shoes and wriggled her toes in the soft, warm sand. As she pulled her sandwich from her handbag, she rediscovered the magazine rolled up in one corner of the big leather satchel.

She had promised Cathy, and she knew her flatmate well enough to know she wasn't going to let this drop. Donna was also just a little curious, and she had nothing better to do for the next half an hour. She took a bite of her ham and cheese on malted brown bread, and began reading.

There were more than a dozen of them. All farmers and all single. Faces both young and old smiled up at her from the pages. At times, Donna found herself smiling back.

Thirty-year-old David was a sheep farmer who believed women were better at caring for animals than men were. He lived in South Australia and wanted a slim wife.

John was fifty and raised cattle in the Snowy Mountains. He was looking for a non-smoking woman with a good sense of humour.

Cathy's vegetable farmer was indeed very good looking. He was also a man who believed women were far better at housework than men. No guesses what he was looking for in a wife, Donna thought.

She shook her head. It didn't really matter what these farmers were like. She wasn't about to answer a letter. Much as she loved Australia, she wasn't planning to get married just to stay here. There was much more to marriage than that. When she got married, it would be for the right reasons.

She flicked over the last page.

He wasn't particularly handsome. His face was lean and angular. His dark hair looked like he cut it himself, which he probably did, as he appeared to live in the middle of nowhere. He was leaning against a wooden fence, and behind him there was nothing. Just blue sky, red dirt and a few scrubby trees that appeared to be wilting in the heat. That was the outback Donna had imagined back in soggy old London.

A dusty wide-brimmed hat dangled from his long fingers. He was dressed for work in a faded blue open-necked shirt and what looked like jeans. His face was tanned by the sun, and there were creases at the corners of his eyes. He was looking at the camera with a strange sort of half-smile. That smile almost broke her heart.

Peter Nichols' letter was brief. He was a widower and the father of two small children. He owned a cattle property near a place Donna had never heard of in the Northern Territory. He described himself as a caring man, with a sense of humour, searching for a similar woman who was willing to take on a ready-made family. There was always room, he wrote, for one more. His wife would lead a hard life in a remote place, but one filled with great natural beauty. She would have none of the benefits of city living — no movies or shopping or Sunday brunches with friends. Instead, she would have the rewards that came with being part of a loving family. That sentence caused Donna to pause. It was a rare thought for a man.

She looked at the photo, seeing the sorrow in his face even more clearly. She wondered how his wife had died. She must have been very young. Such a tragedy. And for the children, too.

If she was going to write to anyone, it would be this man.

She wouldn't send him some bikini photo hoping to catch his eye. This man would want more than that. Instead, she could tell him how much she longed to be part of a big family, like her own family in faraway England. She wasn't concerned about shops and movies. Those things hadn't been enough to keep her in London. Nor were they enough to keep her here in paradise. As for the loneliness of the outback . . . no one could be lonely if they had someone to love. Someone who loved them in return.

If she was to write, that was what she would say.

* * *

'Simon. Isn't this your neighbour?'

Simon Bradford looked up from the account books for his winery. Tania Perry was leaning against his office door, a magazine in her hand. He smiled at her. Tania was the sort of woman who made men smile. Tall and slender, with long dark hair, she looked exactly what she was: a rich man's daughter and part-time model. She was also Simon's part-time girlfriend, an arrangement that suited them both.

'Isn't who my neighbour?'

'Here. In this magazine.' Tania often stayed with Simon for a few days between modelling jobs. She always brought a huge pile of magazines with her. She spent hours reading them. Simon supposed that made sense, given her job. He had occasionally glanced at the pages of glossy fashion photos, when Tania was featured, but mostly he ignored them.

Now he pushed his chair back from the big wooden desk and reached for the offered magazine. The face that stared back at him from the page wasn't Tania's.

'It *is* Leigh,' he murmured.

It was a very different Leigh Kenyon from the one who had been wrestling with fencing wire a few days before. In the photograph she was wearing a dress and make-up and looked like a woman, rather than a farmer. An attractive woman at that. His brow creased as he flicked over the pages and read the headline. **THE FARMER NEEDS A WIFE**. In Leigh's case, that probably meant a husband. What was she thinking?

'Why would she do something like that?' Tania voiced the same thought.

'I really don't know,' Simon answered, still trying to get his mind around what his eyes were seeing.

'She was engaged once, wasn't she?' Tania wanted to know.

'Yes, she was.'

'Didn't he run off with all their money or something?'

'Something like that.' Even if he wasn't still reeling from the shock of seeing his neighbour in a national magazine campaign, Simon didn't feel comfortable discussing Leigh's affairs with his girlfriend.

'What a bastard he must have been.'

Simon agreed, although he didn't say anything. Leigh Kenyon and Jack Thorne had been newcomers to the Hunter Valley, and just making a place for themselves, when Jack had run off. Simon remembered the gossip that had spread through the small community like wildfire. It was said that the couple had won a small fortune on the lottery, and that Jack had absconded with all of it. That wasn't the whole story. Simon knew more about it than any of his neighbours, but he kept his mouth shut. He had his own reasons for disliking Jack Thorne.

'Strange that she needs to do this to find a man,' Tania said. 'She's really quite pretty.'

'Yes, she is,' Simon replied without thinking, then ducked as Tania swung a playful punch at his head. 'Not in your class, of course,' he added, laughing.

'That's better.' Tania stepped between Simon and the pile of letters on his desk. She sat on the polished wood, one leg either side of his chair, and took the magazine away from him. 'I was beginning to feel jealous.'

'Jealous. Not you. Never.'

'Well, neglected perhaps.'

'Oh, I wouldn't want that.'

Simon ran his hands up the satin skin of Tania's long legs, so invitingly displayed under her short black skirt. He grabbed her hips and pulled her forward to straddle his lap. Tania leaned forward and kissed him; a long, slow kiss filled with the promise of more to come. He pulled her closer, his fingers twining through her hair. The magazine lay forgotten on the desk.

Much later, Simon slipped from the bed. They had left the lights on in the living room when they tumbled into bed, and the light filtering into the bedroom fell on to Tania's sleeping form. The sheets had been tossed aside as they made love, leaving her body open to his gaze. Even asleep, she was a remarkably beautiful woman. She was a generous and warm lover, even though she wasn't in love with him. Neither was he with her. They felt affection for each other, and a sexual attraction that was exciting and satisfying. That was enough. When it was time to move on, they would both do so with good memories and no regrets.

That was how Simon wanted it. His only attempt at something more meaningful had ended badly, leaving behind two shattered relationships, and turning away someone who should have been a friend.

Which brought him back to Leigh.

Simon didn't bother putting on a dressing gown as he left the bedroom. There was no one else in the house to see him. No neighbour either. At least, no close neighbours. The nearest house was Leigh's, and that was half a mile away. He moved through the house, turning off the lights as he went. In the living room, he picked up the half-empty glass of wine that he had left behind when he and Tania went to bed. Then he turned off the light, and stood by the glass doors that opened on to his garden, and beyond that, the gentle slope of his moonlit vineyards.

To one side, he could see the shapes of the buildings of his winery. A few security lights clearly outlined the larger buildings, where grapes were crushed and the wine was made. A series of long, low mounds covered the storage areas where his finest wines were ageing slowly, kept cool in underground bunkers, protected by tile roofs covered with soil and living grass. It wasn't exactly a common type of storage, but he found it worked. Hidden from his view was the cellar door — a wine shop and restaurant that catered to the tourists who were becoming almost as big a business as the wine itself.

Simon felt he was justified in his pride. He had built a successful business, which supported more than a dozen families. He had a large and comfortable home, and a beautiful girlfriend. Not bad for a man in his early thirties. Well, mid-thirties maybe. Still, not bad at all.

His gaze moved from the buildings of the winery to the slopes where his vines grew. From there, it seemed inevitable that his eyes should come to rest down the valley, where sometimes he could see the lights of Leigh's house. Tonight, though, there was nothing, just a deeper blackness where the buildings would be.

Now that he was alone with his thoughts, the disquiet he'd felt all evening matured into real concern.

Why would Leigh offer herself in some magazine?

She certainly didn't need to. She was an attractive woman. Her eyes were the most amazing blue. She looked pretty good in a pair of tight jeans, too. Her lips were very kissable. There were times, before Tania, when he might have kissed them, given the slightest encouragement.

It wasn't just the way she looked. Anyone who took the time to get to know Leigh would soon realise that she was quite something. She had courage, the way she had stayed on at the winery after Jack left. She had faced down the gossip and kept going. She certainly wasn't afraid of hard work, and she was good at it too. Despite everything, she was still in business. He bought her grapes every year, and knew just what a good job she was doing.

Simon drained the last of the wine from his glass. He liked Leigh. His feelings were, if not brotherly, certainly protective. After the hell she had gone through with Jack Thorne, he didn't want to see her hurt again. There were times when he almost felt . . . but there was too much history and the shadow of her former fiancé between them. He had seen it in her eyes when she looked at him, so he kept their relationship strictly business.

But this was hard for him to ignore. Why would Leigh be writing to some magazine?

The magazine was still in his office, where Tania had dropped it earlier. He turned on the desk light and examined it more closely. At least it wasn't one of the sleazy men's magazines that were just expensive porn. A lot of this magazine's readers would be women. In fact, that was clearly who the campaign was aimed at. All the other farmers were men. The small woman with the big eyes looked so out of place among them.

Simon couldn't shake the feeling that whoever answered her letter would be bound to hurt her again. No man worth having would answer an ad in a magazine. The letter printed beside the photograph seemed only to emphasise Leigh's vulnerability.

A partner to share . . . Trust is important . . . willing to work towards a dream . . .

She was asking a lot. It was no more than she deserved after the hell she had gone through with Thorne. But Simon doubted she would find what she was looking for through the pages of a magazine. Any man that was right for Leigh would hardly be reading . . . Simon turned the magazine over . . . *Australian Life*.

Not unless someone told him to.

Simon hesitated, as an idea began to form

in his mind. He searched his memory for names. Single men who could be trusted not to hurt her. Every time he thought of someone, he rejected the idea. This one was a bit of a fool. Another had a bad reputation with women. Leigh deserved someone better. Someone . . .

It was either a very good idea, or a very bad one. He wasn't sure which.

If Leigh ever found out what he'd done, she would kill him. But how would she find out? Only two people need ever know. If his idea was successful, she would be protected from the losers who might answer her ad. Who knows, it might work out. That would be a good thing. Wouldn't it?

Simon shivered. Autumn was coming. It was the wrong time of year to wander around the house naked at night. He should go back to bed and Tania's warmth. He dropped the magazine back on the desk and turned out the light.

* * *

'These are good, Molly, really good.' The advertising account manager waved a hand at the photographs spread over his desk.

'Thanks.' Molly reached out to touch one of the photos, but she didn't pick it up. She knew every inch of each one of them. She had planned the shoot, and told each model what to wear and how to stand. She had taken the shots, cropped and manipulated them into the images that the advertising man was now looking at.

'Do you miss being on that side of the camera?' he wanted to know.

'No. Not at all. This is much more rewarding.'

Molly Seaton had started her career as a model. She was fairly tall, and fairly thin, and fairly pretty. At least that was how she thought of herself. The modelling agent she approached had agreed and promptly told her to dye her hair blond and go on a strict diet if she wanted to make it to the top. It hadn't taken Molly long to realise that what she really wanted was to be behind the camera. She wanted to create images, not be a part of them. The decision taken, she had eaten some hot chips and a tub of mango-flavoured ice-cream, then bought a camera. She let her hair return to its natural sandy brown and set about becoming a photographer.

Her experiences in front of the camera had taught her just how competitive the fashion industry could be, but Molly never even entertained the possibility of failure. She shamelessly used the contacts she'd made as a model and bullied a leading fashion photographer into taking her into his team as an unpaid assistant for four months. During those months, she had gradually built up a portfolio of her own images. Her chance came when her boss had cancelled a commission at the last minute. Molly had approached the advertising agency and offered to fill the gap. They were desperate enough to say yes, and Molly's career as a photographer began. That first shoot had been a success, as had the one after and the one after that. In the year since then, her reputation had steadily grown — and now agents and editors called her, instead of the other way around.

'I think our client will be very pleased with these,' the advertising executive said, gesturing towards the photos on his desk. 'Using the theatre was a brilliant idea.'

'They turned out even better than I had hoped,' Molly said.

The agency had commissioned Molly to create advertising images for a fashion house that specialised in street-wear for teenagers. Their styles featured military-type camouflage fabrics, black leather, and studs. The image was aggressive and unconventional. Molly had taken the models to a recently refurbished old theatre, and posed them against the elegant baroque furnishings and fabrics. The juxtaposition was striking.

'They're coming in shortly. Do you want to stay and meet them? Hear what they have to say?' The invitation was a mark of respect for her work.

'Sorry, I can't,' Molly replied. 'I've got another meeting. But call me and let me know how it goes. These are the best shots, but I've got some more if they're interested.'

'Will do.' The agency executive leaned back in his chair. 'You do good work, Molly. I've got another couple of jobs coming up that I'd like you to do, if you're free.'

'I'd love to,' Molly said. 'How about I call you tomorrow? You can tell me what's happening with these shots, and we can talk about the others.'

'Are you sure you don't want a full-time job?' His smile told Molly that he already knew the answer. After all, he had asked the question several times before. Her refusal had not damaged their working relationship. If anything, she suspected he admired her independence.

They shook hands and Molly left.

She was almost bouncing as she walked out into another glorious Sydney day. She wanted to hug someone. A good shoot made her feel like that. A big client offering her a job did too, even if she was never going to take it. She was twenty-two years old, with no mortgage, no husband and no kids. She could afford the uncertainty of freelancing and enjoy the freedom it offered. If she didn't do it now, she never would. Maybe in a few years she might be looking for the stability of a full-time job. Not today. Right now, she was succeeding at her dream career and it felt good.

She walked down George Street, enjoying the crisp autumn air. Her gaze constantly flickered over the office buildings towering above her, looking for some line or perspective that might make a good backdrop for a fashion shoot. She watched the people walking past, noting their clothes, their looks and the way they walked. How she loved Sydney! She had moved here from her parents' home in the Blue Mountains three years ago, and now she could not imagine living anywhere else. She loved the harbour and the bridge and the opera house. She loved the tall buildings and the manicured green lawns. The restaurants and the people and the galleries. Tonight she was going to a reception on board a ferry, which would cruise the harbour as the people on board partied. Her date for the evening was a news cameraman who worked for one of the television stations. They had been out several times since they met at a fashion event a few weeks ago. He was nice and a fun date, but Molly wasn't serious about him. She wasn't ready to be serious about anything but her work right now. Still, he was good company and pretty cute, too. She was looking forward to the party. A perfect ending to a great day!

Molly's good mood was still with her when she reached the offices of *Australian Life*. On the twenty-third floor, she greeted Richard Gordon with a smile.

'Molly.' Richard's face broke into a huge grin. 'It's good to see you. How are you?'

'I'm just great.' Molly knew that Richard had a bit of a thing for her. He'd never asked her out, but the way he smiled told her enough. She tried not to encourage him. He was good looking, and very nice, but she didn't want to get involved in a relationship that might interfere with her work. However, his obvious attraction did make her feel good. Especially on a day like today.

'I loved the shots for the kids' fashion spread.'

'Thanks,' Molly said. 'Whoever said never work with kids and animals was right. The shoot was hell, but the results were worth it. When is it slotted to run?'

'In three weeks,' he told her.

'Great. My mum always likes to buy the issues with my stuff in them.'

'Give me her address,' Richard said. 'I'll get a copy sent to her.'

'Thanks. She'd get a real buzz out of that,' Molly said. 'Is Helen in?'

Australian Life was fast becoming one of her biggest customers. She had done several shoots for them in the past few weeks as Helen set up features for the new-look magazine. Hopefully this meeting would result in another commission.

'I'm here,' said a voice behind her.

Molly turned around. 'Hi, Helen,' she said, then followed the older woman through into her office.

Molly took the offered seat, while Helen took her accustomed place behind the big desk. As always, Helen was beautifully dressed. The suit was classic Chanel, and the shoes were Kurt Geiger. By comparison, Molly was wearing one of her many pairs of blue jeans, and a plain white T-shirt. Black leather boots and a black jacket completed her outfit. She could have felt intimidated by Helen's immaculate style, but she didn't. Molly wasn't easy to intimidate.

'How is the relaunch going?' Molly asked.

'Really well,' Helen said. 'The farmer campaign is creating a lot of interest. The mail room is overflowing.'

'That's good.'

'That's also what I wanted to talk to you about,' Helen continued. 'Are you available to do a shoot with one of our farmers?'

'When?'

'I'm not sure. That depends on the farmers.' Helen held out a folder. 'This is the first lot, published this week.'

Molly opened the folder and flicked through the files. The farmers' details interested her not at all. The photos and the men in them were what mattered.

'They're not too bad,' she said, as she flipped the pages. Their faces were ordinary, but her job was to make the ordinary look like something else.

She lifted one of the photos for a closer look. The man in it was about her own age — dark-haired and blue-eyed in the classically handsome manner. The photo was not good. It looked as if he had taken it himself, by balancing the camera on a fence post. But there was something appealing about the face. Something vulnerable, perhaps, or sad. She turned the photo over. Greg Anderson was his name. He was a canegrower from Townsville. He ran the farm alone, because his father was ill. And he was a silversmith! He sounded an interesting young man for several reasons. 'You are also very cute,' she muttered under her breath.

'Well, what do you think?' Helen asked.

'I could do something with any of them,' Molly replied in her best professional manner as she dropped the photo back on the desk. 'What's the next step?'

'The readers' letters are being passed on as soon as they arrive. We'll stay in touch with the farmers. When one of them invites a woman to visit, I'll want you to go too. Get some shots of them together on the farm for a follow-up story.'

'When do you need it?'

'We've got two more weeks of farmers to print. I'd like to have a couple's story for the week after that.'

'I'm booked for Monday and Tuesday of next week, but after that I've got a bit of a break.' She had been planning to scout some locations for future fashion shoots, but that could wait. 'If something happens, I can be available.'

'Good. I'll be in touch.'

Molly stopped by Richard's desk as she left. 'It looks like I'll be doing a farmer shoot for you,' she told him.

'That's great.'

Molly picked up a copy of the magazine that was lying on the desk. She quickly flicked to the page she wanted. 'See this guy.' She pointed at the photograph of Greg Anderson. 'If there's any choice, he's the one.'

Richard looked at the page. 'Do you fancy him?'

Molly laughed. 'No. Of course not. But he has a good face. I'd like to photograph that face.'

'I'll see what I can do,' Richard promised.

'Thanks.'

Molly left the building still in high spirits. She turned left towards the harbour and the Museum of Modern Art, where there was a photographic exhibition that she wanted to see.

* * *

Helen watched Molly walk out of the door. The girl was very good for one so young, and was getting better with every shoot she did. Helen was keen to keep using her talent for the magazine. Not only that, she liked the photographer. Molly's enthusiasm for life practically poured out of her. Every move she made, every look on her face seemed to say, 'Life is great.' Helen used to feel like that, but she hadn't in a very long time. The thought made her feel suddenly almost middle-aged.

The pile of paperwork on her desk called,

but Helen wasn't in the mood. She felt unusually restless, and didn't know why. The farmer campaign was looking like a huge success. The mail room had already delivered several large bundles of mail to be passed on to lucky farmers. The letters were spread over the big layout desk in the outer office, and her people were going through them now. She should be celebrating. Certainly her team in the outer office were, if not exactly celebrating, certainly enjoying the obvious success of the campaign. There was a great deal of laughter as they sorted through the mail.

Helen took a firm grip on her thoughts. Just because the farmer campaign was doing well, she couldn't afford to be complacent. She had staked her reputation on turning around a failing magazine. She needed another big story to follow the successful launch. Something to show that the magazine wasn't a one-shot wonder — and nor was she.

She unlocked the top drawer of her desk and pulled out a folder. She opened it to reveal some typed pages, and a few photographs. The typed pages were the first draft of a feature story. The photographs, bought at great expense from an American paparazzo photographer, showed a major Hollywood star on holiday with another equally well-known star. Both men were married, but the photos displayed a level of intimacy that left the reader in no doubt as to the relationship between the two. When the photos had been originally offered to her, Helen had been suspicious. There had never been any rumours about the two actors. Both were family men and thought to have two of the strongest marriages in the movie industry. This was a scoop of quite exceptional proportions. Within minutes of the magazine hitting the streets, *Australian Life* would be featuring in media reports around the globe. The photo would be reproduced and the magazine quoted in a dozen languages. Her name would be brought to the favourable attention of the media world's heavyweights.

Then why was she sitting on the story?

No more than a handful of people knew it existed. Helen had the only copy of both the photos and the text. It was the perfect lead for the issue following the farmer campaign. A strong new story would build on the initial launch momentum and should push her sales to record heights and justify the bold gamble she had taken when she walked into this office a year ago. Yet she had been unable to commit to using the story. It couldn't be that she had any qualms about the two men and their right to privacy. They were both public figures who courted the media when it suited them to do so. She shouldn't be concerned about the effect the revelations would have on their careers, or their families. That wasn't her problem, was it? Besides, if the men had been cheating on their families, didn't they deserve everything they got? In printing the story, she would just be doing her job — and doing it well.

A burst of laughter from outside her office cut through her thoughts. Helen looked out through the glass panels. Her staff had gathered around the layout desk. The odd items of clothing and bottles of the latest cosmetics that usually covered the desk had given way to piles of envelopes. Letters from farmers. As she watched, a letter was passed from hand to hand, accompanied by another surge of laughter. Helen felt an irrational surge of anger. What was going on?

'What's so funny?' she asked as she walked into the outer office.

'Some of the letters,' one of the girls replied. 'Helen, you've got to read them.'

'Listen to this,' said another. ''I'm not handsome, but I really am a nice guy. And you wouldn't have to have sex with me until you were sure!' What a loser!'

'You reckon that's bad?' her colleague interrupted. 'How about the replies?' She began reading a letter. ''Dear Editor, I've never had a boyfriend. I've never even been kissed properly. It's because I am fat and ugly. And not clever. But I am a nice person, so please send my letter on to a farmer. Send it to one who didn't have too many replies. Then there's more chance he'll pick me.''

Once more the group dissolved into laughter. Except Helen.

'I think that's enough.' She spoke quietly, but the response was instant. Her staff knew her well enough to understand when she was serious.

She pulled an unopened letter at random from the pile and held it up. 'Don't laugh at these people,' she said. 'They might not be as clever as you. They might be fat, or desperate, or maybe just plain lonely. Whatever and whoever they are, they deserve to be treated better than that. They deserve a bit of respect.'

There was murmured assent from the group.

'Good. Now, I want every one of those letters sorted. Every farmer gets every single letter addressed to him. Got it?'

More murmurs.

'And any letter not addressed to a particular farmer gets the standard reply.'

Helen didn't wait for a response; she

turned and walked back into her office and closed the door behind her. As she did so, she realised she was still holding a letter in her hand. She tossed it into her open briefcase. She wasn't sure why she was so annoyed. Was it simply because her people were laughing at the letters? If they were guilty of treating the letter-writers badly, what about her? She was the one shuffling lives about like so many playing cards. Her eye fell on the folder with the grainy but devastating photo on top. She was worst of all. She was planning to publish a story that might destroy two men she had never met. Not to mention what it would do to their families. And for what?

For the first time in her career, Helen suddenly felt unsure of herself. She was good at her job, that much she knew. But was it the right job? Was this what she had worked for all these years? She remembered the girl she had been, devouring any book she could find with something like wonder, and swearing that one day she too would be a writer. At university, she had vowed that she would change the world with her words. Had it come to this — manipulating people's private lives for the sake of sales figures?

Didn't the actors have a right to their secret? Everyone had secrets. No one knew that better than she.

Helen snatched up the file from her desk and almost threw it into her briefcase. She didn't understand where these unsettling thoughts had come from, but she had to get past them. She was standing on the threshold of a whole new phase in her career, and she wasn't about to let a few sentimental moments destroy years of hard work. She looked at her watch. It was still quite early, but she would head back to her flat. She had a briefcase full of work. Perhaps she'd be able to concentrate better once she was away from the curious glances being sent her way by her now silent staff as they worked at the big layout desk.

It wasn't going to be that easy. Helen was still feeling very unsettled when she sat down to work later that evening at the big desk in her living room. Her North Shore flat had big sliding glass doors opening on to a balcony with a glorious view that featured the great iron 'coathanger' that spanned the harbour. When the weather was nice she often worked out there, but tonight she wasn't in the mood. She settled herself at the desk with a small glass of wine near her hand. When she opened her briefcase, she saw the unopened letter sitting on top of her papers.

She lifted it out. She meant to leave it unopened and return it to the growing pile in the office next morning. She certainly didn't want to read it. Not when she was feeling like this. But before she could stop to think, her fingers were reaching for the letter-opener in her top drawer.

What a nice picture, she thought as she pulled the contents from the envelope. The photograph showed a man crouched in front of a very young foal. He wasn't wearing a hat, and his face was lit by sunlight. His entire concentration was on the creature in front of him. The foal was reaching out to sniff the man's face, its every muscle poised for flight. Both man and foal were obviously unaware of the photographer. That was what made it such a great shot. It wouldn't have done for her magazine, of course. She had selected only good clear shots of the subjects facing the camera, their attention on the lens and the readers who would see them through that lens.

This was very different, but she found it compelling.

The letter, when she finally opened it, was written and printed from a computer.

Dear Ms Woodley,

Please allow me to introduce myself. My name is Matt Redmond. I am forty-two years old, and breed Australian stock horses near Scone in New South Wales.

Helen glanced back at the photograph. Matt Redmond had a good strong face. It was a face that would have improved with age. She guessed he was better looking now than he had been at twenty, before his face developed the lines of maturity and experience. Not that he would ever have been unattractive. He was handsome: no doubt always had been and probably always would be.

She read on.

I am divorced, and the very proud father of Alison, who has this year begun studying veterinary science at university. Now that my daughter is no longer here, the homestead seems very empty.

My time is spent in the peaceful surroundings of the farm, and my work is devoted to breeding and training horses that are both beautiful and intelligent.

Life would be more complete if I had someone with whom to share it. This someone would appreciate the beauty of the land. She would share my joy at the birth of a healthy young animal, and pride at watching it grow.

It may sound like a cliché, but I am told I have a good sense of humour. I enjoy reading and classical music. I do not smoke. I like a glass of red wine with dinner or a beer on a hot day.

I would like to find a similar soul and share everything I am and everything I have with her. I look forward to hearing from you,

The signature was smaller and neater than she would have expected. It did, however, match the words, which were more expressive and thoughtful than she would have anticipated from a man, especially a farmer.

Helen sat back in the chair, and looked once more at the photo. She couldn't explain it, but she felt as if something had touched her. Maybe it was just the handsome face. More likely it was his words. Simple and unaffected, they had struck home to her. She was moved by his obvious love and pride in his daughter. Even more affecting was the thought of him spending his days bringing new life into the world, and watching it grow. How lucky he was. That was a feeling she would never know.

She put the letter and photo aside, and reached into the briefcase for the work she needed to do. But the folders remained unopened, as she turned back to Matt Redmond's letter. She read every word again and sat for a long time just staring at the photo. Matt Redmond would not go into her magazine. Even if the photo had been suitable, she could not bring herself to give him to the gaggle of editorial assistants and layout artists and printers who would then pass him on to be ogled by the readers. Not this man. He deserved better than that.

Helen reached into her desk drawer and pulled out a writing pad. She picked up a pen, and wrote the first words of a letter. She would reply to Matt Redmond. Just a short note to explain why he had been passed over. Something about lack of space in the pages. Short and impersonal.

Fifteen minutes later, she was well into the second page of the letter.

3

The filly's neat black hooves beat out a steady rhythm on the hard ground. Matt Redmond moved with the swaying of the horse's back, his hands gentle but firm on the reins. They were moving at a steady canter through the short grass of the home paddock, but Matt could feel his mount's impatience. The air was crisp with the first hint of autumn, and the healthy young animal wanted to run. He could feel a similar desire in his own veins.

'Okay, little one. Let's do it.'

He eased his weight forward in the saddle, and clasped his legs tighter against the filly's sides. Her ears flickered, and her stride lengthened.

'That's it.'

Encouraged by his gentle urging, the horse broke into a gallop, her long legs flashing over the ground. Matt leaned slightly forward in encouragement, then gave the filly her head. She flicked her tail and started to run. In seconds she was at full gallop, her breath coming loudly as she strained for extra speed.

She's very fast, Matt thought, a little surprised. This was the first time he had given the newly broken youngster a chance to really stretch out. Now he gave himself up to enjoying the feel of the fresh breeze on his face and the horse beneath him.

A few minutes later, he gently brought the filly back to a canter, and finally to a walk. He didn't want to overdo it. Her nostrils were flared, her sides heaving a little as she gulped down great draughts of air.

'That was pretty fast,' Matt crooned as he stroked the brown neck that was slightly damp with sweat. 'But you enjoyed it, didn't you?'

As if in reply, the filly stretched her nose towards the earth, then snorted loudly and shook herself, the dark hair of her mane flicking wildly. Matt chuckled as she began walking again, her neck extended in a sign that she was relaxed and happy. They walked slowly towards the line of tall gum trees that marked the fence. Matt switched the reins to one hand, and pulled his battered old brown Akubra from his head. He swung it back along the filly's side, then forward along her neck. She flicked an ear, but ignored him. Well pleased, Matt wiped the thin sheen of sweat from his brow with the back of his hand and put the hat on again. A few days ago, the swinging hat had caused her to shy away in a panic. Matt felt the deep satisfaction of knowing his training was working. He looked about for a new challenge to give her.

They were standing at the edge of the long gravel driveway leading from his front gate to the cluster of buildings that Matt called home. Tall, straight gum trees lined the driveway. The grass between them was short and tinged with brilliant green, the result of good rain the week before. Looking down the drive towards the road, Matt saw the white mail van just pulling away from his gate.

'Okay, Granny,' he said to the horse. 'Let's go get the mail.'

Granny was a strange name for a filly not yet three years old. Her registered name was Ygraine. Or rather, Willaring Downs Ygraine. All his stock carried his stud name as a prefix. His daughter Alison named the foals, each year selecting a different theme. The year Granny had been foaled, it was the legend of King Arthur, and she had named the dark brown foal with the four white socks after Arthur's mother. Somehow, Ygraine had migrated to Granny, much to Alison's disgust. This year, Alison wouldn't be here when the foaling started. She was already settled in Sydney, pursuing her dream of becoming a vet. Proud as he was of her, Matt had to admit he was missing her. Sydney wasn't that far away from Scone, but he suspected Alison was already well involved with both her studies and a new social life. Which was as it should be. He didn't expect to see her back at Willaring Downs until the end of the first semester. That seemed a long way away.

Granny suddenly slid to a stop, snorting wildly and rolling her eyes. A dozen yards away, a motorcycle raced down the highway, the high-pitched roar of its engine breaking the silence of the day. Matt focused his concentration once more on the job in hand. Every moment with a young horse was a lesson. The hat. Opening the gates. Vehicles on the highway, and now collecting the mail. The teaching never stopped. Matt loved every moment of it and could not imagine spending his life in any other way. With patience and care, he calmed the filly, and coaxed her to walk over to the white-painted oil drum that served as his mailbox. He could feel her tense as he leaned over and reached inside the drum for a bundle of envelopes bound with an elastic band.

'Well done,' he told Granny as he turned her head for home. 'We'll just drop this off at the house.'

Nestled among the trees just a hundred yards from the river bank, the house was timber, painted white and surrounded on all sides by a wide veranda. Matt's father had built the house when he established Willaring Downs, named after the aboriginal word for the possums that lived by the river. Since his parents had retired to the coast, Matt and Alison had lived alone in the big house. Alison spent a few weekends a year with her mother in Queensland, but her life had always been here, with her father and the horses. Looking at the big house now, Matt realised once more how empty it seemed without her.

He swung himself from the saddle at the gate in the white picket fence. The fence had originally been his ex-wife's idea, but Matt had come to like it. The hitching rail near the gate had been his idea. Quickly he flicked Granny's reins over the post. He stroked her nose, and headed for the front door. He didn't need keys. The door was seldom locked, and never when he was home. He took off his hat as he stepped into the relative darkness of the front hall, and closed the door beside him. He wanted to wait a few minutes and see how Granny behaved alone. He moved to the window to watch, idly flicking through the envelopes as he did so. There was the usual assortment of bills and junk mail. Some forms from the Stock Horse Association, of which he was a member. And a white envelope addressed in a neat handwriting that he didn't recognise. Curious, he opened it.

Dear Mr Redmond,

I am writing to say that unfortunately your letter and photograph will not be published in Australian Life. *This is not in any way a reflection on yourself or your letter, but rather due to issues of space. I am sorry if you are disappointed.*

Matt's forehead furrowed. His letter and photograph? What was this all about? He looked at the second page. It was signed Helen Woodley. He didn't know the name, but she apparently knew something about him. He continued reading.

In your letter, you mentioned that your daughter Alison is beginning her university studies. I hope she enjoys the adventure ahead of her.

Alison! A suspicion began forming in Matt's head. Somehow Alison was involved in this.

A sudden movement outside the window attracted Matt's attention. Something had startled Granny. The filly pulled back against the reins holding her, her eyes rolling with fright. Matt dropped the letter and turned for the door. By the time he was outside, the horse had recovered from her fright and settled. Matt untied her and led her back towards the stables. It was almost time to find Granny a new home, and he knew someone who might be interested. He would e-mail him this evening. And after that, he would phone Alison and find out more about that strange letter.

Matt didn't think about the letter for the rest of the day. With Alison gone, he had more work than ever to do around the stud. He was looking to hire some help, but hadn't yet found the right person. He was interviewing a potential jackaroo tomorrow. The lad was just twenty-one and had grown up on a New Zealand stud farm. Matt hoped that he would prove suitable. In the meantime, he had to muck out the stables, feed and exercise all the horses as well as do the general maintenance. More than enough to fill the daylight hours. When darkness fell, it was bookkeeping and paperwork.

It was almost nine o'clock when he finally sank back into the comfortable leather chair in his office, and phoned his daughter's mobile. Alison answered on the second ring.

'Hi, Ali.'

'Dad!'

'I hope I caught you in your room studying hard,' Matt said.

'Actually, I'm just walking back from the library,' Alison told him. 'If you'd called a few minutes ago you wouldn't have caught me. I left my mobile on last week, and when it went off, I thought the librarian was going to kill me.'

'I hope you're not out alone this late at night?' The question was out before Matt could stop it.

Alison sighed dramatically. 'No, Dad, I'm not. I've got a friend with me. A big strong football player.'

To Matt that sounded just as bad. 'Ali, I got a strange letter today — and I think you can tell me something about it.'

'A letter?'

'Yes, from the editor of a magazine called *Australian Life*.'

'Oh.'

The tone of his daughter's voice told Matt what he needed to know. 'Come on, Ali — confess.'

'Oh, Dad, it was a joke really. I sent your name and photo to the magazine. It was running a thing to find wives for farmers.'

'Ali!' Matt wasn't sure whether or not he was angry. 'I don't need a wife, and if I did, I could find one for myself.'

'I know. It's just . . . ' Alison's hesitation seemed to be endless.

'It's just what?' Matt asked gently.

'Well, Dad, I've never known you to even go on a date. And I thought, with me down here . . . Well, I thought . . . I thought you might get a bit lonely,' she finished in a rush.

Matt smiled into the telephone. Since the day she was born eighteen years ago, his daughter had never failed to amaze and delight him.

'It's nice of you to worry,' he told her, 'but I am a big boy. I can look after myself.'

'I know. So, tell, what did the editor say?'

'She said she was sorry they won't be publishing my letter and photograph.'

'Rats! I was sure they'd pick you. What a shame.'

'No, it's not,' Matt told her. 'It's a good thing. Please promise me you won't do something like that again.'

Having received her promise, Matt started asking Alison about university and her studies. A few minutes later, as he was about to end the call, he remembered to ask which photo she had sent to *Australian Life*.

'One I took last year. Remember we took those shots of the new foals? You were with Hyperion.' Alison had named the last crop of foals after characters from Greek mythology.

'I remember.' Matt shook his head. 'Do me a favour? Next time, ask before you try to fix me up with a date.'

'Okay.' She sounded just a little abashed.

'All right then. Now, you watch out for that footballer.'

'I will,' she laughed down the phone. 'Love you, Dad.'

'I love you too. Bye.'

After he hung up, Matt realised his daughter had been right. About several things. He was lonely without her. And he hadn't been on a date for longer than he cared to remember. After the divorce, there just hadn't been anyone.

He picked up the letter, and read it again.

* * *

Sitting here, I feel a bit like the Banjo Paterson poem. You are 'Clancy of The Overflow' . . .

And he sees the vision splendid of the sunlit plains extended,
And at night the wondrous glory of the everlasting stars.

While I, of course, am in the dusty, dirty city — dreaming of changing places.

* * *

Matt walked through to his large airy living room, and sought for a volume on one of the overflowing bookshelves. He opened the book, and read again the poem that he had so loved as a child.

I had written him a letter which I had, for want of better
Knowledge, sent to where I met him down the Lachlan, years ago;
He was shearing when I knew him, so I sent the letter to him,
Just on spec, addressed as follows: 'Clancy, of The Overflow'.

A picture formed in Matt's mind of a woman sitting at an empty desk, surrounded by blank walls that cut her off from the teeming city around her. He could see her head bent over the letter she was writing, but he couldn't see her face. He could, however, sense that she was very much alone.

Matt shook his head. It wasn't like him to be so fanciful. Still, there was no doubt something in the letter touched him. Perhaps he could understand the loneliness of the writer. He should reply. It would only be polite. He wandered back into his office, where the computer still hummed softly. He could probably e-mail the magazine. But that was too impersonal. He reached for a pen and paper.

Dear Helen,
I should correct a slight misunderstanding . . .

* * *

'This is utter nonsense. What on earth possessed you?' Robert Anderson's voice was unnaturally loud in the stifled hush of the hospital. He waved the magazine at his son. 'You have embarrassed yourself. And you have embarrassed me.' He slammed the magazine down on the faded green cotton of the bedcover.

Greg looked at his own face staring back at him from the page. They chose him? Until this moment, Greg hadn't known that *Australian Life* had featured him in their pages. He wanted to pick it up for a closer look, but his father's obvious contempt stopped him before he could move.

'Dad, I just saw the ad and thought it might be a laugh,' he said softly, trying to deflect what he knew was coming.

'A laugh? A laughing stock more likely.' Robert snorted with derision. 'How am I supposed to hold my head up at the Sugar

Growers' meetings after this?'

You're not, Greg wanted to shout. Don't you understand that you'll never go to another one of those meetings? You'll never grow another stick of cane. You'll never leave this room. You will spend the rest of your life surrounded by cold lino floors and faded pastel walls. And I'll never get to leave!

He swallowed the words along with his anger and pain and simply opened the briefcase to produce the weekly accounts. His father seized them and promptly ignored his son.

Greg picked up the magazine that his father had forgotten. He wondered who had brought it in to show him. One of the nurses, probably, and while he wished Robert hadn't seen it, Greg was absurdly pleased that the magazine had chosen him. He flicked through the pages, noting the other farmers featured with him, including a woman who grew wine. They must have had dozens, maybe even hundreds of farmers apply. And they chose him. Obviously the magazine editors didn't share his father's opinion of his worth.

Greg slid the magazine inside his briefcase, and glanced across at the man on the bed. Robert's face had taken on a dull pallor, brought on by his illness and lack of sunlight. He was still refusing to acknowledge his condition or to plan for the future. He wouldn't admit to weakness, or even normal human emotions. Greg could never remember seeing his father show pain or fear. He had never seen him cry. He suspected that Robert hadn't even cried when his wife died. Greg remembered nothing about his mother, and his father never spoke her name. The few old black and white photos that Greg treasured showed a young woman with long blond hair and a smile that seemed to leap off the paper. She was always dressed in flowing skirts, and had a vaguely hippie air. Greg had often wondered what such a woman could possibly have seen in Robert Anderson. Perhaps his father had once been open and loving. He would never have been a hippie, but he might have had a sense of humour. Greg still wondered how different his life might have been if his mother hadn't died.

He slid his hand inside the pocket of his jeans to grip the silver charm. Except for the photos, all traces of his mother had long since vanished from the house. But Fay Anderson had left him something. In all the photos, she was wearing silver jewellery. Earrings and bracelets. In one photo Greg could see the glint of a silver pendant around her neck. He believed with all his heart that his talent for making jewellery was a legacy from his mother. He also believed that he would somehow be failing her if he didn't use that talent. But his dreams of leaving the farm and becoming a professional silversmith had come crashing down the day his father collapsed.

His father seemed to have fallen asleep. He was doing that more often now. His heart was failing, and there was nothing the doctors could do about it. Nothing Greg could do either but give up his dreams and stay. He wasn't doing it for love. Any love he felt for his father had long since died under the sting of the older man's bitterness and contempt. It wasn't a sense of duty. If anything, his duty was to fulfil his mother's legacy. Perhaps it was fear. Perhaps Robert Anderson was right, and he was a coward.

Careful not to wake his father, Greg gathered up the papers and letters spread across the bed. He slid them back inside the briefcase and quietly left the room. He walked quickly along the sterile corridors, past doors that opened on to more rooms just like the one where his father lay. With a sigh of relief, he opened the front doors and stepped out into the fresh clean air and blazing sunshine. When he reached the car park, he tossed the case on to the front seat of the car, and got in behind the wheel. Before he reached for the ignition, he pulled the charm out of his pocket. The silver oval was small enough to fit into the palm of a woman's hand. A series of gracious curves crossed the polished surface, creating shadows as Greg angled it to catch the sunlight. The piece had no function. It served no purpose but to be a thing of beauty. Greg could still feel the wonder that had touched him as it emerged from the casting process. He had become a jeweller that day.

He closed his fingers tightly around the glowing metal and raised his fist to his lips. He would find a way out. He had to.

When he arrived back at the farm, he didn't even glance at the rows of dark green cane. He gave no thought to the dozens of small jobs needed to keep the farm running. He went straight to his workshop. Workshop was probably too grand a title for the corner of the shed that his father had reluctantly granted him for what Robert described as a 'namby-pamby hobby'. Greg hadn't cared what his father called it; at least he had a place to work. Since his father's illness, he had spent more and more time in the workshop. It was the only place where he was truly happy.

He pulled the silver charm out of his pocket and placed it in its usual spot on the shelf above his workbench. Then he sat down to work. Greg had never wanted to be a canefarmer, but that didn't stop him taking his inspiration from the land. He was working on a series of designs inspired by the fires that burned the cane each year. His sketchpad was covered with rough ideas, and the first wax moulds were looking promising. They would soon be good enough to cast in the precious metal that was safely locked in the house. Greg pulled one of the fine stainless-steel tools from a box. He examined the end carefully. Dentists used the same tool for fixing teeth, but he had an entirely different use for it. First he needed to heat the end.

Greg was so engrossed in his work that he didn't hear the car approach. The blare of the horn startled him out of his concentration.

'Damn.'

He hated being disturbed when he was working, particularly when it was going well, as it was now. Carefully he placed the wax mould on a piece of cloth. He turned off his burner and put down the tool he was using to etch the surface. Wiping his hands on a cloth, he walked out into the yard. The dusty red mail van had stopped halfway between the shed and the house.

'Hi, Greg.' The driver waved a hand as he walked to the rear of the vehicle.

'Tom. What have you got for me?'

The driver disappeared behind the rear doors for a few seconds and emerged with a box.

'You'll have to sign for this one.'

'Sure.' Greg took the offered paper. The box contained jewellery supplies he couldn't buy locally. Chemicals, some more tools. He was eager to get it back into the workshop.

'That's not all.' The mailman was reaching once more into the back of the van. He pulled out an open cardboard box. Inside were white linen mail bags that obviously held bundles of letters.

'What . . . ' Greg spluttered.

'All for you,' Tom said, laughing. 'Must be something to do with that magazine.'

'Oh. You saw it too?' Greg didn't know why he was surprised that people had seen it. After all, that was the whole idea.

'Yeah. My wife reads that magazine.' Tom put the box of letters down on the driveway, and both men stood looking down into it.

'How many?' Greg asked in a daze.

'Almost a hundred.'

Greg didn't know what to say.

'I suppose they're all from women wanting to marry you.' The mailman was nearly sixty years old, and had a well-worn face that seemed to say the world had no more surprises to offer him. For the first time since

Greg had known him, he looked stunned.

'I guess so,' Greg said.

The older man slapped Greg on the shoulder and got back behind the wheel. 'Good luck,' he called as he drove off.

Greg carried both boxes into the house. For once, he didn't eagerly investigate his box of jeweller's supplies. He set it to one side, almost forgotten as he tipped the bundles of letters on to the kitchen table. Slowly he removed the elastic bands that held the bundles together and spread the envelopes across the table. They were all addressed to him care of *Australian Life* magazine. Most were hand-written, although a few had printed labels. Greg didn't quite know what to do next.

'Well, I guess I just start opening them,' he said to the empty room.

He pulled an envelope at random from the pile. As he opened it, a photograph fell out. The girl was dark-haired, and she was naked! Shocked, he dropped the photo. It lay face up on the top of the pile, the naked girl smiling sweetly up at him. Whatever Greg had expected, it wasn't that. He picked up both the photo and the unread letter and shoved them back inside the envelope. He wasn't a prude. Nor was he a virgin. But he just did not want to read a letter from some girl who would send a naked photograph to a stranger.

Cautiously he opened the next envelope.

At least this one had clothes on. A good thing too, Greg thought. She was fat. Not just a bit fat. She was huge! He knew he was being unfair, but he didn't read her letter either. He set it to one side and had a third try.

The photo showed a girl about his own age. She wasn't pretty, but she wasn't ugly either. Greg felt a surge of relief. At least this one wasn't scary. He unfolded the three hand-written pages and started to read the letter.

I would like to get away from the city. I've been busted here for shoplifting. And smoking grass. Maybe if I get away I can start again.

Greg shook his head and folded that letter too. He probably should feel sympathy for the girl. No one knew better than him how hard it was to break away. But he had problems enough of his own. He couldn't take on any more.

Feeling deeply disappointed, he began tossing the unopened envelopes back into the box. His father had been right. Sending in his photo had been a mistake. He was stupid to think that anything good could have come from what was, after all, a cheap stunt to sell magazines. He wasn't going to find the solution to his problems this way, and he didn't think he could cope with reading any more letters like the three he'd just opened.

At last all the letters were back in the box. Greg stood looking down into it. He felt like a coward.

'All right,' he said out loud. 'Just one more.'

She was beautiful. Her blond hair fell to her shoulders. Greg just knew her eyes would be blue.

Dear Greg,

I feel a bit strange writing to someone I have never met because of a story in a magazine. I wonder if you felt strange too, when you sent in your photograph.

Greg liked that. The girl understood.

My name is Jasmine Lewis — but people call me Jasi. I am 22 years old and I live in Melbourne. I work in an art store — because I really love art. Paintings fascinate me. I don't think I could ever be a painter, but I love being around them.

This was getting better with every line. His father had never understood Greg's need to create beautiful objects. Perhaps Jasi would. His heart sank a little when he read that she lived in Melbourne. That was a long way, and such a lot of money for a plane fare.

I don't know if we'll get along. And I don't think either of us should make any promises. But I would like to meet you.

The photo was lying on the table in front of him. Greg picked it up and looked at it again. He saw the faint blur of a silver pendant at her neck. That was the sign he needed. This time, he wasn't going to be a coward.

Her letter did not include a phone number, which proved she was sensible and cautious. It did, however, mean he would have to write to her. A letter might take a couple of days to get to her, so he should do it right away. Greg went looking for pen and paper. He wouldn't do this one on the new computer. When he had found what he needed, he sat for a few seconds, staring at the blank sheet of paper. This letter had to be just right! He had to find the words to make that lovely girl want to be with him. As phrases ran through his mind, he began absently doodling on the paper, sketching intricate patterns that might one day be worked in precious metal.

* * *

A single loud metallic clang echoed unnaturally through the vast silence of the outback. After a few moments, a second clang rang out. Then a third. The noise was becoming louder and faster as the breeze caught the metal blades of the windmill. From deep inside the earth, a gurgling noise echoed through the pipe, and the first few spits of water dropped from its open end on to the sunbaked concrete, evaporating almost immediately. A few more drops followed, stained by the rust on the pipes. Then came a trickle. Finally, as the windmill gathered speed, a jet of clear life-giving water burst from the cast-iron pipe and fell into the open concrete tank.

Peter smiled. He shoved the spanner into the back pocket of his faded jeans, and tossed his hat on to the ground. The water rising from the vast underground basin was slightly warm, but still very sweet. Stepping forward, he thrust his head under the flow, letting it wash away the sweat and dust from the back of his neck. He splashed the water over his face, enjoying the reward of several hours' work to repair the windmill. He cupped one hand under the flow and took deep draughts of the water. It had a slightly earthy taste. Red rock and soil. It tasted better than the sweetest wine.

He stood up and shook his head, sending droplets of water flying. The damp stain on the concrete was spreading, but the water still hadn't covered the bottom of the tank. It was several metres in diameter and rose almost a metre above ground level. It was designed to water large numbers of cattle during the forthcoming muster, and would take days to fill. Peter looked up at the clear blue sky above him. The wet season was over. The boggy dirt roads were starting to open, and soon his contract mustering team would appear. He was almost ready for them.

Peter whistled, and a few seconds later his blue cattle dog emerged from the shade of the trees at a flat run. The dog skidded to a halt at Peter's feet and stood looking up at his master, his tongue lolling as he panted in the heat.

'Get in there,' Peter told him, and pointed to the water tank.

In a trice the dog was up and over the concrete edge, biting and lapping at the water pouring out of the pipe. Peter grinned as he watched his dog's antics, then he swept his hat up off the ground. He didn't bother dusting it off. The broad-brimmed Akubra had seen far worse than a little dirt. It was battered and stained and almost a part of him. He walked back to the trail bike that was standing in the shade of a cluster of scrubby trees, whistling softly to himself as he put his tools back in the saddlebag. He swung one long leg over the bike and kicked the engine into life. The roar of the engine brought his dog running. Without breaking stride, it leaped on to the back of the leather seat, bracing itself against Peter's back for the journey. He could feel the damp from the dog's coat as it leaned against him.

The track from the muster yards back to the homestead was dirt, with two deep gouges to show where trucks had passed over the years. In the dry season it was just good enough for a cattle truck to use. On a motorcycle, it was easy. Peter held the bike at a steady thirty kilometres an hour for the twenty-minute journey back to the homestead. As he rode, his eyes roamed constantly over the harsh landscape, finding familiarity in every jagged red rock outcrop and every stunted tree. When he arrived back at the cluster of buildings that had been his home all his life, he rode the bike straight to the machinery shed and parked inside. The dust of his arrival hadn't begun to settle as he strolled back outside, heading for the house.

He'd taken just a few steps when movement caught his eye. Jenny and Ken were sitting on the wooden bench in the shade of one of the acacia trees near the house. Their heads were close together in conversation. He was too far away to hear the words, but he did hear his sister laugh at something her husband said. There was such joy in her voice. Then Ken took her in his arms and kissed her, a long, lingering kiss full of love and passion and promise. Peter turned away. Seeing them together only made his heart ache more for his own love lost. After seven years, the pain of Karen's death still haunted him every day. Jenny and Ken had been his lifeline during those long, bitter years, and now they were both leaving.

His little sister had been his shadow for as long as he could remember. Growing up in such a remote place, Peter and Jenny had been as close as brother and sister could be. She had held him while he cried for his wife, then taken on the task of caring for the twin babies Karen had left behind. But Jenny was more than just his sister now. She was Ken's wife. The former jackaroo had become a key part of the day-to-day running of the station. He could ride any horse that carried a saddle, and fix anything with an engine. He was also Peter's best friend. The three of them together were both a family and a business.

But changes were coming to River Downs Station. Peter didn't like change — at least not these changes.

Jenny and Ken would soon be parents. It was right that they should head east to make a life for themselves and the family to come. That didn't make their going any easier for him. He would have to hire a new jackaroo, but no matter how good the kid might be, it would be a long time before he could even begin to take Ken's place in the working life of the station. A nanny for his kids was proving a far more difficult task. If they couldn't find someone suitable, the twins might have to go to boarding school. The mere thought was almost more than Peter could stand.

And neither a nanny nor some kid from the east could begin to assuage the loss of his closest friends.

He had lived all his life in this vast wilderness, and never for one moment considered it lonely. Now the spectre of loneliness was all around him. Without his family around him, he was starting to wonder if his love for this rugged land would be enough to sustain him. And if it wasn't . . .

Shaking off that thought, he started walking towards the house. Jenny and Ken had already vanished inside. As he opened the insect screen that protected the front door, he heard their voices from the open kitchen window.

' . . . don't like this,' Ken said.

'I know,' Jenny replied. 'But it will work out in the end, I'm sure of it.'

'When are you going to tell Peter?'

'Tell me what?' Peter asked as he walked into the kitchen to find Ken perched on the kitchen bench as normal, while Jenny fixed dinner.

'About the new nanny,' Jenny replied, almost too quickly.

'You've found someone?' Peter asked eagerly.

'I think so.' Jenny turned away to look for something in the refrigerator. 'She wrote in response to the ad. We've exchanged e-mails. I think she'll be perfect.'

'Well, tell me about her.' Peter filled a glass with cold water and dropped on to a stool.

'Her name is Donna Boyd. She's a teacher,' Jenny said. 'On a sort of working holiday.'

'This is no holiday.' Peter was concerned. 'I wouldn't want her to leave just as the kids were getting used to her.'

'She won't do that.'

'How can you be certain?'

'She sounded genuine,' Jenny said. 'She's a rural girl. Her father has sheep. She knows what to expect.'

At his spot on the bench, Ken suddenly collapsed into a coughing fit. Shaking his head, he reached for a glass of water.

'Anyway,' Jenny hurried on, 'I think she'll be great . . . for the kids. I've already talked to her about coming out here. She can be here on the mail plane the week after next. But I have to let her know tomorrow so she can make arrangements.'

'That's a bit quick, isn't it?'

'Peter Nichols.' Jenny turned to face him, her hands on her hips. 'Don't you start finding excuses to delay this. It's way past time we found someone. I want to give the poor girl a chance to settle in and learn the ropes around here before I go.'

'Okay!' Peter held his hands up in mock defence. 'I know when I'm beaten. If you think she's the one, make the arrangements.'

'Right.' The tone of his sister's voice told him that the subject was closed. 'Now, you had better tell the kids — so they have time to get used to the idea.'

He found the twins exactly where he expected them to be. In a large run behind the house, his cattle dog bitch was nursing a litter of puppies. Five little blue and white bundles of fur were clambering all over his children, who lay in the dust of the run, their faces wreathed with smiles. The puppies were almost six weeks old. Soon they'd be weaned and sent on to their new homes. Peter's work dogs were well known, and the puppies had been spoken for long before they were born. Each was destined for a life on a cattle property. But for now, they were puppies doing what puppies do best — playing with children.

'Hi, kids.' Peter stopped outside the gate.

'Hi, Dad,' the twins chorused in unison. They extricated themselves from their playmates, who quickly waddled back to their mother, thrusting their noses under her belly looking for their dinner.

'Do all the puppies have to go?' asked Sara, looking up at him with deep brown eyes that were the very mirror of her mother's.

'I'm afraid they do,' he told her as he opened the gate to let them through. 'You know that Chipper's pups are always in demand.'

'That's because she's a champion,' Chris declared.

'That's right.' Peter smiled. 'She's a champion working cattle dog. And the pups are going to be cattle dogs too. They wouldn't be happy if they couldn't work.'

The twins nodded, their young faces serious and thoughtful.

'Now, I've got something to tell you,' he said as he led them towards the house. The three of them took seats on the wide shady veranda, and the twins waited expectantly.

'You know that Aunt Jenny and Uncle Ken are moving east in a few weeks,' Peter said.

The twins nodded, their smiles fading. They would miss the aunt who was the closest thing to a mother in their lives.

'You know that we are going to find a new jackaroo to help me work the station after Uncle Ken is gone.'

'But he won't be as good a stockman as Uncle Ken,' Chris announced firmly.

'Well, you never know. Let's wait and see,' Peter said, touched by his son's loyalty. He ruffled the boy's hair. 'There's someone else coming too. A nanny.'

'A nanny?' Chris looked horrified. 'But I'm nearly nine. I don't need a nanny.'

'What's she like?' Sara asked.

'Well, her name is Donna, and she's very nice. She's a teacher, so we could always say she was your teacher rather than your nanny. Does that sound better?'

The twins exchanged a glance, and nodded. It was set.

Later that night, as he lay in bed, Peter

realised there were a hundred things he should have asked Jenny about this Donna Boyd. How old was she? Where was she from? Peter was very protective of his kids. They had lost their mother so young that they knew her only from photographs. Their beloved aunt was about to leave. He didn't want them to have another trauma in their lives. Still, he trusted Jenny's judgement. She loved his kids as much as he did. She would make sure that this nanny — or rather, teacher — was right. And tomorrow he'd ask to see her letter and e-mails.

His mind made up, Peter rolled over, turning his back on the empty part of the bed, and closed his eyes.

* * *

Leigh sat in her car, feeling rather foolish. For more than twenty minutes she had been parked in a busy Sydney suburban street. All around her, people were hurrying in and out of shops, laden with bags of groceries and other household goods. Teenagers were lounging about, indulging in the unfathomable activities of their species. A slowly passing driver cast a questioning glance her way, as if hoping she might move on, opening up a parking space. Leigh ignored them all, her attention firmly fixed on a shop just a few metres away. All morning, people had been walking in and out of that shop. Sometimes they came out empty-handed. More often they came out with bags that obviously contained bottles of winc. Not surprising, really, as the sign above the door said 'Ian Rudd, Wine Merchant'.

The same Ian Rudd had written the letter that sat on the passenger seat next to Leigh. She almost reached for it, to read it again, then stopped herself. What was the point? She already knew it by heart.

> *Dear Miss Kenyon,*
>
> *I am not sure why I am writing to you. Such an act is out of character for me, but your photograph and story in* Australian Life *touched me. Working in the industry, I know how difficult it must be for a woman alone to run a winery, and I admire you for that.*

Leigh had been sitting at her kitchen table when she read those words. She had opened about half of the bundle of letters delivered by the postman that day. She didn't bother opening the rest. If she had truly started this because she wanted a date for the Hunter Valley Winegrowers' Dinner, then she had found him. A wine merchant would be perfectly at home there. The colour photograph that accompanied the letter showed a man in his early to mid-thirties. He might not look like Brad Pitt, but he was certainly very presentable. He would be the perfect partner for the dinner, and that was all she really wanted. She had no expectation of anything else.

That was when it dawned on her that perhaps Ian Rudd had expectations beyond just a dinner date.

The answer was blindingly simple. She would drive to Sydney and meet this wine merchant. She could talk to him, and come to some sort of arrangement. And if she didn't like him, then she could call the whole thing off. It wasn't as if she was afraid to go alone to the dinner. Or to face Simon Bradford without a man at her side.

Now that she was here, however, she seemed afraid to walk into a shop.

He might not even be there. In his letter he wrote that he divided his time between his retail store in North Sydney, and visiting wineries as part of his wholesale trade. This whole trip might have been a waste of time. But she would never know unless she went inside the store. She hadn't driven for two hours to leave without at least trying. She opened the car door.

Before she crossed the road, she took a moment to check her appearance. Deciding what to wear for this meeting had seemed inordinately difficult this morning. She had changed three times before settling on a knee-length denim skirt and a green knitted top. It was, she thought, smart but not too business-like. Nor did it look like she was trying to attract male attention. At the same time, she felt she looked — well — not unattractive.

The shop was quite narrow, but very deep. It was dim after the bright sunlight outside, and even through her nervousness Leigh was able to immediately appreciate that this was a true wine-lover's heaven. The low light would help preserve the wine in good order. The bottles that lined the walls were laid carefully on their sides, to keep the corks moist. She recognised some of the labels. The shelves held some of the very finest wine.

Two other people were inside the shop: a couple standing by the service counter, flicking through some brochures. There was no sign of Ian Rudd, or any other member of staff. Leigh moved along the shelves, touching bottles of wine but not seeing them. She glanced over her shoulder at the counter, and the open door behind it. Once she thought she heard a voice from the back room. She felt like a nervous schoolgirl. Her palms were sweaty.

Get a grip, she told herself, but it didn't help. The man waiting at the counter glanced her way.

'The owner is looking for some information for us,' he said. 'Sorry to hold you up.'

'It's fine,' Leigh croaked in a voice that seemed to have dried up.

Enough, she thought. She was getting herself into a state over a man she had never met. Just because she hadn't had a date in three years. And wasn't about to, either. She would go to the Winegrowers' Dinner on her own. She had done it before and it hadn't killed her. It was time to forget the stupid magazine and go home.

Ian Rudd walked through the back door.

He didn't look like Brad Pitt — he looked better. His photograph did not do him justice. His hair was blond and his eyes were blue, but such a simple description didn't even begin to suggest how drop-down-dead gorgeous he was. He was dressed in a simple linen shirt and trousers, but they sat well on him. He wasn't tall, but then neither was Leigh. When he spoke to his customers, his voice was low and calm, and seemed to reach across the room to her.

Leigh couldn't take her eyes off him. Her stomach clenched in a feeling she recognised as pure lust. She wanted to touch him, to run her fingers across his chest. To feel his breath against her cheek. She wanted . . . She turned away, and studied the wine in front of her without seeing it. Colour was rising in her face. She hadn't felt like this since that bastard Jack Thorne left her. In fact, she didn't remember that her ex-fiancé had ever made her feel quite like this.

She couldn't handle this. She had to get out of here.

'Can I help you?'

The voice close behind her seemed to slide across her ear like a caress. The other customers were leaving, and now Ian Rudd had turned his attention to her. Leigh fought to get a grip on herself. He didn't know who she was. She would simply buy a bottle of wine and leave. She carefully set her face into a neutral smile and turned around.

'I was just looking . . . ' Her voice failed as she gazed directly into those sparkling blue eyes.

'I'm sorry . . . ' A slight frown creased his brow. 'Are you Leigh Kenyon?'

There was no point denying it. It was too late to run away. She nodded.

'I recognise you from your photo. It's nice to meet you.' He held out his hand. 'You read my letter?'

'Yes.' Leigh put her hand in his, and the

world seemed to close in around them. He didn't let it go.

'And you drove down here to meet me?'

'I . . . had a business meeting in Sydney,' Leigh lied, 'and thought that as I was here . . . '

'I'm glad you came.'

An eternity seemed to pass before Leigh suddenly realised she was still holding his hand. Carefully she extricated herself.

'Anyway, I . . . ' She had no idea what to say next.

Ian came to her rescue. 'Have you had lunch?'

Lunch? How could he think of eating at a time like this? She shook her head.

'Well, let me treat you.' He held up a hand to forestall the protest that was on the tip of her tongue. 'I won't take no for an answer. Nothing fancy. There's a coffee shop just around the corner.'

'That would be nice,' Leigh admitted weakly.

'Then it's settled. Just give me a moment to let my assistant know.'

He smiled and vanished through the door to the back of the shop.

Leigh felt as if she had been hit over the head with a brick. A gold brick. She was stunned, but at the same time she felt more excited than she had in a very long time.

Ian was back in a few minutes.

'I have a truck coming today with supplies, so I can't be out too long,' he explained.

'That's fine,' she said.

In silence they walked the short distance to the coffee shop. Leigh had never been so aware of the warmth of the sun on her face or the feel of the breeze in her hair. The restaurant featured an outdoor section, with large plants growing in terracotta pots and brightly coloured umbrellas sheltering white tables. A few people were already eating. Ian guided her to a table in a quiet corner.

'This looks nice,' she said, looking at the menu because she was afraid that if she looked at Ian, he would see how flustered she was.

'I eat here sometimes when I have reps round,' he explained.

The waitress hurried over. She was young and pretty, and the look on her face made it clear that serving Ian was a pleasure, not a hardship. Leigh felt a twinge of something that could almost be jealousy.

'So, what would you like?' Ian asked.

You, she wanted to reply. Instead, she glanced at the menu again, but the words seemed strangely out of focus.

'I . . . ' She had no idea. 'What do you recommend?' she asked, almost in desperation.

'The salads are very good.'

She ordered mango and avocado. Ian calmly ordered a chicken salad, then asked her if she wanted wine.

'No thank you,' Leigh said. 'I have a long drive in front of me.'

'Of course. In that case, I also recommend the fresh fruit juice blends.'

He ordered pineapple and orange. Leigh did the same because making another decision was totally beyond her. The waitress walked away, and Leigh realised that she and Ian would now have to talk to each other.

'I feel a bit — '

'I just want to — ' he said at the same time.

They both stopped.

'You first,' Ian said.

'I just wanted to say that I feel a bit foolish now about writing to that magazine. I really don't know why I did it. I've never done anything like that before,' she confessed.

'And I wanted to say that I've never done anything like that before either — and I feel a bit embarrassed.' Ian smiled. 'Would it be easier if we pretended we just met by accident today when you walked into the shop?'

'It might.'

'Well then . . . Good afternoon, my name is Ian Rudd.'

'Pleased to meet you. I'm Leigh Kenyon.'

She held out her hand for him to shake.

He took it in both of his and held it for a long moment, before letting go.

'So, Leigh, tell me what you do for a living.'

'I own a winery in the Hunter Valley.' Leigh fell in with the game.

'Good heavens. Fancy that. I'm a wine merchant — how's that for coincidence.'

Unable to keep a straight face any longer, Leigh started to laugh. Ian joined her and the ice was broken.

'So, Leigh, tell me about your winery,' he said.

By the time their food arrived, they were deep in conversation about grapes and wine. It was a shared passion, about which they were both very well informed. Leigh's nervousness had vanished, and she even found herself enjoying her food. The conversation flowed easily until long after the meal was finished. Finally Ian glanced at his watch.

'Leigh, I really have to go. I'm sorry, but I have this shipment. It was due half an hour ago . . . '

'I've got to go too,' Leigh said. 'I want to get back while there's still enough daylight to get some work done.'

Ian paid the bill, and they started walking back the way they had come. As they rounded the corner, Leigh saw the large truck parked outside Ian's shop. A man was loading cases of wine on to a trolley to take inside.

'Ah — that would be your shipment.'

'It would, but I still have time to walk you to your car.'

As they got closer to the truck, Leigh noticed the label on the wine boxes, and for an instant her step faltered. Ian was buying large amounts of wine from Simon Bradford.

'Leigh?' Ian took her arm. 'Is something wrong?'

'No. I'm fine,' Leigh said, dismissing her momentary loss of composure. Of course he bought Simon's wine. Bradford Wines was a major producer. Ian would be a strange sort of wine merchant if he didn't buy from Simon's winery. There was no cause for her to be concerned. Lightning did not strike twice in the same place. Simon was no threat to her now.

She smiled at Ian to cover the moment, and together they crossed the road to her car. She unlocked the door, then turned to him.

'Thanks for a lovely lunch.'

'My pleasure. When can I see you again?'

Leigh felt a small thrill at his words. Did the attraction she feel run both ways?

'Well . . . ' She decided to take the plunge. 'In two weeks' time there is the Hunter Valley Winegrowers' Dinner. It's a big deal. Black tie. Dancing. If you're free . . . ?'

'I would love to come.'

Leigh almost sighed with relief.

'But two weeks is a long time. Do you think that maybe this weekend we could get together?'

Leigh's heart sang. 'That would be nice.'

'I don't have your number,' Ian said.

'Do you have the Wine Federation Growers' Guide?'

'Of course.'

'Then you have my number.'

Without any further hesitation, she opened the door of the car and slipped behind the wheel. Once she was there, she was safe from any possibility that he might kiss her goodbye. Or that she might kiss him back and give away far too much. Ian stepped back and waved as she pulled away. Leigh concentrated on her driving until she was on the freeway heading north. Then she let her mind wander, lingering over those moments when he had smiled, and his eyes had held hers. She could pretend that the lunch was nothing more than a business gesture between two people in the same industry. But that wasn't the case, and she knew it. It wasn't the winery owner who was so keen to see him again. It was the woman who was . . . dare she say it . . . head over heels in lust with Ian Rudd.

4

'Ladies and gentlemen, we have begun our descent into Townsville airport. I ask you now to please place your seat back in the upright position. Any electrical devices . . . '

The announcement droned on. Molly Seaton turned to the girl sitting next to her, who was staring out the window, twisting a lock of long blond hair in her fingers.

'We're almost there. How do you feel?' she asked.

'I'm really nervous,' Jasi replied with a half-smile.

I'm not surprised, Molly thought. You've just given up your job and flown more than two thousand kilometres to be with a man you've never met. Both of you have expectations of marriage. What will you do if it doesn't work out? More importantly, what will you do if it does?

'You shouldn't be,' she said out loud, trying to comfort the poor girl. 'You said he was nice when you talked on the phone.'

'Oh, he was. He was just wonderful,' Jasi gushed. 'But I'm scared he won't like me.'

'What's not to like?' Molly smiled at her.

'You're friendly and bright and very pretty.'

'Do you honestly think I'm pretty?'

'Yes.'

'Wow. That's really something coming from someone like you. Someone in the fashion business.'

Here it comes, thought Molly, the inevitable question from every girl with a pretty face and dreams of being a star. She had long ago learned how to politely suggest that not every such girl could be a model or an actress. But Jasi had gone back to staring out the window and torturing her hair. Molly sighed to herself and checked that her camera bag was firmly stowed under the seat in front of her. She and Jasmine Lewis had met a couple of hours ago at Sydney airport. *Australian Life* was paying for Jasi's trip from Melbourne to meet Greg Anderson in Townsville. In return, Greg and Jasi had agreed that Molly could spend a few days with them, taking photographs for a story for the magazine. Molly made a mental note to thank Helen Woodley's assistant for getting her the subject she'd requested on her last visit to the magazine offices. Greg and Jasi would make a good couple — at least to look at.

The plane landed and taxied to the terminal. As the seatbelt sign pinged off,

Molly put a restraining hand on Jasi's arm.

'Jasi, let me go first.'

'You first? Why?'

'Well, I need to find Greg. I want some shots of him waiting for you to come through the door,' Molly explained. 'More importantly, I want the shot of the two of you meeting for the first time.'

The poor girl was so nervous, she would have agreed to anything.

Molly put a comforting hand on her shoulder. 'Can you wait till the very end? Be the last person off the plane?' That would give her five minutes, maybe a bit more, to get ready.

Jasi nodded.

'Okay.' Molly picked up her bag and headed for the door, leaving Jasi sitting alone in her business-class seat as the economy passengers started streaming out from the back of the plane.

He was waiting just outside the gate. Molly recognised him in an instant. He was as good looking as his photo had suggested. This afternoon, though, his handsome young face was creased with concern as he anxiously scanned the arriving passengers. He was dressed in what Molly guessed were his 'going to town' clothes. A broad-brimmed hat hung from his hand. Molly thought he probably wasn't even aware that he was slowly turning the hat round with clenched fingers. She decided she should put him out of his misery.

'Greg Anderson?' She held out her hand. 'I'm Molly Seaton, photographer for *Australian Life*.'

'Hello.' His voice betrayed his nervousness as he shook her hand. 'Is Jasmine . . . Jasi . . . with you?'

'We travelled up from Sydney together.'

His shoulders sagged with relief. Did he think she wasn't coming? Molly wondered.

'Where . . . ?'

'I asked her to give us a few minutes,' Molly said. 'I want to get a couple of shots of you waiting.'

'Oh. All right.'

Molly's camera bag was, as always, slung over her shoulder.

'What do you want me to do?' Greg asked, looking even more nervous, if such a thing were possible.

'Just stand there,' she told him. 'I'll do the rest.'

As she moved around him, checking light and backgrounds, it seemed to Molly that he had already forgotten her. His whole attention was once more focused on the doorway to the air bridge. She took a few quick shots. She doubted that she would use them, but she was thorough. They also gave her a chance to get a feel for the setting and his face before the more important shots when Jasi appeared.

The last few passengers were straggling through the gate. Greg moved a little closer, and Molly positioned herself so her lens could see part of Greg's face and the blonde figure moving hesitantly off the plane. As Jasi stepped into the doorway, Greg's features were lit up by a broad, welcoming smile.

Molly started snapping shots.

Ignoring the photographer and the clicking of the camera, Greg stepped quickly forward. He reached out to take Jasi's hands and brought the girl close to him. He was much taller than she was. He continued smiling down into her eyes as he held both her hands in his. A tentative smile lit Jasi's face.

'Hello,' she said. 'I'm Jasi.'

'Welcome to Townsville, Jasi. I'm glad you came.'

Molly watched the encounter through the lens, mentally urging the pair to kiss.

They didn't.

She had all the shots she needed. Greg and Jasi were still standing self-consciously together, ignoring her.

'Greg, Jasi.' Molly slipped her camera back

into her bag. 'Shall we get our luggage?'

'It's this way.' Greg took the lead as the three of them made their way through to baggage reclaim.

Molly's luggage consisted of the stout metal carry-case for her photographic gear and laptop, and a small rucksack of clothes and personal items. Jasi's large suitcase suggested she was planning a long stay — or, thought Molly, many changes of outfit.

Taking Jasi's case in hand, Greg led the way again out through the sliding glass doors into the blinding sunlight and searing heat. Molly felt the sweat break out immediately on her forehead. As they walked across the car park, the heat of the sun-softened bitumen surface soaked through her shoes.

'Wow, it's hot,' Jasi said. 'I thought it would be starting to get cooler by now.'

'It never really gets that cool this far north,' Greg told her.

'Well, I like the heat.' Jasi smiled bravely as Greg stopped in an empty parking space and reached into his pockets for his keys. 'But I am looking forward to the air-conditioning in the car.' She was looking at the late-model blue sedan they were standing beside.

'Ah . . . ' Greg looked discomforted. 'This is my car — it doesn't have air-con.'

Jasi's face fell as she turned around to look

at the old white ute. 'Oh.'

'But it won't take us long to get home,' Greg hastened to assure her.

'That's fine.' Jasi beamed up at him. 'I've never ridden in a ute. This could be fun.'

Molly silently cheered the girl. She was trying so hard when she was clearly feeling very nervous. Greg too was doing his best. As she hefted her rucksack into the back of the ute, Molly noticed it had been freshly washed. No doubt to impress Jasi.

Greg opened the passenger door, and a wave of heat flowed out of the vehicle on to their faces. 'I'm afraid it will be a bit of a squeeze,' he told the women apologetically.

Jasi got into the car, and slid to the middle of the seat. Molly got in beside her, cradling her camera bag on her lap. 'Sorry,' she said to Jasi. 'Habit. I just can't put it in the back.'

Greg moved swiftly around the front of the car and slid in next to Jasi. He was right. It was cramped with the three of them in the front seat. And hot.

'It will cool down a bit once we get underway,' he told them as he wound his window down.

He started the engine and headed for the exit. He pulled the car into the line of exiting traffic and in a few moments found himself at the automatic gate.

'Oh, no!'

Both girls turned to face him.

'What's wrong?' Molly asked.

'I forgot to pay at the machine,' Greg admitted. 'And I'm in the pre-paid queue.'

Molly glanced back. Another car was right behind them. And another behind that. There was no way they could move aside and let the others through.

'There's a pay station just over there,' Greg said. 'I won't be long.'

He ducked out of the car and waved an apology to the waiting drivers as he sprinted for the pay station.

Molly looked at Jasi. The younger girl looked like she was about to burst into tears from a combination of nerves and heat and stress. An impatient blast of a car horn from the queue behind them didn't help.

'You know, he's just as nervous as you are,' Molly said.

'Do you think so?'

'I know he is. He's trying so hard to impress you.'

Jasi smiled faintly. 'He is nice.'

'Yes, he is,' Molly agreed. 'And very cute.'

Jasi's smile grew even broader. 'He's gorgeous!'

They both looked out the window, to where Greg was digging in the pockets of his jeans trying to find coins for the machine.

'Nice bum,' Molly added.

Jasi giggled.

'You think I didn't notice?' Molly said. 'Every female within a mile would notice.'

If Greg wondered why both girls were laughing when he got back into the car, he didn't ask.

During the drive to the farm, he kept up a running commentary for Jasi on the places they were passing. Molly stared out the window, leaving Greg and Jasi as alone as was possible for three people squeezed into the front of a ute. Not that they seemed to need much encouragement.

Just as the camera bag was never far from her hand, so the professional photographer in Molly was always at the ready. The big red sandstone hill that dominated the town had already caught her attention. The hill itself was spectacular, and she imagined the views from the top would be even more so. The midday light was harsh, but in the evening, the softer light would work wonders with the brilliant arc of sky, particularly if it was cloudy. She was here to do a job for *Australian Life*, but there was nothing to stop her branching out to do a little private work while she was here. She would ask Greg to take her back to that hill. If she could drag him away from Jasi.

Their journey ended when they turned down a long gravel road. Tall, dark green cane hedged the driveway, so thick it seemed to create a solid wall. Greg pulled up in front of a large white-painted timber house, with broad covered verandas all the way around.

Jasi slid out the driver's-side door to stand next to him.

'Welcome to the farm, Jasi.'

Listening to him, Molly thought his voice lacked the pride or sense of ownership she would have expected, but Jasi didn't seem to notice anything strange.

'The house is big,' she said, 'and I love the veranda.'

'It's fairly typical of houses up here,' Greg told her. 'The wide verandas tend to keep the house cool. Come on inside.'

Greg carried Jasi's case. Molly followed behind with her own things. She wasn't planning to take any more photos today. She would take some shots around the farm tomorrow, when she'd had time to look for the best locations. Greg led them straight into the kitchen, obviously the centre of the household. It was just like any other kitchen — but bigger. This one room was almost the size of Molly's tiny studio flat in Sydney. The stove was huge, and the refrigerator could have held enough food for a small army. A vast wooden table sat at one end of the room. On it lay a small, brightly wrapped package.

Greg took the package and handed it to Jasi.

'This is for you.'

'Oh.'

Molly looked at it. It was the right size and shape for a jeweller's box. The sort of box that would hold a ring. One glance at Jasi's face showed Molly that she wasn't the only one who thought that. Well, according to the magazine, Greg was looking for a wife. That was why Jasi had come. If everything worked out, there would have to be a ring involved somewhere. But surely Greg hadn't . . . not this soon.

Jasi's hands trembled as she tore away the wrapping. The box was covered in some soft black fabric. She hesitated for a second, then opened it. Unable to stop herself, Molly craned her neck to see.

The ring was nestled in more of the black fabric. The silver band was wide and flat and etched with a complex pattern of curves. Nestled in the middle was a single pale blue stone.

It was beautiful, but it wasn't an engagement ring.

'I made it for you,' Greg said hesitantly.

'When you said you would come here to meet me. I hope you like it.'

Molly thought Jasi hid her disappointment well. The girl slipped the ring on to the third finger of her right hand, and then she kissed Greg on the cheek as she thanked him and told him she loved it.

Molly felt an unexpected surge of relief.

* * *

Sixty-four e-mails waited in Helen's inbox when she turned on her computer. A light day. As she settled herself down to check them, she wondered whether e-mail was as much of a boon to business as everyone said. It seemed to her she wasted a lot of time each day dealing with things that might otherwise have never crossed her desk. Perhaps it was time she let Richard Gordon filter this mail, as he did the old-fashioned kind.

The fifth mail was from Molly Seaton, sent just after midnight the night before. How like Molly to be working that late. Barely scanning the text, Helen opened the attached images.

The first shot showed Greg Anderson meeting his chosen girl at the airport. Helen had expected a shot of a kiss — but looking at it closely, she decided this was better. The right half of the picture showed Greg's handsome face, a mixture of fear and delight as he stared at the pretty blonde girl walking through the doorway in the distance.

Her face mirrored the same emotions. It was a very powerful image, exuding both romance and sexual tension.

The second image was a close-up of the girl's hand. She was wearing a silver ring set with a pale blue stone. The ring was intricately and cleverly wrought. Helen clicked back to Molly's e-mail. Of course. Greg Anderson made jewellery. The ring was his gift to the girl who had travelled so far to meet him. This was shaping up to be a good story. Helen mentally reviewed her staff of writers, selecting one who could do the piece. There was no need for the writer to fly to Townsville. She could do the interviews over the phone. Molly would provide the shots and she could talk to the writer as well. Give her a feel for the atmosphere between Greg and . . . what was her name . . . Jasi.

Quickly Helen sent off her reply.

Helen's day was, as always, busy. It wasn't until late afternoon that she was able to close her office door and take the plain brown folder from her locked drawer. She opened it and looked again at the enclosed photographs of the two Hollywood stars. The paparazzo who had taken the shots had captured the two men in a very compromising pose. There was no chance they could explain that embrace as just friendship. It was a scoop guaranteed to send Helen's circulation into the stratosphere; and along with it her reputation. Yet she had still not been able to commit to using the story. She didn't know why. She might tell herself that the farmer campaign was taking too much of her attention, but that wasn't true.

Helen got up and went to stare out the window. Sydney Harbour lay below her, in all its glory. Ferries and pleasure craft cruised past the shining white arches of the opera house. She had come a long way from the tiny town in Western Australia where she had been born. Despite the fact that her parents were still there, she hadn't been back for years.

Unconsciously, Helen's hand moved to lie against her stomach. Her father was a hard man, with an uncompromising and old-fashioned morality. He had never forgiven his only child for a mistake made when she was very young. He hadn't exactly thrown her out of his home, but his coldness and her mother's reflection of it had long since driven Helen away. Her occasional phone calls at Christmas and on birthdays were a chore she did not enjoy. She told herself she didn't need her parents any more. Her career was all she needed.

She was 'the editor', a title she had fought hard to win. Her life began with her work, and mostly ended there. Social occasions were seldom for pleasure. Attendance at the theatre and charity balls was as much part of her job as deciding when — or if — to publish a story. So if her work defined her, did she really want that definition to be based on an exposé about the private lives of two actors? An exposé that would destroy their careers and tear their families apart?

Helen shook her head. Surely she wasn't developing a conscience?

The phone was a welcome interruption to the line her thoughts were taking.

'Helen,' her assistant's voice sounded uncertain, 'I'm sorry to disturb you, but there's a caller wanting to talk to you.'

Richard always screened her calls. He normally knew exactly who she would and would not talk to, just as he knew that when her door was closed, she didn't want to be disturbed.

'Who is it?'

'Her name is Alison Redmond.'

Helen searched her memory. 'I don't know anyone by that name.'

'She sounds quite young,' Richard told her. 'She says you and her father are . . . friends.'

Helen caught the hesitation in Richard's voice. In twelve months as her assistant, he had never taken a personal call for her.

'I don't . . . ' Helen stopped.

Alison Redmond. Matt Redmond's daughter. The university student who had written the letter to the farmer campaign on her father's behalf. Helen's eyes flickered to her briefcase. The letter actually written by Matt Redmond was there. She had received it two days ago, and not yet replied. She wanted to write back to him, and that was as disturbing to her as her indecision over the scandalous story that lay on her desk. She wondered why the girl was calling her.

'Put her through,' she told her assistant as she settled herself back in her leather chair.

'Hello . . . Miss Woodley?' The girl did sound young, but not the least intimidated to be speaking to a national media figure.

'Hello, Alison. How can I help you?'

'You know who I am?'

'Yes, I do. Your father mentioned you in his letter.'

'Well, that's why I'm ringing,' the girl hurried on. 'Dad told me about the letters. He seemed interested . . . I mean . . . he seemed to like . . . No . . . '

Helen said nothing. She wasn't going to make this too easy for her.

'Anyway,' Alison started again, 'Dad is here in Sydney. He brought some stuff down for me. I just thought that maybe the two of you could . . . '

Helen couldn't hold back a laugh of genuine surprise. 'Alison, are you trying to set your father up on a date with me?'

'No! Well, sort of. I guess. Yes.'

Helen was speechless. She didn't know whether to laugh out loud or to hang up. She had to admit, the girl had courage.

'Does your father know you've called me?'

'Not yet. He's outside getting . . . Oh shit! Oh, sorry. He's coming back. Miss Woodley, please talk to him.'

Helen heard some indistinct noises down the phone. There was a murmur of voices in the background, then a muffled exclamation.

'Miss Woodley, it's Matt Redmond here.'

His voice fitted his photograph perfectly. It was deep and rich, slow but still vibrant. Despite the awkward situation, it was a voice filled with confidence and certainty. Helen felt instinctively that she would like the owner of this voice.

'Hello, Mr Redmond.'

'I must apologise for my daughter,' the voice continued. 'Alison lets her heart rule her head at times. She shouldn't have disturbed you.' Despite his words, his tone resounded with love for his child.

'Please, Mr Redmond, think nothing of it. I am just surprised that she managed to talk her way past two receptionists and my assistant to get to me. She must be a remarkable young woman.'

'She can be quite persistent.'

Helen found herself smiling. 'Would you . . . ' She hesitated, then rushed on before she could talk herself out of it. 'Would you like to have a drink with me? It seems a shame that such persistence should go unrewarded.'

In the few moments of silence that followed, Helen could hear Alison's indistinct voice questioning her father. Helen steeled herself for the answer. Of course he would say no. And that was a good thing. What was she thinking, inviting him for a drink?

'I would love to have a drink with you.'

Helen just caught the muffled shout of teenage glee at the other end of the phone.

'I'm likely to be working quite late tonight,' she said quickly. 'Perhaps it would be easiest if you could meet me here.' That would also be safest, she thought. A quick drink in a nearby bar, then she could plead the pressure of work and return to her office.

'That will be fine,' Matt said.

Helen gave him the address, and ended the call; a touch abruptly, perhaps. She leaned back in her chair, wondering what had possessed her to invite the man for a drink. There were barely enough hours in the day for all the work she had to do. There wasn't room in her life just now for a man, and certainly not for a farmer. He was a horse-breeder. What would she have in common with him?

She reached for her briefcase and took out his letter. Well, they had poetry in common. And he wrote very well. As she did. Why, once she had even thought of herself as a writer, rather than an editor. But that was a long time ago. She hit the call button to the outer office.

'Richard, please alert security that Matt Redmond will be coming here to see me later this evening.'

'Yes, Helen.' Even her perfect assistant couldn't hide the surprise in his voice. 'Do you want me to stay so I can show him up? Or in case you need — '

'No, Richard. I'll be fine.' She closed the intercom, knowing full well that Richard would be almost bursting with curiosity. She wasn't going to enlighten him. Even if she did, he would find it hard to believe that she was having a drink . . . it wasn't a date . . . with one of the farmers. It was hard enough for Helen herself to believe.

Shaking her head, she turned her attention back to the folder on the desk in front of her. She still could not commit to running the expose. If she was going to hold that story, she had to find another front page.

The rest of the afternoon took an aeon to pass, as Helen struggled with the front pages of her next editions. Greg Anderson and his romance with his mail-order girl might just be strong enough for a lead. She had a couple of other options too, but not one was as strong as the story that lay inside the brown folder.

She sent Richard home shortly before six. He seemed reluctant to go, and Helen knew that was curiosity, rather than any great need or desire to stay at his desk. She was not going to have him, or anyone else on her staff, witness the meeting with Matt Redmond. It wasn't that she was embarrassed. Or was she? Her first strictly social encounter since she took this job was with a farmer she had met only by mail. Put like that, it did seem . . . She was ready to call Matt and cancel. Plead the pressures of work. If he was only in town for the day, he'd have to go home and that would be that.

If only she had his mobile phone number!

As if called by the thought, the phone on her desk rang.

'Yes?'

'It's security here, Miss Woodley. There's a Mr Matt Redmond to see you. I was told you are expecting him.'

'That's right,' Helen replied. 'Thank you. Please show him where to go. Don't bother coming up with him. I'll meet him at the elevator.'

'Yes, Miss Woodley.'

Helen got to her feet. If she hurried, there might just be time to go to the bathroom. She should at least comb her hair. Perhaps put on some fresh lipstick. But even as she reached for her bag, she knew that there wasn't time. For the first time in years, she was facing a meeting feeling less than prepared!

The man who stepped from the elevator was tall and well built under a jacket that was not particularly fashionable yet suited him perfectly. He waited as the door closed behind him, looking around with casual interest. Everything about him said he was a man who did not belong in a glass and chrome office amid the city's high-rise towers. He needed sunlight and open spaces. Yet he didn't look awkward or out of place. At most, he appeared mildly curious about the workings of the world he had just stepped into. He had the look of a man who was totally comfortable with himself, whatever his surroundings.

He hadn't seen her yet. Helen straightened her skirt and opened the door of her office. She fixed her most professional smile on her face and walked briskly over to him. The eyes that turned towards her were a deep brown, and the smile that tilted the corners of his mouth was more honest than her own.

'Mr Redmond.' Helen extended her hand. 'It's nice to meet you.'

He didn't so much shake her offered hand as simply hold it for a few seconds while he looked at her with a directness that she found slightly disconcerting.

'Please call me Matt.'

Without the distorting effect of the telephone, his voice held a rich timbre that was very appealing. Helen found herself wondering if he ever sang. His eyes were a deep brown, set in a face tanned by long hours in the sun. He gave every impression of being a strong man. Not just physically, although clearly that was the case. He also seemed to emanate a vast inner strength.

'Helen,' she responded automatically as she gently disengaged her hand. 'Thank you for coming to the office.' She hated the way she sounded — like she was greeting a business contact.

'It was no bother,' Matt replied. 'And we have made my daughter very happy.'

Helen smiled, remembering the teenage glee echoing down the phone. 'I heard her cheering.'

'She thinks I need to get out more.'

'It's in the nature of teenage girls to worry about their fathers.'

'In this case she might be right.'

'What about her mother?' Helen asked before she could stop herself.

'She lives in Queensland. Ali spends some time with her, but mostly she's been with me at Willaring since the divorce.' Matt paused and looked around the office. 'What about you? I imagine this takes up more of your time than it should.'

'I love my job,' Helen responded automatically, then paused. 'You're right. It does take up a lot of time.' Even to her own ears, her voice was tinged with regret. That surprised her. The conversation had become personal very quickly.

'I'll just be a moment,' she said almost brusquely, 'then we can go somewhere for a drink.'

'That sounds fine.'

Helen's office was very large, as befitted the

editor of a national magazine. Matt moved to the window, to gaze out at her spectacular view of Sydney Harbour and the bridge. Helen walked to her desk, wondering why it was that the office suddenly seemed quite small. Even when she was standing on the far side of her desk, Matt still seemed very close.

'That's a very impressive view,' he said.

'One of the perks of the job.' Helen dismissed it as she started to shut down her computer. Then she stopped and looked out the window. Her voice was softer when she spoke again. 'It is lovely, isn't it? I confess, I do love it.'

'I have to wonder,' Matt continued, 'how it would have looked to the first settlers two hundred years ago. Before the trees were cut down. Before the high-rise buildings and the bridge.'

'I think that would have been pretty impressive too,' Helen said, smiling at the thought. 'But I'd miss the bridge. I've become rather fond of that big chunk of metal.' She tossed some papers in her open briefcase.

Matt turned to watch her. Helen suddenly became very self-conscious. She was wearing a black suit with a short tight skirt and a white silk top. Her shoes were black and elegant. She knew she looked good, but found herself wishing she was dressed differently. Like someone who wasn't trying quite so hard.

'Is it everything you wanted it to be?' Matt asked.

'I'm sorry?' Helen didn't understand.

'All this.' Matt indicated their surroundings. 'I imagine you had to work pretty hard to get here. Is it everything you wanted it to be?'

She was about to automatically answer yes, then looked at the folder in her hand. Inside lay the photos that were causing her so much concern. If the job was everything she wanted it to be, why was she having all this trouble with one story?

'Matt, can I ask your opinion about something?' The words were out before she could stop them.

'Of course.'

She shouldn't discuss the story with anyone. And certainly not with this man whom she barely knew. But she was going to.

'I am having trouble deciding what to do with this.' She held up the folder.

'What is it?' he asked.

'A story. A very big one. A scoop that will send my sales figures rocketing.'

'But there's a problem?'

'Not really a problem.' Helen took a deep

breath. 'It's about two famous men. Their relationship.'

'I see.' Matt showed surprisingly little curiosity. Helen waited for him to ask who the men were. He didn't.

'It will destroy their families.' Helen hurried on, aware of Matt's eyes on her face. 'Possibly their careers.'

'Why would you want to do that?' Matt seemed genuinely puzzled.

'I don't.' That was the truth. 'But it is a big scoop. It's my job to make the magazine successful. This would do that.'

'But at what cost?'

'They're celebrities. They make money out of their public personas. That makes them fair game.' Even as she said it, Helen realised how cold it sounded. She also wondered if she really believed it.

Matt's voice was very gentle. 'I didn't mean the cost to them.'

The words struck too close to home for comfort. Helen had no answer. Avoiding his eyes, she tossed the file in her drawer and turned the key in the lock.

Helen led the way to the elevator. The door opened almost instantly. Neither spoke on the short journey to the ground floor. Helen's mind was racing. What should she do now? She had planned to take Matt to a nearby bar. It was small and trendy and noisy. The perfect place for a casual drink with someone she probably wouldn't see again. But she had quickly changed her mind. Matt was not one of the trendy media types she normally spent time with. It had been a very long time since she spent an evening with someone for strictly personal reasons.

'Where would you like to go?' she asked as they stepped through the sliding glass doors from the gleaming marble foyer into the street.

Matt looked around at the crowded footpath and the street jammed with cars.

'Somewhere quiet. It would be nice to talk. Somewhere with a view of the water, or perhaps some fresh air.'

Helen hesitated. She knew suddenly exactly where she wanted to take him. She hadn't been there in such a long time. It probably was not what he was expecting, but she had a feeling he'd like it. 'I know just the place.'

'Do we need a reservation, or does your job help you get the best tables?'

Helen held out an arm to flag a taxi. 'Where we're going, there's always room for anyone.'

Following Helen's softly spoken instructions, the cab took them over the great iron bridge, and immediately turned off the freeway to curve back past the huge stone pylons. It pulled to the kerb directly under the broad bridge span.

Matt looked up as he got out of the cab. From above came the muted rumble of traffic on the bridge approaches.

'Not what I expected,' he said.

'It gets better. Follow me.'

Enjoying the moment, Helen led Matt to a row of shops that lined the narrow road leading down towards the water. The takeaway fish and chip shop was next to the bottle shop. Dispatching Matt to buy beer, she ordered dinner.

Together they walked down the long grassy slope of the park, listening to the muted sound of the traffic on the bridge. They settled on a wooden bench with a view across the water towards the opera house. It was getting dark, and the lights on the opera house gave it a radiant glow. Lights from ferries and other small boats moved slowly on the dark water, and on the other side of the harbour the high-rise buildings of the city centre provided a spectacular backdrop.

'This should be old newspaper,' Matt said as he unwrapped the fish and chips.

'That's against the law these days,' Helen said, 'but I think it tasted better when it came wrapped in yesterday's news.'

As they ate, they drank a beer each and talked about inconsequential things. The view. The bridge and opera house. Helen couldn't remember when she had last talked for so long about things unrelated to her work.

They were not alone under the bridge. Nearby, a young woman was sitting bent over a book under one of the park lights. She had obviously been reading as the sun went down, and was loath to stop. Finally she pulled her mobile phone from her pocket and opened it to shed just a little more light on her final pages. She closed the book with a sigh of satisfaction and left, unaware that behind her, Matt and Helen were watching.

'That used to be me,' Helen said, 'but I didn't have a mobile phone. I used a torch.'

'You like to read?'

'I don't get much time to read just for pleasure these days.' As she spoke, Helen felt a twinge of regret. 'As a child, I read anything I could get my hands on. Went through a lot of batteries for that torch, reading under the bedclothes after my mother had turned the light out.'

Matt chuckled. 'Me too. I still read a lot, but now I can leave the light on.'

'Being a grown-up has its advantages.'

'Yes, it does.'

'At one point, I was going to be a writer,' Helen mused softly.

'Isn't that what you are? A journalist?'

'I suppose,' Helen said doubtfully. 'I really wanted to be a novelist. Write the great Australian novel. I even started a couple of books.'

'What happened?'

'The world got in the way. Dreams don't pay the bills.'

'You shouldn't be so willing to give up on your dreams,' Matt said.

'Did you ever have a dream that didn't turn out the way you hoped?' she asked quietly.

'I think everyone does,' Matt replied. 'But that doesn't mean you have to give up on it. Not if it's important.'

As the words fell into the gentle darkness, Helen knew he was right. She had given up her dreams. Was it too late now to find them again?

'You read poetry,' she said at last. 'That's a little unusual.'

'Is it?' Matt asked. 'You read poetry too, so perhaps we are both a little unusual.'

Helen had no answer for that, or for the long, slow smile that accompanied the words. It didn't seem to matter. They sat for a while longer in comfortable silence.

At last Matt looked at his watch. 'I hate to end this, but I should go. I have a long drive ahead of me.'

'Are you driving all the way back to Scone tonight?'

'That's a farmer's life. I have to be there to feed and work the horses in the morning.'

Reluctantly Helen got to her feet. They walked in silence up the hill to the road.

'I'll get you a taxi,' Matt offered.

'There's no need. I live just over there.' Helen indicated her apartment building.

'So that's how you knew where to get the best dinner in Sydney,' he joked.

'I haven't done this in far too long,' Helen said. 'Thank you for giving me an excuse.'

'You are most welcome. But you know, you shouldn't need an excuse.'

A taxi turned into the street and slowed hopefully as it approached them. Matt held up his hand.

'I have to go back across the bridge to pick up my car.' He turned to Helen, and took her hand in his as he looked down at her and smiled. 'Thank you for a lovely evening.'

'I enjoyed it too,' Helen said. Matt's dark eyes held hers, and she felt a sudden warmth curl through her body. She smiled slowly. Matt leaned down and touched his lips to her cheek.

'Good night,' he said softly, and got into the taxi.

As Helen watched the tail lights vanish around the corner, she felt something very like disappointment. Or perhaps regret. She touched her cheek, which still felt warm from Matt's kiss. In the glamorous world of the media, a kiss on the cheek was much like a handshake. A mere greeting, often devoid of any real meaning. But those few moments when Matt's lips had brushed her cheek had been very different. A brief touch had stirred something in her. And when he held her hand . . . Helen suddenly realised that it had been a very long time since another human being had touched her with any real meaning. It was strange . . . but good. She looked up the road, but the taxi had vanished. It was too late to call Matt back.

Helen turned her feet towards home. Maybe it was a good thing that he was gone without any talk of meeting again. There wasn't room for a man like Matt in her life. When she was younger, she might have dreamed of a home and a family, but that dream had been shattered by her own mistakes a long time ago. She might regret its loss, but despite what Matt had said, that was one dream she could never get back.

* * *

She had exaggerated his attraction. She must have. He was handsome, certainly. And nice. He had great eyes, and an even better smile. But . . .

Leigh looked at the face staring back at her from the mirror. The Leigh Kenyon in the mirror had blow-dried her hair. She was wearing mascara. And a skirt. Again! This wasn't her. This was some other person. Some other person who was about to check her watch for the umpteenth time in the last half-hour. Some other person who was as excited as a schoolgirl on her first date.

It was almost noon. Ian Rudd should be here any minute.

He had called her on Tuesday. And again on Thursday. Yesterday he had rung, he said, just to confirm their lunch date. As if she would have forgotten!

Leigh took one last look at her reflection and left the bedroom, vowing that she would not change her clothes again. She had done it twice already this morning. The evidence was strewn all over her bed.

She turned around and went right back into the bedroom. She picked up the discarded clothes and hung them back inside the wardrobe. Not that Ian was going to get anywhere near her bedroom. It was just lunch. He wasn't even staying for dinner. He'd explained on the phone that he had to get back to Sydney for some family occasion. Staying the night wasn't even a consideration. Leigh tidied the bedroom anyway. It was something to do while she waited. If she didn't do something, she would probably change her clothes again.

In disgust, she slammed the wardrobe door and walked out of the room. Resisting the urge to stand by the window and stare down the drive, she went into the kitchen. When she had invited Ian for Saturday lunch, she hadn't really thought about what they'd eat. Maybe a quick sandwich, after which she would show him around her place. Talk to him about her plans for bottling her own vintage and having a cellar door for sales to visitors. It wasn't a date. Not really. More a meeting of colleagues.

Why then had she prepared a feast? Prawns with avocado. Grilled asparagus with flavoured oil and parmesan shavings. Green salad with a balsamic dressing. Home-made bread. A selection of unusual cheeses and a bowl of fresh fruit salad that would feed a family of four for a week.

She had excused herself by saying that it was fun to plan a meal for two after so many months . . . years of cooking for one. Eating alone was fine for a night, or a week. After a month, or a year, she hated it. Since her rat of an ex-fiancé had left, Leigh had eaten alone. Worked alone. Slept alone. That brought her back again to Ian Rudd, and how devastatingly attractive she found him. Even his voice on the phone had sent a warm shiver through her. Maybe her body was trying to tell her something. Maybe that was why she was wearing this white cotton gypsy skirt and strappy top. She wanted . . .

Leigh marched out of the kitchen and headed for the bedroom, and the safety of blue jeans and a T-shirt. She would find some shoes, too. Bare feet seemed too casual . . . too intimate. She didn't make it. Through the living room window, she saw a car pull up next to the house.

It was too late now.

Not wanting to appear too eager, Leigh stayed where she was, and watched through the window as Ian slipped from behind the wheel of his car. He was casually but well dressed in dark trousers and an open-necked linen shirt. He stretched to relieve the cramp of the long drive, and the soft fabric of his shirt curved suggestively around his stomach and shoulders.

Leigh felt a churning low in her stomach.

She couldn't fool herself any longer. All her resolutions dropped away. She wasn't sure which frightened her more — the thought that he might feel the same compelling attraction that set her every nerve jangling, or the fear that he did not. She couldn't hide any longer. She walked to her front door, took one long, steadying breath, and opened it.

Ian was collecting a rucksack from the back seat. His face broke into a smile when he turned and saw her. He crossed the yard and took the stairs to her veranda in two long, quick strides.

'Hi, Leigh.' He leaned over to kiss her cheek, in the manner of a friend or acquaintance.

'So you found the place all right?' she asked, turning to lead the way indoors, hoping to hide the colour that had risen in her face at the gentle brush of his lips on her skin, and the merest hint of a subtle aftershave.

'It was easy,' Ian replied.

The living room seemed ridiculously small with him in it. He was just standing there, close to her, smiling at her with those lovely blue eyes. She could simply reach out her hand and touch him . . .

'Would you like something to drink . . .

coffee or something?' she asked quickly.

'No, I'm fine, thanks. But . . . ' He opened the rucksack and produced a bottle of white wine. 'I brought this — for lunch.'

'Thank you.'

'And this — for you.' He offered her a book.

She took it. *Women of Wine*, she read on the front cover. *The Rise of Women in the Global Wine Industry*.

'I thought you might find it interesting.'

'I'm sure I will. Thank you.'

She smiled up into those blue eyes again, and for a year or two they simply looked at each other.

'I think maybe that wine should go in the fridge,' Ian suggested at last.

'Of course. I don't know where my head is.' She turned and bolted into the kitchen. She did know where her head was . . . she just didn't want Ian to know.

'That looks nice.'

Leigh almost dropped the bottle of wine. She carefully set it in the fridge and turned to see Ian leaning against the doorway of her large open kitchen-cum-dining-area, studying the table she had set for lunch with a crisp white tablecloth and a small vase of red and yellow roses.

'Do you want to eat now?' she asked, fully

aware that it was barely midday.

'To be honest, after the drive I've done I'd like to stretch my legs a bit. You did promise me a tour.'

'That's a good idea.'

Trying not to feel like she was running away from the disturbingly charged atmosphere of her kitchen, Leigh opened the back door and slipped her bare feet into some flat sandals. They walked into the bright sunlight, and she felt able to breathe again.

'Where would you like to start?' she asked.

Ian smiled a long, slow smile. 'Wherever you like.'

The double meaning was impossible to miss. Leigh's heart seemed to skip a beat. Once she might have flirted right back at him. Perhaps even initiated something. But that was a long time ago. Before Jack Thorne had walked into then out of her life, leaving her confidence in tatters. Before she had locked away her dream of love and resigned herself to living alone. She no longer knew how to respond to the invitation.

'Let's go this way.' She reluctantly turned away. 'I can show you the vines — and the new area I'm planning to plant later this year.'

'Lead on.' If he had been expecting something else, his voice didn't show it.

They walked in silence along the path that

led up the slope from the house to the nearest vines. Leigh was very conscious of the breeze that teased the hem of her skirt, threatening any minute to fling the soft fabric high enough to cause her to die of embarrassment. How she wished she had changed into those blue jeans!

'I see you've pretty much finished the pruning,' Ian said as they drew level with the first row of vines.

'Yes.' This was safer ground. Talking about grape vines couldn't be considered flirting. It wasn't the slightest bit sexy. 'Now all I can do is wait and hope for the right weather.'

'Did you do all this yourself?' Ian sounded impressed.

'Yes.' Leigh didn't want to explain that her former fiancé had been part of this. Before he won that lottery. Before he was rich. Before he cheated. 'The previous owner was getting old. Some of it was a bit run-down when . . . when I first bought the place. It's been a lot of work bringing it back.'

'You've done a great job. Why did you decide to be a winegrower?'

'It's a silly story really,' Leigh said. 'I had a friend at school who was from an Italian family. They drank a lot of wine. My friend and I used to sneak behind the house and try it.'

Beside her Ian chuckled.

'One day her grandfather caught us. He had been a wine maker back in Italy. He gave us a lecture about wine, and began to teach us how to appreciate it, which mostly involved not stealing it.'

Ian laughed at the image she painted. He had a nice laugh. Warm and genuine.

'Anyway,' Leigh continued, 'that got me started. The more I learned, the more wine fascinated me . . . and this is where I ended up. All I have to do now is make it work.'

'I don't doubt that you will.'

Leigh felt a warm glow at the admiration in his voice.

They walked a little further along the pathway, discussing the growing of grapes and the making of wine, until they reached the crest of the hill.

'Are those your vines too?' Ian asked, indicating the lines of vines on the next hillside.

'No.' Leigh fought to keep the bitterness out of her voice. 'They are part of the Bradford Winery.'

'They make good wine,' Ian observed.

'Yes.' Leigh was hesitant. 'I saw the truck at your shop last week. Is Simon Bradford a friend of yours?'

'We do business together, of course.' Ian

turned to face her, his brow creased. 'From the tone of your voice, I gather you have some problem with him.'

'Well . . . ' Leigh took a firmer grasp of herself. 'Simon and I have . . . history. That's all.'

'Oh?' Ian sounded intrigued.

'It's nothing. We get on all right as neighbours. He buys grapes from me. That's all there is. Really.'

'Okay.' Ian smiled broadly. 'Let's forget him, then. You mentioned the other day that you were planting a new area. Where is that?'

'It's this way,' said Leigh, eager to change the subject.

She led the way to the slope where her new trellises stretched taut and shiny in the sunlight, waiting for vines.

'You did this alone?' Ian asked.

'Yes.'

'Wow. I am impressed.' He turned to face her. 'You are really quite something.'

He was standing very close, smiling down at her. Leigh closed her eyes to acknowledge the compliment, but as she opened them, she was looking for more than just his admiration of her skill with a pair of fencing pliers.

Ian reached out and took one of her hands in his, turning it over so he could look at the palm. He ran his fingers over the fading marks of the blisters caused by her labours. For one long moment, it seemed he would lift it to his lips.

He didn't. He cupped her hand in his for a few seconds longer, then released it.

'I have an idea,' he said, moving slightly away from her.

Leigh also stepped away a pace, feeling almost bereft. 'An idea for what?'

'Planting vines is hard work.'

'I know that.'

'But I know how to make it easier. I have a wine-tasting group at the retail store. I think some of them would love to try their hands at planting.'

'I don't understand.'

A smile spread across his face as he explained. 'You could invite the wine club to participate in the planting. I've seen it done before. They plant the vines. It would be a good idea to have some sort of newsletter or web page where they can follow the progress of the plot. When you make the first vintage using those grapes, we can do a special tasting. They can be the first offered the chance to buy the wine — and they will buy it, because they have an interest in it.'

It was a brilliant idea, and Ian's enthusiasm was catching.

'I could even involve them in naming the

plot — or the vintage,' Leigh said.

'Great idea.'

'And I'd get all that hard labour for free.'

Ian laughed out loud. 'Leigh — you're not quite getting it. These people will pay for the privilege of planting your vines!'

'Pay?'

'That's right. To be part of the birth of a new vintage would be a special outing. A bus from Sydney. Lunch up here. They could taste and buy some wine — yours if you have some; if not, I'll arrange something.'

'I can provide lunch,' Leigh enthused. 'I'm working on my cellar door now. Come and see.'

It seemed so natural to take his hand to lead him back towards the buildings. He showed no surprise, or desire to break the touch.

Leigh led the way to a square brick building set to one side of the larger winery buildings. She ignored the large glass doors at the front, and made for a smaller door round the back.

'This was the former owner's sale outlet,' she explained as she led the way into the building, groping for the light switch. 'It hasn't been used for a few years. But it won't take too much work to get it ready.'

The large room was almost empty. A few

dusty chairs and tables were stacked in one corner, and a large wooden bar dominated the far end. Part of a kitchen was visible through the open door behind the bar.

'I will paint it. I was hoping to get some local artists to display work on the walls. The bar needs work, but . . . '

Ian was standing close beside her, his face alive with pleasure and excitement. It was so good to share her dreams with someone who understood.

'It will be great,' he told her, and he dropped an arm across her shoulders in a friendly hug.

The touch of his warm skin on her bare shoulders drove all thoughts of wine and tour buses from her mind. She kept her eyes firmly fixed on the other side of the room, afraid of what would happen if she turned to look at the man standing beside her. He began to move his arm — not away from her, but in a gentle caress. His fingers stroked her shoulder, then trailed softly and sensuously across her back. Leigh could barely breathe. She moved her head as he ran his fingers gently along her neck. At last she turned to face him.

His blue eyes were no longer shining with enthusiasm or laughter. They glowed with far deeper feelings. He stepped close to her, gently cupping her face in his hands. He kissed her.

It was a long, slow, warm kiss that reached down into the part of her that had been frozen for so long. Leigh wasn't conscious of moving; she only knew that her hands were on Ian, revelling in the feel of firm muscles under the soft linen shirt. In response to her touch, he pulled her closer, his hands sliding down to her waist.

After a long, long time, Ian broke the kiss and stepped away. He took a deep breath, and smiled down at her. Leigh's own ragged breathing slowly eased, and she smiled back.

Ian took one of her hands, and this time he did kiss it.

'Now,' his voice was husky, 'you promised me lunch. I think that might be a good idea about now.'

Leigh nodded, too shaky yet to trust her voice, and led the way out of the room.

As they walked back towards the house, Ian talked about the winery, her plans for the future, the possibility of working together. Leigh thought she gave appropriate answers, but her mind was racing down a different path.

What was she doing? She barely knew him. What was worse, they had met through a magazine. She had only spent a couple of hours in his company; why then was she wishing he didn't have to return to Sydney that night? She had not shared her bed since her former fiancé had left. Yes, there were times when she had felt the frustration, when her body had cried out for a lover's touch. But that was no reason to fall into bed with the first handsome man she met.

Except he wasn't. She had met other handsome men, some of whom had made their interest very clear. Had she just been after a good-looking man to sleep with, there was always Simon Bradford right next door. No, she was searching for something else, and maybe, just maybe, Ian could give her that. He was different in some way she couldn't define, and she wasn't certain she even wanted to fight the feelings he aroused in her. It was so good to feel like a woman again.

Back inside the house, Leigh set about serving lunch, while Ian opened the wine. She was standing at the bench, preparing a dressing for the asparagus, when she became aware that he was standing very close behind her. He put his hands on her shoulders, and kissed her gently on the back of the neck.

'I have a confession to make,' he said in her ear.

'What's that?' She didn't turn around, but her hands stilled in their task.

'I'm afraid I lied to you.'

For one horrible instant, Leigh froze, her hands shaking as she waited for the next words.

'I don't have to go back to Sydney tonight,' Ian continued. 'I just said that so I would have an excuse . . . if things didn't go so well.'

Leigh turned to look into his eyes. She liked what she saw there.

'As lies go,' she said, 'I think I can live with that one.'

'And?'

Leigh raised herself up on the tip of her toes, and kissed him.

* * *

'Are you certain you want to do this? Really, really certain?'

The words echoed in Donna's head, too loud to be drowned out by the steady drone of the aeroplane engine.

Was she certain? Donna looked out the window of the tiny plane. On all sides, an endless red plain stretched to the horizon. The land appeared lifeless, apart from a few scrubby trees that seemed small and stunted in the vast emptiness. Low hills and outcrops of jagged red rock were the only features in the immense landscape. To eyes accustomed to the greens and yellows of the English countryside, this was a desert. It seemed beyond imagining that anyone could live here. Yet somewhere out there was a place called River Downs Station. Donna wondered about that name, in a land devoid of even a hint of water. Even more she wondered about Peter Nichols, the man who would be waiting for her at the end of this flight. Peter Nichols and two small children for whom she had ventured into this inhospitable place.

Really, really certain?

No. She wasn't certain.

After that initial letter, she had exchanged e-mails with Peter. He had told her all about his children and his home. He had barely mentioned his late wife beyond saying she had died in a tragic accident. Between the crisp lines of text on the computer screen, Donna had easily read the great love he had for his children and for the hundreds of square miles of near desert called River Downs. His words had evoked in her a desire to meet the twins and to experience the wild beauty that he described so well.

As for Peter himself? Donna was less certain about him. His e-mails might have given some small insight into his character, but was that enough to decide if there could be a relationship between them? Donna didn't know. She did know that she had to try. If she didn't, she would spend the rest of her life wondering what might have been. She had handed in her resignation the next day and begun planning her journey.

Peter's e-mails had talked about isolation, but she hadn't realised just what he meant until today. The maps she studied hadn't prepared her for the journey that had begun early this morning beside the blue Pacific Ocean, and was continuing now, some seven hours later, over the parched outback. The energy and enthusiasm with which she had started out had been slowly eroded by distance and heat. Four hours in a commercial jet took her to Darwin, and her first taste of the draining heat and humidity of the north. Somehow she had found her way from the modern terminal to a corrugated-iron shed at the far side of the airport to meet a cheerful man in shorts and a peaked cap. He described himself as a bush pilot. Donna had never heard the expression before, but it didn't take long for her to figure out just what he meant. He had strapped her into the co-pilot's seat of his single-engine Cessna, explaining that the passenger seats had been removed to make way for the cargo that filled the back of the plane. Then he had launched the aircraft into the brilliant blue sky. It was noisy, making talking difficult, but that didn't bother Donna. She was content to simply stare from the window at the passing vista, watching the shadow cast by the plane as it moved across land that gradually turned from green to brown to red.

About two hours into the flight, the plane suddenly dipped and began to descend at a rapid rate.

'Are we there?' she queried the pilot.

'River Downs? No. This is just one of my stops. I have to drop off mail and supplies. It won't take long.'

'I see.'

'River Downs is still a couple of hundred kilometres further south.'

A couple of hundred kilometres further? Into the desert? Donna found that impossible to imagine. She leaned towards the window, hoping to get a glimpse of the homestead below. It might give her some idea of what was waiting for her at the end of her long journey.

She saw nothing but red earth and scrubby trees. No buildings and nothing that looked even vaguely like an airport. Still the aircraft dropped lower. Donna wasn't afraid of flying. She had crossed half the world by air. But as the plane banked sharply, she felt a twinge of fear. They were dropping, and there was still no sign of an airstrip.

The pilot pointed at something on the ground. Donna looked again. He couldn't mean that thin straight line of bare dirt! That wasn't an airstrip. Was it? Her knuckles turned white from gripping the seat as the plane bucked and bounced its way to the ground, rolling to a stop at one end of the airstrip. She climbed gladly out of the plane for a few minutes of fresh air and solid ground.

A man was waiting for them beside a battered old utility. Like the bush pilot, his skin was brown and cracked from exposure to the sun, and like the pilot, he was a man of few words.

'G'day.' He touched a finger to his dusty hat as he acknowledged Donna.

'Hello.' Donna smiled politely, conscious of the man's curious gaze.

She could hardly believe how hot it was standing in the sun. She could almost feel her skin burning. The golden tan she had acquired on the coast wouldn't protect her from burning under this scorching sun. She had always liked her thick wavy hair, but now she lifted the dark mass away from the back of her neck, wishing she could cut it all off and let some cooling air touch her skin. But the air wasn't cooling at all. Her skin was just as hot where it was exposed to the air as where it was covered by her clothes. She could feel a trickle of sweat running down the centre of her back, and her forehead was already damp. She had thought that a light cotton skirt and top would be appropriate in the heat, but nothing would help in this furnace. In fact, she was beginning to wish she was wearing something that protected more of her skin from the sun.

'Not often you see tourists out here,' the man continued, his curiosity obviously getting the better of his reticence.

'She's heading for River Downs,' the pilot volunteered.

'Yeah? What for?'

Donna opened her mouth to answer, then realised she had no answer to give. She could hardly tell this stranger that she was answering a magazine ad for a wife. That made her sound like a mail-order bride — and she wasn't. Was she? If not that, then how did she explain her journey of thousands of kilometres to be with a man she had never met? She muttered something about a holiday from England, and walked away saying she needed to stretch her legs after the cramped conditions in the plane. That excused her from further questions.

Fifteen minutes later, she climbed back

into the plane, sweating profusely from her minimal exercise and still no closer to finding an answer for the man in the dusty hat — or for herself. The question gnawed at her, and the rest of the journey passed with her attention turned inward. The pilot's voice, when he spoke again, came as something of a shock.

'I'm just going to buzz the homestead.'

'Sorry?'

'I'm going to buzz the homestead to let them know you're here. I'm sure they'll want to send out a welcoming committee.' He smiled at her.

'We're here?'

'Yep. Look out the window. You'll get a pretty good view.'

Donna strained against the restricting seatbelt. The plane was rapidly losing height, dropping towards a small cluster of buildings. She saw what she thought was the main house. There were a couple of large buildings that would be barns. Sheds, she corrected herself. They don't have barns in the outback. They have sheds. Several dirt tracks led to and from the buildings, and she could see some yards and wooden fences. There was not much else. Even around the house, everything was brown. There was not even a hint of green lawn.

Donna had read as much as she could about the Northern Territory in the days before her departure, but that hadn't prepared her for the reality that lay below her. No words could describe the vast emptiness of the outback. Intellectually she had known where she was going, and what she would encounter, but this was beyond her wildest imagining. She felt a rising panic. She couldn't do this. She most especially could not do this based on a few e-mails from a man she had never met. What had she been thinking?

The fear that caused her hand to clench on the seatbelt around her hips had nothing to do with the lurching of the plane as the Cessna banked sharply. The buildings vanished under the wing. A few seconds later, a thin line of red dirt appeared and the Cessna dropped steeply towards the airstrip. It seemed but a moment before they pulled up beside a small iron shed, and the engine sputtered into silence.

It took the greatest of efforts for Donna to remove her seatbelt and climb down the narrow aircraft steps. Her subconscious seemed to think that if she stayed on board, she could fly away from whatever waited for her. She could go back to her cosy flat by the beach. Or even back to her homeland on the other side of the globe — where the land was green and people were everywhere.

The heat hit her like a hammer blow. Even this late in the day, the sun was almost painful as it seared her skin. The pilot seemed not to notice as he hefted her bags from the back of the plane. He carried them a few metres and set them down in the shade beside a large open tin shed, which sheltered a plane not unlike his own. Without a word, he returned to unload some boxes of cargo.

Shading her eyes against the sun's glare, Donna turned slowly around. It felt as if she and the pilot were the only living souls for a thousand kilometres. The scrubby bush around them was still. Not even the smallest breeze disturbed the dust-covered tufts of thin brown grass. The airstrip boasted two buildings. There was the small tin shed with a closed door and no windows, and the aircraft hangar, if the simple structure could be given such a grand name. In the distance, she heard the lonely cry of a crow. The only other sound was the ticking of the cooling Cessna engine.

The pilot was beside her.

'I'd like to wait and catch up with Peter,' he said, 'but I haven't got time. Say 'hi' for me.'

'You're leaving?' The words came out as a horrified whisper.

'I've got to keep going. I've got two more

stops to make before it gets dark.'

'But . . . ' Donna was unable to form words. The only other person in this wilderness was about to go. To leave her . . . alone.

'Don't worry,' the pilot said cheerily. 'Someone will be here soon.'

He climbed back up the stairs and with a final wave vanished inside the plane.

The Cessna engine roared into life. Donna caught a whiff of aviation gas. Then the small plane was rolling down the airstrip, raising a cloud of red dust. It lifted a few metres off the ground, then roared upwards. In a few seconds, it was a diminishing dot against the blue sky. A minute later, even the sound of its engines had faded.

Donna stood rooted to the spot, watching the dust slowly settle back to the ground.

'What if no one comes?' she whispered, but there was nobody to hear her.

5

'Damn it!'

Peter gripped the wheel tightly as the old ute hit a hole in the track and bounced wildly. He was driving far too fast, but he needed to get to the airstrip quickly. The mail plane had been early, and he was late. He cursed the broken generator that had delayed him. The new nanny had been sitting out there for well over an hour. The poor girl must think he had forgotten her.

The ute bounced through the open gateway and on to the dirt strip. Peter drove straight down towards the tin sheds where the girl should be waiting. Stirring up a cloud of red dust as his vehicle slid to a stop, he got out and looked around.

Two suitcases sat on the earth near the hangar; but of the girl there was no sign.

'Hello!' he called. Perhaps she had gone looking for a cooler spot to wait.

When a minute passed with no answer, Peter reached through the open window of the vehicle and honked the horn several times. His only answer was the startled cry of a nearby crow.

Where had she gone?

Squinting against the sun's glare, he turned slowly around. Surely she could not have gone far. His sister had told him the new nanny was from a shccp propcrty. Shc must know the ways of the outback. She would not be stupid enough to set out on foot. Would she?

Peter didn't wear a watch. He didn't need one. After a lifetime on the land, he knew exactly how many hours of light there were in any day. Out here, that was all that mattered. He glanced at the sun. There was a little over an hour of daylight left. He hefted the suitcases into the back of the ute. Then he raised his hands to his mouth, and gave a piercing cry.

'Coo-ee!'

His only answer was a deathly silence.

Peter slipped behind the wheel of the ute and started the engine, his mind racing as he dropped it into gear and headed back the way he had come. He hadn't seen her on the track, so she must be going cross-country. She would have seen the homestead from the plane. It didn't look too far to walk. He knew better. Distance was deceptive from the air. Anyone trying that walk faced some pretty rough going, the possibility of some dangerous wildlife, and above all the heat. She would be carrying a water bottle. Or would she? Peter suspected that any fool who would attempt such a walk in unknown country might just be stupid enough to do it without water. The thought caused him to press a little harder on the accelerator.

Jenny and the kids came racing out of the house as he pulled up outside.

'Where is she?' the twins demanded in unison.

'I don't know,' Peter said. 'She's walking.'

The twins fell silent. Even at their age they knew what that meant.

'Chris. Sara. I want you both to stay here with your Aunt Jenny.' Peter turned to his sister. 'Where's Ken?'

Before Jenny could answer, her husband appeared in the doorway behind her. 'What's wrong?'

'I think she's walking from the strip.'

'Cross-country?'

'Yes.'

'Are you going to take the plane up?'

'No time. It'll be dark soon.'

Without another word, Ken reached back into the house for his hat.

'Jenny, if we're not back by dark, I want all the lights on. Here. Down the yards. The shed. Anything she might see.'

Jenny nodded, her face creased with concern.

Peter turned away and strode towards the machinery shed. Ken was a few steps ahead of him when they reached the motorcycles. They would be better off with horses. On horseback they might hear her call. But the horses were somewhere in the home paddock, and there wasn't time to get them.

'I'll work south from the fence,' Peter told Ken. 'You go north.'

'It's only about an hour since the plane came. She can't have gone far.'

The two men started their machines and headed off without another word. They were both thinking the same thing. You didn't have to go far in this country to get lost. If she set out in the wrong direction, she would find only scrub and red rock. No buildings. No people. And the only tracks were made by cattle. If she followed one of those, it could lead her further and further from safety. Without water, and if she wasn't wearing a hat, she wouldn't last long. If she fainted, they could pass within a few metres of her and never know it.

They had to find her before darkness made their task impossible.

As he searched, Peter's attention was divided between keeping his bike upright in the rough going, and scanning the scrub for some glimpse of the girl. He was trying to strike the difficult balance between the need to hurry, and the risk of going too fast and missing her. He had no idea what she was wearing, but could only hope it was white. If she was dressed in dark green or brown, he'd never see her. In his mind, he tried to visualise River Downs as the girl had seen it from the air. Peter had flown in and out of the station hundreds of times. He knew every inch of the place like the back of his hand. But how would a stranger see it?

The plane would have approached from the north, placing the homestead to the left side of the strip. But if the pilot had done a circuit, the girl could have become confused. When she set off to walk, she might have gone totally in the wrong direction. If she had turned to the west, there was nothing in front of her but desert. If she ever got that far.

Peter stuck to his set search area for another fifteen minutes and found nothing. The shadows were lengthening, and darkness wasn't far away. He was becoming more certain than ever that she had turned west, away from the homestead. He stopped the bike and took a long, slow breath. If he was wrong, it would make matters worse. But he wasn't wrong. He was sure of it.

He turned the bike and twisted the throttle. The machine leaped forward, too fast for safety on the rough ground. Peter didn't care. He knew where she was — at least, he thought he did.

* * *

Her head bowed against the heat, Donna resolutely put one foot in front of the other, because to do otherwise would be to admit she had made a terrible mistake. She should have reached the homestead by now. Or a fence. Or some sign of human life. The buildings that she had seen from the plane were no great distance from the airstrip. Back home in England, she would have walked that in half an hour, without raising a sweat. She was certainly sweating now. She had hoped the temperature would drop as the sun went down — but that wasn't the case. It was just going to get dark, and she didn't want to think about that.

One foot in front of the other. Her feet were killing her. Back home, a night out in high heels could make her feet ache. But not like this. This was a whole other world of pain. This was the agony of feet sorely abused, and blisters that were beginning to bleed. Her soft flat pumps were no protection against the jagged rocks and the scorching sand.

Donna forced herself to take another step. Why had she answered the letter in that stupid magazine? Why had she made this journey? And why hadn't Peter Nichols been waiting for her at the airstrip? If he was serious about starting some sort of a relationship, then the least he could have done was be there to meet her. What sort of a man would drag her all this way, and then leave her to fend for herself in the outback? Donna bit back any stray thoughts that perhaps she had made matters worse by setting off on her own. She wrapped her anger around her like a protective shield and kept walking.

A distant sound cut though her haze of exhaustion and pain and stopped her in her tracks. It sounded like an engine.

'Hello!' she shouted. 'Hello.'

Her voice cracked on the second call. Her throat was too dry to try again.

She was walking along the sandy bottom of a dry river bed. She had stumbled down into it what seemed like hours ago and had not been able to muster the energy to climb back out. The bottom of the gully also offered fairly easy going, compared to the rough ground above. And surely the gully would lead to a main river. There would be water, and where there was water, there would be people.

Donna looked again at the sides of the gully. If someone was out there looking for her, she had to climb out. The stone and earth banks looked as high as Mount Everest, and as difficult to climb. She took a deep breath and staggered to the bank and looked up. It wasn't that high — maybe two metres — but it was steep. A few large trees lined the gully, and exposed roots criss-crossed the bank. There were rocks that would offer a foothold. Donna wrapped her fingers around a root and began to pull herself upwards. Her feet scrabbled for purchase on the slippery bank. Her left foot found a solid rock. Ignoring the pain as a sharp edge cut through her shoe, she reached above her head for another root. Slowly she pulled herself upwards until she heaved her head and shoulders over the edge. Panting with exertion she looked up — and froze.

Something was moving through the long grass just in front of her. Slow and sinuous and deadly.

'Don't move!'

The low, forceful voice came from her left. Donna remained frozen.

The snake hesitated, and raised its long, narrow head. Donna could see its forked tongue flickering.

A loud explosion shattered the silence.

Donna screamed and flinched. She started to lose her footing on the bank and began to fall backwards.

A strong hand caught her wrist.

'I've got you,' the deep voice said, and Donna was pulled upwards. A second hand grabbed her around the waist and pulled her away from the bloodied snake, writhing in its death throes.

'It's all right. You're safe now.'

Instinctively, Donna turned towards the tall man at her side and buried her face in his chest, sobbing in shock and fear and exhaustion. The man said nothing. He just held her.

As her breathing began to return to normal, she pulled away. She brushed the tears from her face and looked up into a pair of brown eyes and the same tanned face that had smiled at her from the pages of the magazine.

'You're Peter Nichols.'

'I assume you are Donna Boyd.'

Donna nodded, and for a few seconds they just stood there. He was a full head taller than her, and looked every inch the bushman. His skin was tanned, his body lean and hard inside the blue jeans and checked cotton shirt. One hand held a shotgun, carried with ease by his side. He wasn't wearing a hat, but his dark hair was flattened against his head as if he had only just removed one. Donna was suddenly very aware of her own sweat-streaked clothes, sore feet and what must be a very dirty face. This wasn't how she had imagined their first meeting.

'Why weren't you at the airstrip?' It wasn't the best way to start their acquaintance, but the question was out before she could stop it.

'I am sorry.' He looked as if he meant it. 'I was fixing a generator. And the plane was early. I did come for you, but you were gone. You shouldn't have tried to walk.'

'I know that now.' Donna looked down at the dead snake and shuddered. 'Was that dangerous?'

'Very. King brown. There are a lot of them around the gully.'

She shuddered again.

'Let's get you out of here.'

Donna followed slowly, her eyes casting about for slithering movements among the rocks.

'It's all right. The sound of the shotgun will have driven any others off.'

Donna wasn't taking any chances.

A motorcycle stood not far away. Peter slid the shotgun back into a holster strapped to the side of the bike. A rectangular canvas bag with a metal handle was clipped to the handlebars. He removed it and passed it to Donna.

It took a few moments for her to realise what it was. She unscrewed the cap, and lifted the water bag over her head. She struggled for a few seconds as the canvas sagged in her hands, the liquid inside it sloshing about, then she grasped the bag by the handle and tilted it. The water that gushed out over her face was warm, but it was the best thing she had ever tasted. Coughing a little as some of it went up her nose, she took several deep swallows, then she handed the water bag back and watched as Peter skilfully guided a steady stream into his own mouth, drinking his fill without spilling a drop.

He returned the water bag to its place on the bike, and recovered the dusty hat that had been left on the seat. With the ease of much practice, he swung one leg over the bike.

'Have you ridden one of these before?'

Donna shook her head.

'It's easy. Hop on behind me.'

Donna stepped up to the bike. It might be easy for him, with his long legs and blue jeans. It wasn't quite that easy for her with her cotton skirt. Cautiously she swung one leg over the bike and slid on to the leather seat.

'Rest your feet there.' Peter pointed. 'Now

move closer to me.'

She slid forward till only a few centimetres separated them.

'No. All the way. Put your arms around my waist.'

She moved closer again, her skirt sliding up to expose her thighs. Peter didn't seem to notice and Donna was too tired to care.

'Hold tight.'

With a sudden movement, he kicked the motorcycle into life. The roar of the engine blotted out all other sound. After a quick glance to make sure Donna was all right, he twisted the throttle and the machine jumped forward.

At first they were travelling through trackless scrub, so their progress was slow. After about ten minutes they reached a narrow track, and Peter revved the engine. The bike sped through the bush. Donna sat with her arms wrapped tightly around Peter's waist and her cheek pressed in between his shoulder blades. The noise and the speed isolated her from everything but the warm, firm feel of his body, the touch of his cotton shirt against her cheek, and his rich, earthy smell.

Donna didn't know how long that ride lasted. She only knew a sense of profound relief when Peter stopped the bike in front of a large wooden house. She hopped off the machine, glad of the feel of solid earth under her feet. Slowly she turned around to take in her surroundings. Her new home, if that was what it was to be, was like nothing she had ever seen before.

The cluster of buildings covered an area larger than the farm where she had grown up. There were several huge tin sheds, which seemed to house a diverse collection of machinery. Wooden stock yards stood empty. Several smaller outbuildings gave no hint as to their use. The house was huge. Made of timber, it was surrounded by a wide veranda. The roof of the house was made of the same corrugated metal as the walls of the sheds. The edges curved low over the veranda, and she realised this would create a shady respite from the heat of the sun. Huge round tanks of the same metal sat beside the house and the sheds. Water tanks, she supposed. Water would be an issue out here. The tall iron skeleton of what she knew to be the windmill on a water bore stood beside the house.

Her reading had covered all this, just as it had described the heat and isolation. But reading wasn't the same as being here. It felt like she was stranded on some distant planet, and the man standing beside her was as alien as the surroundings. Her head started to spin.

'Are you all right?'

Peter's arms went back around her shoulders at the same moment as the door of the house crashed open and two small balls of concerned noise hurtled across the dust towards them.

'Dad. You found her.'

'Is she all right?'

'Where was she?'

'Enough!' Peter's voice cut through the clamour. 'Miss Boyd is tired. She needs to sit quietly for a bit. Inside!'

The twins turned and ran back to hold the door open. Peter led Donna into a brightly lit kitchen, where a pregnant woman was waiting beside a table covered with the remnants of a meal.

'I'm so glad you're all right.' The woman took Donna's hands and led her to a chair. 'We were worried. I'm Jenny, Peter's sister.'

'We thought you were dead!' the small boy announced.

'No we did not,' Peter told his son. 'We just thought she might be lost.'

'Were you lost?' a quiet voice asked.

Donna looked at the concerned young face. This must be Sara. Despite her own shock and exhaustion, Donna's heart went out to the little girl who had already seen too much loss in her life.

'Well, Sara, I tried to walk from the airstrip, but I went the wrong way.'

'Okay, kids. Give Miss Boyd time to catch her breath.' Peter turned to Donna. 'You'll have to excuse them. They have been so excited about getting a new nanny.'

'A new . . . nanny?' Donna thought she must have misheard.

'I'm sure Jenny told you she and her husband are leaving. The kids were afraid they would be left here with just me.' He smiled broadly and ruffled his son's hair.

'And the new jackaroo,' the boy reminded him. 'When are you going to hire him, Dad?'

'I'm their new nanny?' Donna looked about wildly. Something was wrong. In his e-mails, Peter had said nothing about being a nanny. They had talked about the twins, certainly. But Donna had thought she was coming to join Peter's family — not work for him.

'I think — ' She started to speak, but Peter's sister caught her eye and shook her head slowly. There was some message in her eyes, but Donna was unable to read what it was. She was totally confused. Something was very wrong. She had travelled thousands of kilometres under false pretences. Now she was stranded in the back of nowhere with the man who had tricked her.

After such a long and difficult day, it was too much for Donna to take in. She started to rise from her chair, and the room began to spin. In a flash, Jenny had an arm around her.

'Come with me and I'll show you to your room. You need to rest for a while. We can talk about all this later.' Jenny guided her from the kitchen, down a long hallway and into a bedroom.

'Donna,' she said as she seated both of them on the bed, 'it's all my fault.'

'I don't understand,' Donna said.

'This mix-up. It was me. I'll explain it all to you later. When Peter and the twins aren't around.'

'I should tell them I'm not a nanny.'

'No. Please. Not now,' Jenny pleaded with her. 'I will fix it. Honestly. Just don't tell them yet.'

In the cool quiet of the room, Donna wanted nothing more than to fall back on to that soft bed and sleep for a day or two. She looked long and hard at Jenny. Lines of concern were etched into her pale face. She was perched uncertainly on the edge of the bed, her hand held protectively over her bulge. Donna guessed that there was something Jenny wasn't telling her. But she also felt that she could trust her — at least for now.

'All right,' she whispered. 'But tomorrow we have to tell them everything.'

'We will. I promise. Now, you rest,' Jenny said, backing towards the door.

The last thing Donna heard was the sound of the door closing.

* * *

'You've got to get the temperature of the solder just right,' Greg told Molly as he bent over his workbench. 'Too hot or cold, and it won't work.'

Molly leaned forward for a closer look. In one hand Greg held a pair of small long-nosed pliers; in the other, a soldering torch. In between was a selection of thin silver wires that he had earlier cut and twisted and filed into the shapes he needed. The assurance with which he handled the white-hot flame was fascinating. Molly had come to take photos of him in his workshop, but her camera lay untouched on a chair while she watched him work.

'I've been studying wings,' Greg continued. 'You know, a bird's wing is nothing without its feathers. There are just bones, like our arm bones. It's the feathers that give the wing its shape. Make it beautiful.'

He reached for another piece of wire, and

moved it carefully into position while talking almost to himself 'Now a bat's wing is different, almost like a human hand — with long thin fingers that hold the wing membrane. They are really quite beautiful.'

'You're turning a bat's wing into a piece of jewellery?'

Greg chuckled. 'I guess that doesn't sound very appealing.'

'Maybe to fans of horror films and goth music.'

'Perhaps I'd better come up with a different description.'

Greg carefully put his tools to the side and sat back. He took a magnifying glass to examine the piece in front of him.

Molly leaned closer. A tracery of fine silver lay on the worktop. Greg had shaped a wing that didn't really look like a wing. It was inert, yet something in the lines of the piece gave the impression of speed and flight. It was different from anything she had seen before, and it was beautiful.

'That's lovely,' she said.

'Do you really think so?' Greg's eyes searched her face, as if her opinion was the most important thing in the world to him.

'Yes, I do,' she assured him with total honesty.

He smiled at her, and Molly smiled back.

For a few seconds their eyes locked, then Greg turned back to his work. Without realising it, Molly moved a little closer to him. She liked to watch him work. When he worked, he lost his self-consciousness and doubt. His hands moved with assurance and skill. He had strong, steady hands that were still somehow sensitive to the most subtle changes in the precious metal he was working. She wondered how those hands would feel on her skin. Gentle but strong.

Molly stepped back in shock. What was she thinking? To hide her confusion, she turned to pick up her camera. She put it to her eye, seeing nothing as she fiddled with the lens. She had no place thinking of Greg like that. He was the subject of a shoot. That was all. Telling herself that she was merely touched by his artistry, she took a firm grip on her camera and an even firmer grip on herself.

'Do you mind if I get some shots while you are working?' she asked.

'No. Go right ahead.' Greg didn't look up from his work as he answered.

Molly glanced around, looking at light and angles. She moved to one side and snapped off a couple of quick shots.

As she was lining up another, she noticed the piece of silver on the shelf above the workbench.

'What's that?' she asked.

Greg knew what she meant. He picked it up and placed it gently in her hand. 'It's a piece I made a while back. One of my first cast pieces.'

Molly studied the silver disc and the graceful lines and curves that adorned it. 'It's beautiful.'

'Thanks. It's sort of become my good-luck charm.'

'Does it work?' she asked.

'Maybe.' He flashed her a quick smile and reached out to take the charm from her hand. As he did so, his fingers gently touched her palm. It happened again. That sudden disquieting ache somewhere inside her. Molly wondered if Greg felt it too.

She quickly stepped away and picked up her camera again. She put her eye to the viewfinder and played with the focus.

'How did you get started?' Asking the question would make this seem more like an interview. More like a job. Less intimate.

'Well, my mother died when I was very young.'

'Oh, Greg!'

'In a car crash. It was a long time ago. I don't remember her. Dad didn't keep anything that reminded him of her. But I have a photo. An old black and white one. I used to stare at it for hours as a kid. In the photo, my mother is wearing silver jewellery. A pendant and some earrings. I guess it all started with that.'

Molly zoomed in close on Greg's face as he talked. He was as handsome as any model she had photographed. But more than just his face showed through her lens. His passion for his work spoke to the camera. And also a deep sadness, that she supposed was related to his mother's loss. The shutter clicked as she ran off several quick shots. Not for *Australian Life*. These shots were for Molly.

'When I was at school,' Greg continued, seemingly unaware of the camera's scrutiny, 'I had an art teacher who also made jewellery. Her style was very different to this, but she encouraged me. She taught me what she knew and then helped me find a course at the technical college. Since then, I've just been experimenting.'

'Pretty good experiments,' Molly told him.

Greg put aside his tools and picked up his charm. He looked down at it, turning it over in his hand.

'I've always thought that whatever talent I have for this is a legacy from my mother. I feel close to her when I'm doing this.' He stopped speaking and looked up at Molly. 'I imagine that sounds . . . '

'It sounds fine.'

A moment of silence and mutual understanding was broken by the sound of a voice calling from outside the workshop.

'Greg? Are you in there?'

Molly started almost guiltily at the sound of Jasi's voice.

'Come in, Jasi,' Greg responded.

A blast of sunlight as the door opened heralded Jasi's arrival. The girl was dressed in a light summer skirt and a strapless top. Her blond hair was caught carelessly on top of her head, yet she looked stunningly pretty.

'What are you making?' she asked as she moved to Greg's side.

'It's going to be a brooch,' Greg said as he leaned back to show her the work.

'It looks a bit like a wing,' Jasi said.

'Yes. An angel's wing.' Greg directed the words at Jasi, but he caught Molly's eye as he spoke. Molly smiled at the shared joke, then felt just the smallest twinge of guilt. This was supposed to be about Greg and Jasi.

'It's pretty,' Jasi said.

'Well, thank you.'

Jasi picked up the silver disc that Greg called his lucky charm. She turned it over in the palm of her hand. 'Do you only ever work in silver?' she asked.

'I like silver,' Greg told her. 'I enjoy

working with it. I thought you liked it too. You wear silver jewellery, don't you?'

'Sometimes.' The merest hint of a pout touched Jasi's lips. 'But for something special, I think gold is better. Don't you? I was hoping you might make something for me in gold.'

'Oh. Well . . . I suppose I could try,' Greg said slowly. 'I don't know if it would be any good, though. I'm not practised in working with gold.'

'It will be wonderful.' Jasi carelessly tossed the silver disc on to the bench and hugged Greg.

Molly turned away and pretended to check her camera. She had seen the hurt in Greg's eyes at Jasi's careless dismissal of his prized charm. Molly had also seen him look at Jasi's hand. The girl was not wearing the ring he had given her.

'I thought it might be time you stopped work for a while,' Jasi was saying. 'I've made us some afternoon tea.'

'All right. A break right now would be good.' Greg got to his feet. 'Coming, Molly?'

'You go ahead,' Molly said. 'I want to get a couple of shots of the workshop. I'll be with you in a few minutes.'

'All right.' Greg picked up his charm, and tucked it in the front pocket of his jeans.

Molly watched Greg and Jasi walk back towards the house. The girl slipped her hand into Greg's and smiled up at him. They made a very good-looking couple, but Molly didn't like what she was seeing. In just two days, Jasi seemed to have decided she was here to stay. She was acting as if her future with Greg was already decided. Greg was obviously flattered by her attention. What young man wouldn't be? But Molly wondered if he shared Jasi's certainty about a future together. Greg was very talented, but also very vulnerable in his talent. He needed time and space to develop his art, and Jasi didn't look like the sort of girl who would give it to him. It was none of Molly's business, but she wished Greg hadn't chosen Jasi.

* * *

Greg and Jasi entered the house through the front door. This felt a little strange to Greg. For most of his life he had come in and out through the kitchen. It was Jasi who had changed this. Inside, the dining room table had been set. This too was a change. Greg and his father had eaten at the kitchen table for as long as he could remember. Now the heavy dining room curtains had been thrown back to let the light into the little-used room.

A crisp white tablecloth covered the big wooden table. An etched glass vase sat in the centre of the cloth, some flowers adding colour to the setting.

'This looks great,' Greg said.

'Thank you.' Jasi smiled up at him, her blue eyes shining. 'I hope you don't mind. I explored the cupboards a bit and found all these lovely things that look like they haven't been used for ages.'

Jasi was right. They hadn't been used in a very long time. In fact, Greg couldn't remember the blue-patterned plates or the vase ever being used. They might even have been his mother's things, left gathering dust since her death. He squeezed Jasi's hand. She was trying so hard to do everything right. He liked the way she brightened his home, and the Lord knew it needed brightening. She didn't understand his art, or his need to fashion beautiful things in silver, but that didn't matter. He liked the way she looked and smelled and he liked the way she made him feel, when she looked up at him with those blue eyes. That was exactly what he needed.

On an impulse, Greg put his arms around her. He pulled her close and kissed her, a long, gentle kiss.

As they pulled apart, Jasi reached up a

gentle finger to stroke his cheek. She smiled from under her eyelashes. 'I'll go and get the tea.'

Greg nodded, and as he did so, he saw Molly standing in the doorway. Unaware, Jasi headed for the kitchen, leaving Greg and Molly standing on either side of the dining room. Greg felt distinctly uncomfortable and just a little bit guilty about kissing Jasi when just a few minutes ago he and Molly had . . . Had what? Molly was simply here to take photographs. If they had felt something when their hands touched, it was just the artists in them connecting. He shouldn't feel bad just because Molly saw him kiss Jasi. After all, Jasi was the girl he had chosen.

The ringing of the telephone came as a great relief. Greg almost bolted for the office. He answered the call automatically, his mind still struggling with unexpected confusion. Two words restored his focus.

'I'm sorry,' he said. 'You're from *Australian Life*?'

'That's right,' replied the woman on the end of the line. 'The magazine is planning to run the story about you and Jasi in a couple of weeks. Helen Woodley, the editor, has assigned me to write a piece that will go with Molly's pictures.'

'Oh.'

'I won't be coming up there. I will just need to spend some time on the phone with you, and with Jasi. Ask you some questions . . . '

'I see.'

'That's all right, I hope?'

'Yes. Yes. It's fine.' Greg realised he sounded like an idiot. This was what he had agreed to. It was just sooner than he thought. He and Jasi had only started to get to know each other. He hadn't even told her about his father. 'I was just hoping . . . '

'Yes?' The woman on the phone waited.

'Could we have a couple more days?' Greg asked. 'I mean, well, things are going really well. And if we had just a little bit more time . . . well, it might make a better story.'

'Oh, really? Is there something . . . ' The woman on the phone let the question hang.

Greg knew what she was asking. He knew he was leading her on. But he needed time.

'Well, I can't promise anything . . . ' he said, hating the teasing sound in his own voice.

'I understand,' the reporter said. 'We can possibly postpone it to another issue. I can call back in two or three days, if that will help.'

'Yes. That would be good.' Greg felt a surge of relief.

'All right. Molly was scheduled to fly back tomorrow, but maybe she can stay an extra day or two — if you think it would be worth her while.'

It hadn't occurred to Greg that as soon as the story was done, Molly would leave. He suddenly realised that he did not want to see her walk out of his life.

'I think it would be good if she stayed,' he said with complete honesty.

* * *

Helen had been driving for almost four hours when she saw the mailbox. Well, the white oil drum that served as a mailbox. The important thing was the sign. Someone had written 'Willaring Downs' in dark green paint along the side of the drum. As she turned off the highway on to the curved gravel drive, Helen found herself wishing the journey was just a little bit longer. Up until now, she had been so focused finding her way that she hadn't given any thought to what might happen when she arrived. Now she wanted just a few more minutes to prepare herself.

She still wasn't quite sure why she had said yes to Matt Redmond. She had been absurdly pleased when he called three days before, to thank her for their evening watching the harbour lights from underneath the bridge. At first she had assumed the call was just old-fashioned courtesy. Good manners. The invitation to spend the weekend at his Scone horse stud had come as a surprise, but not as much of a surprise as her immediate acceptance. She didn't have the time or the inclination for any relationship, let alone with some horse farmer who lived two hundred and fifty kilometres away. So why did she have this feeling of nervous anticipation in her gut?

The driveway led to a cluster of buildings. To her right was a large house, with a wide shady veranda and a neat lawn. It was well kept, and was guarded by a white picket fence. That fence made her lips twitch in a smile. She would not have thought Matt was a picket fence kind of a guy. The gravel drive led past the house and curved to a cluster of stables and sheds, which, to Helen's inexpert eye, looked as neat and prosperous as the house. She changed down a gear and allowed the car to slow as she looked around her, taking in the line of tall gums by the river, the neatly fenced paddocks with their grazing occupants.

Helen wasn't sure where she should stop. Would Matt be waiting for her at the house? Or would he be at the farm buildings? She knew enough about life on the land to realise that this appearance of prosperity was achieved only by long hours of backbreaking work.

She decided to park near the house, and got out of the car into a world that was entirely different to her own. Apart from the ticking of her cooling engine, there was no sound of traffic. No sound of another human being. She could hear birds calling, the wind in the gum trees and even the occasional sound of nearby horses. The late-afternoon sunlight glowed softly on the white-painted buildings. It was at once both peaceful and yet full of life. She closed her eyes and breathed deeply, enjoying the warmth of the sun and the taste of fresh, clean air. Even the smell of the earth was good.

When she opened her eyes, Matt was standing a few feet away, watching her.

'Oh.' She almost blushed, feeling like a schoolgirl caught doing something against the rules. 'Matt. I was just . . . '

'I know,' Matt said, smiling. 'It gets me too. Every time I come back from the city. The sounds. The smells.'

'It's wonderful,' Helen breathed.

Matt nodded, then, after the smallest hesitation, stepped close and kissed her cheek. 'Welcome,' he said.

Helen looked up into his face and felt her nervousness drop away. 'It's good to be here,' she said.

She followed him as he carried her overnight bag into the house. She smiled as he removed his hat, then opened the door for her to enter ahead of him. She was unused to such courtesy, and decided she rather liked it.

The inside of the house was spacious and tidy, but it was not, as Helen had expected, totally masculine in feel. While Matt took her bag through to the guest room, she looked around her. Packed bookshelves lined the living room walls. Some shelves held silver trophies, no doubt won by the horses in the framed photographs that sat next to them. There were deep, comfortable chairs and bright curtains. That must be his daughter's influence, Helen decided. A large aboriginal painting hung on one wall. Through an archway, she glimpsed a light, airy kitchen. The house was friendly and welcoming. She could easily feel at home here.

'Are you tired after the drive?' Matt asked as he came back into the room. 'Would you like a cup of tea, or a cold drink?'

'No thank you,' Helen replied. 'To be honest, after almost four hours sitting in the car, what I'd really like is to stretch my legs.'

'Well, you're in the right place,' Matt said.

'I'll give you a tour.'

He led the way from the house towards the stables and yards. As they walked, Helen was content to let him do the talking, listening with intcrcst as he told her about the history of the property, about the horses she saw grazing in the paddocks, about his plans for them. He obviously had a deep and abiding love for the land and the animals. Watching him, Helen couldn't help but think back to the photograph that had launched the Farmer Needs a Wife campaign in *Australian Life*. The pretty blue-eyed boy with the streaked blond hair was as far from Matt Redmond as it was possible to get. The photo was a fraud. The man walking beside her was the reality — a reality she found very attractive.

It was getting dark when they came back inside the house. Helen found the bathroom, and after freshening up, she emerged to find Matt in the final stages of preparing dinner.

'Pasta and salad?' she joked. 'I had you down as a steak and potatoes sort of a man.'

'Just you wait for tomorrow night,' Matt said as he set the plate in front of her, and reached for a bottle of wine.

They touched the rims of their glasses.

'So tell me,' Matt asked as they ate. 'What do you think of all this?'

'It's just lovely,' Helen said. 'It must be a lot of hard work.'

'It is,' Matt replied. 'But the work isn't so hard when you love what you're doing.'

'I imagine it isn't.' Helen spoke quietly.

'Don't you feel the same way about your job? I should think that to rise to your level, you must be good at it. I always thought that only people who love what they do are really good at it.'

'I used to love it,' Helen said. 'When I was a young reporter, I was going to change the world. Unmask the bad guys. Fight the important fights.'

'What changed?'

'I guess I did,' Helen said. 'I grew up. I learned that it's not easy to change the world. Or even your little corner of it. So now I'm finding wives for lonely farmers.' She smiled to take any sting out of the words. 'And revealing the personal secrets of the rich and famous. It's not quite the dream.'

'Have you had a tough week?'

'They're all tough,' Helen said.

'Have you decided what to do about that story? The one about the movie stars that you mentioned?'

'No,' Helen said. 'If my boss knew I was sitting on something like that, he'd kill me. If he knew I'd told you, I'd probably lose my job. I probably deserve to.'

'Why *did* you tell me?'

'I think I was trying to impress you.' Helen smiled up at Matt.

He shook his head. 'That wasn't what impressed me,' he said.

Helen could see the invitation in his eyes. Her insides were churning, and she suspected that this time she really was blushing. This was the moment to let him know that she was equally impressed. But it had been so long, and she wasn't sure how to. If this was a movie, she thought, someone would knock on the door, or the phone would ring to rescue me.

She took a deep breath. She had to say something, but had no idea what it should be.

The phone rang.

* * *

Matt was very tempted to let it just ring. He didn't want this evening interrupted. But the machine's clamour was insistent. He shrugged and stood up.

'Hi, Dad.'

'Ali?' His daughter's voice should not have come as such a surprise.

'Who else?'

'How are you? How's school? Studying hard?'

'It's great, Dad. Stop worrying.' Ali laughed down the phone.

Matt glanced over at Helen and grinned ruefully. Helen smiled and, taking her wine glass, stepped outside on to the veranda to give him privacy.

'Dad,' Ali was saying, 'I was thinking about coming home tomorrow.'

'Coming home?'

'Yes. A friend is driving up that way, and there are some things I need to pick up. He would drop me off about lunchtime and pick me up again on Sunday.'

Matt was silent. This was a complication he hadn't expected.

'Dad?'

'Ali, you know I'd love to see you, but . . . '

'Dad,' Ali's voice was concerned, 'is there something wrong?'

'No,' Matt hastened to assure her. 'It's just that I have . . . plans this weekend.'

'Plans?'

'Yes, plans.' He wasn't sure what to tell his daughter; he didn't want to keep secrets from her. But there was nothing to tell. Yet. And if the weekend didn't work out . . .

'Dad! It's her, isn't it? You're seeing Helen Woodley again!'

Matt moved the phone back from his ear, glad that Helen had stepped outside. His daughter sometimes got a bit loud when she was excited.

'Well . . . Yes. I am.' He wasn't going to lie to Ali, but he wasn't going to volunteer any more information than he absolutely had to.

'That's great! When? Where? Tell me everything.'

'No. I will not tell you everything.' Matt chuckled down the phone. 'And if you want to come home this weekend, of course you can. I'd love to see you.'

'Ah — that means she's coming there!'

'Ali!'

'She's there already, isn't she? Oh my God! Did I interrupt something? Dad . . . '

'Enough!'

'All right, Dad. I'll go away now. And don't worry. I won't suddenly arrive on the doorstep. But I will expect you to call on Monday and tell me everything.'

'I will do no such thing.'

When Matt joined Helen on the veranda a few minutes later, he sat down next to her on the top step. 'I'm sorry about that.'

'Your daughter?'

'Yes. She wanted to come up tomorrow to pick up a few things, but has decided she doesn't need the stuff as urgently as she thought.'

'You told her I was here, and she didn't

want to be a third wheel?'

'She figured it out for herself, but that was the general idea.'

'Your daughter is a very smart young woman.'

'Yes, she is.' Matt didn't try to hide the pride in his voice. 'You never had children?'

In the silence that followed, he glanced sideways. Helen was staring at the wine glass in her hands, swirling the last remnants of her drink slowly around the bottom of it.

'I'm sorry,' he said. 'I don't mean to pry. If you . . . '

'No,' Helen assured him. 'It's just one of those questions that people ask all the time. I always say that things didn't quite work out that way.'

'I see.' Matt could sense there was a lot more to it than that.

'Well,' Helen said brightly. 'As you cooked dinner, shall I see if I can make us some coffee?'

'Thank you,' Matt said. 'I could come and show you where everything is.'

'No. You wait here. I'll yell if I can't find anything.' Helen vanished through the door.

Matt stayed where he was, looking out towards the moonlit stables and yards. He wanted to kick himself. He had obviously touched a raw nerve. And just as Helen was starting to relax. During the past few hours, he had felt the tension slipping away from her, but now it was back. He hated to see those tight lines around her beautiful eyes.

Helen Woodley was the most attractive woman Matt had met in a long, long time. It wasn't just that she was sexy — although she most certainly was, particularly in the tight jeans she was wearing. It wasn't just that she was intelligent, although Matt suspected she was probably smarter than he was. Nor was it just her sense of humour. Or the way her mouth moved when she smiled. It was all of those things and something else. Matt sensed something deep inside Helen that drew him to her. He didn't know what it was, but he did know he wanted to get closer to her. A lot closer.

'How do you take your coffee?' Helen's voice floated back through the open door.

'Black. No sugar.'

She sounded better, he thought. Helen might be the editor of a national magazine, with a reputation for toughness, but he could tell that part of her was vulnerable and even a little scared of the sort of intimacy he had in mind. He would wait. He had a feeling it would be worth it.

'Do you have plans for tomorrow?' Helen asked brightly as she sat back down beside him.

'I do.' Matt was willing to match her mood. 'Do you ride?'

Helen laughed. 'I did. But that was a long time ago, when I wore pigtails and a school uniform.'

Matt almost spilled his coffee.

'Well then,' he said, ignoring the image his overactive imagination threw at him, 'tomorrow I will introduce you to Granny.'

'Granny?'

'She's a horse. I'll explain tomorrow. I think the two of you will get on just fine.'

'I don't have any riding boots,' Helen pointed out.

'That's no excuse. I'll bet Ali's will fit you just fine. Are you game?' Matt turned to look Helen full in the face. She was smiling and he knew they were past whatever memory had come back to haunt her.

'I am.'

They talked a little more as they drank their coffee, but it wasn't long before Matt caught Helen trying to stifle a yawn. He glanced at his watch. It wasn't quite ten o'clock.

'It's all this fresh air,' he told her. 'Why don't you get some sleep?'

'I think I will turn in,' Helen said sheepishly. 'Good night.'

'Good night.' Matt kissed her cheek again, and opened the door for her to pass inside.

* * *

Leigh could see her reflection in the glass door and she liked what she saw. Earlier in the week, she had set out in search of something to wear this evening. A classic black cocktail dress, with shoestring straps and a jacket. She never found it. At the very first shop she fell in love with a strapless golden dress that hugged her body like a lover. The dress was simplicity itself: shiny satin the colour of ripening wheat and embossed with tiny tulips. A smattering of sequins glinted on the satin belt and on the gossamer-thin wrap covering her shoulders. Her carefully painted toenails peeped out from beneath the diamante straps of shoes with heels so high she risked her ankles with every step.

It was young and fun and oh so very sexy. Leigh loved it. She loved the way she looked. She loved the way she felt and she loved the way Ian could barely keep his hands off her. She felt a delicious tingle of anticipation.

Leigh could hardly believe the luck that had made her choose Ian from the dozens of replies to her letter in *Australian Life*. He had turned her life around. Turned *her* around. The woman reflected in the glass door was no longer the bitter workaholic of two weeks before. The old Leigh Kenyon had struggled to go it alone after being abandoned by a faithless fiancé. Now she was Cinderella, about to go to the ball. And this year, she would have her prince at her side. No more raised eyebrows from those who had heard the story of Jack Thorne's betrayal. No more pitying glances from the likes of Simon Bradford.

Tonight was her night.

Ian appeared, walking back from the car park. He looked particularly handsome in his dinner jacket. But then he looked good in everything he wore — or didn't wear. Leigh almost blushed at the direction her thoughts suddenly took. The previous weekend, Ian had stayed not only Saturday but Sunday night as well. Leigh hadn't been with a man since Jack had left, and Ian seemed to have awakened a part of her that had been lying dormant for far too long. They had made love, and slept in each other's arms, and she had awakened to a new world. She had no idea how one weekend could have changed so much, but as Ian slipped his arm around her to lead her through into the hotel, she knew that she wanted it to continue.

The ballroom was a delight. Balloons and streamers hung from the ceiling, moving gently as if keeping time to the music played by the band on the stage at the far end of the room. The tables were covered with starched white cloth and gleaming silver — with vine leaves and bunches of grapes forming colourful centrepieces. Around the tables, at the bar and on the dance floor, colour swirled as people greeted each other with smiles and laughter.

'This looks great,' Ian said, smiling down at her.

'Doesn't it,' Leigh agreed.

'I think champagne is in order, don't you?'

The bar was crowded. Leigh waited as Ian made his way through the crush, pausing as he did to greet friends and acquaintances, many of whom were also known to Leigh. She felt a deep glow of happiness. She and Ian shared so much. Their work. A sense of humour. And as for physical compatibility . . . She felt herself blushing at the thought.

'Leigh, you look wonderful.'

The deep voice so close to her ear made her jump. She turned to find Simon Bradford standing close beside her.

'Hello, Simon,' she said, stepping as far back as the crowd would allow.

Simon didn't say anything more for a few moments as he looked at her, his eyes moving slowly from her face, down the length of her body to those red toenails, then back again.

Leigh felt a sudden shock — almost as if he had actually touched her.

'You look . . . amazing.' He seemed to be struggling for words.

'Thank you.' He looked pretty fine too, she thought. But then he would. He was the annoyingly perfect Simon Bradford. And for some reason, tonight he was even more annoying, with that disconcerting way he was looking at her, admiration on his face.

'Well, Simon.' Ian's voice was a most welcome sound.

'Ian.' Simon reached out to shake his hand. 'I was just telling Leigh how wonderful she looks.'

'She certainly does.' As he spoke, Ian handed Leigh her glass of champagne, then slid a hand around her waist, and pulled her towards him. Leigh saw Simon's smile fade just a little, and she stepped closer to Ian. Simon looked slightly taken aback by the sign of intimacy. Leigh felt a small glow of triumph.

'I've been looking forward to this evening,' Ian continued. 'An appropriate end to a good season.'

'Yes, it was a good year.' Simon's response seemed automatic and disinterested. 'If you'll excuse me, Tania is looking for me.'

Leigh watched him move through the

crowd to where his girlfriend was waiting. Tania was wearing an emerald-green designer gown that set off her height and curves to perfection. She looked every inch the model, and quite spectacular.

'You know, she can't hold a candle to you.' Ian's voice was soft in her ear. 'There's not a man in this room who doesn't envy me at this moment — and that includes Simon Bradford.'

Leigh looked up into Ian's handsome face. The curve of his smile and the light in his eyes showed he meant every word. She reached up with her free hand and grabbed hold of the front of his jacket, tugged gently to pull him towards her, and kissed him.

'Are you sure you want to stay?' Ian teased. 'We could just go home and . . . '

'No,' Leigh responded with a laugh. 'I want to talk to people, and laugh and dance . . . '

'Then you shall.' Ian took her hand and guided her into the throng of people.

They were still greeting mutual friends when they were asked to take their seats for dinner. Each of the large round tables was numbered and set for ten people. Leigh was just settling into her chair when she spotted Simon Bradford and his girlfriend heading towards her.

'Oh no!' she whispered.

'What is it?' Ian asked, then followed her gaze. 'You really don't like Simon, do you?'

'I hate him.' Leigh's vehemence surprised even herself.

'Why?'

'It's a long story,' Leigh said.

'We can always change tables,' Ian offered.

Leigh squeezed his hand. Simon and Tania had stopped to speak to someone. There was time for them to move without making it too obvious. She was about to say yes, then changed her mind.

'No,' she said firmly. 'There's no need.'

There wasn't any longer. Her fiancé's betrayal, and Simon Bradford's part in it, was a long time ago. It was well past time she moved on. Ian was beside her, his face full of concern . . . and something else. If not love, at least the beginnings of something very like it. She could handle Simon Bradford now.

'Are you sure?' Ian asked.

'Very sure.'

Simon and Tania were moving again. Simon nodded at Leigh and Ian, and moved past to sit at the next table. Despite her new-found self-assurance, Leigh was glad. She didn't want even the smallest shadow to spoil this night.

The dinner was excellent. It began with delicate Parma ham and melon, followed by salmon and asparagus. Wine and conversation flowed freely around the table, with Ian always there smiling at Leigh, flirting with her outrageously. She even allowed herself to sample the white chocolate mousse. She decided that a good day's work in the vineyard would ensure the lovely gold dress fitted next time she wanted to wear it.

Dinner gave way to speeches. The outgoing association president said a few words. So did the incoming president. But as after-dinner speeches went, they were remarkably short. Then came the dancing. Ian pulled Leigh on to the floor, taking advantage of the slow rhythm of the music to draw her close. Leigh didn't argue. She let her body melt against his as his arms went around her.

'Thank God for the music,' he whispered in her ear.

'Why?'

'Because it was killing me, sitting at the table with you, unable to do this . . . ' He lowered his head and brushed his lips gently against her ear. 'Or this.' The hand cradling her lower back moved across her waist in a teasing caress, pulling her close against his lower body so she had no doubt as to where his thoughts were leading.

She should tell him to stop. Warn him that they were in public. But she didn't care. She slid her hand off his shoulder, inside his jacket, to lay the palm against his chest. Through the soft fabric of his shirt, she would swear she could feel his heart beating. It must be the wine, she thought, or there's something in the air, but she felt like she was floating in his arms.

A few minutes more, and the band switched to a faster number. Ian did not let her go.

'You know, this *is* a hotel,' he whispered, running one finger ever so softly over the soft skin of her bare shoulders.

Leigh looked up into his handsome face, seeing the desire there. Her whole body felt as if it was glowing. This was her night. Tonight she could be and do anything and everything she wanted. And at this moment, there was nothing she wanted more than to make passionate love with the man holding her.

'They won't have a room,' she said. 'They would have been booked out days ago.'

'They were.' Ian pulled a key from his pocket. 'All they had left was the bridal suite. I hope that's all right.'

Leigh nodded. Ian pulled her close and, oblivious to the people around them, he kissed her long and slow.

'Just give me a moment,' Leigh almost

gasped as he let her go.

'Don't be too long.'

Leigh's knees were shaking as she walked back to the table. She collected her bag and wrap and headed for the ladies' room. Once inside, she barely recognised the woman who looked back at her from the mirror. She wasn't vain. She knew that she was an attractive woman. But the person who gazed back at her now was more than attractive. In her sexy dress, her eyes sparkling and face glowing, the woman in the mirror was beautiful. Leigh could not remember a time when she had ever been happier.

The sound of the door opening caused her to look away from the mirror, straight into the eyes of Simon Bradford's girlfriend Tania.

'Hi, Leigh.'

Leigh didn't know Tania well. She had come into Simon's life fairly recently, well after the time that Leigh and her fiancé had been friends with their neighbour. Well after the time that Jack Thorne had betrayed her. She couldn't hold that against the model, who seemed nice.

'That's a lovely outfit,' Tania continued.

'Well, thank you.' Leigh smiled. 'Nothing much compared to that designer number you're wearing, though.'

'Don't you believe it,' Tania said as she

checked her flawless make-up. 'Every man in the room has noticed you this evening.'

'Thank you,' Leigh said politely, beginning to wonder how she could escape without seeming rude. Ian was waiting.

'Your date is gorgeous. Did he answer your letter to that magazine?'

Leigh was taken aback by the question. 'Well . . . yes, he did. I didn't realise you knew about that.'

'I read a lot of magazines.' Tania smiled. 'It goes with the job. We were very surprised when we saw your photo.'

'We . . . ?'

'Simon and I.'

'Oh.'

'You did very well.' Tania smiled.

Leigh couldn't stop the smile. 'Yes. Yes, I did.'

Both women were laughing in a friendly fashion as they left the bathroom. Leigh looked about for Ian. He was standing in a corner of the room, half hidden by the band members, who were taking a break. Leigh headed eagerly towards him.

'I don't think that's any of your business.' Ian sounded angry.

Leigh stopped mid-stride. Who could he be talking to?

'Do you expect to sleep with her tonight?'

Leigh recognised the second voice at the same instant that she saw Simon Bradford step up to confront Ian, his face dark with anger.

'Simon, I said stay out of this.' Ian spoke slowly and clearly. 'It is between Leigh and me.'

Leigh was about to move forward, to stand by Ian's side, but Simon's next words stopped her dead in her tracks.

'You've already slept with her? Haven't you?' The words were hissed as much as they were spoken. 'Damn you. I told you to answer her letter. I didn't tell you to sleep with her!'

The music and laughter faded. The lights dimmed and the room stood still. Leigh's heart stopped beating, and began to crack open.

'You might have started this . . . '

Ian's voice was terribly clear in the silence that had engulfed Leigh's world.

' . . . but that doesn't give you the right to tell me what to do.'

'No . . . ' The word was torn from Leigh's throat.

Both men spun around to face her.

'Leigh . . . ' Ian took a step towards her, his face creased with concern.

She stepped back. 'Tell me it's not true.'

'Leigh, it's not how it sounds.'

'No? Then how is it? Tell me.'

Ian hesitated.

'Don't lie to me, Ian. Whatever else, just don't lie to me. Did you write to me because he told you to?'

'I won't lie. Simon did call me. He told me about your letter in that magazine.' Ian's eyes were fixed on her face as he hurried on. 'But that's all. I swear. When we met, I really felt — '

'Stop. I don't want to hear anything more.' Leigh took a long, slow breath. She felt the earth crumbling beneath her feet.

'Leigh, please listen to me. I understand how you — '

She shook her head. She didn't want to hear what he was saying. He might claim to be telling her the truth, but how could anything be the truth when their very first meeting was based on a lie? Tears welled up in her eyes. She had really thought that this time it would be different. Thought that Ian was different.

Simon spoke. 'Leigh, I just — '

'You bastard!' She turned to her neighbour, anger swirling in to mix with the pain in her heart. 'What gives you the right to interfere in my life?'

'I wasn't trying to interfere. I was — '

'What? Just what were you trying to do,

Simon?' Her anger was her armour as she faced him. 'It's your fault Jack and I split up. Were you feeling guilty? Trying to find a replacement?'

'I don't know what you mean,' Simon said.

'Come on, Leigh. Let's go somewhere and talk.'

She felt Ian's hand on her arm. She flinched and stepped away. Just a short time ago, his touch had made her body sing, but now she just felt soiled.

'Don't touch me. I don't want to see you again. Just leave me alone, both of you.'

Leigh turned. She ignored Tania, who was still standing beside her, a stunned look on her face. Tania wasn't the only one. All around the room, faces were turned towards the small group by the stage. Leigh's anger collapsed to be replaced by humiliation. First the business with Jack Thorne, and now this! She tried to hold back the tears and cling on to her composure, at least until she got out of the room. But she didn't have enough pride left. Halfway to the door, the tears were running uncontrollably down her face. She gave up all pretence at dignity, and fled at a stumbling run.

6

I am sitting in my dingy little office,
where a stingy
Ray of sunlight struggles feebly down
between the houses tall,
And the foetid air and gritty of the dusty,
dirty city
Through the open window floating,
spreads its foulness over all.

The words of the poem wandered through Helen's mind as she sat at her desk. Unlike Clancy's correspondent, her office was far from small or dingy, and her windows didn't open. Her air was temperature-controlled and refreshed by the building's air-conditioners, but still she felt the meaning of Paterson's words. It was Monday morning and she did not want to be sitting here at her desk, working. She wanted to hear *the murmur of the breezes and the river on its bars*.

And as for Clancy of The Overflow — well, Matt Redmond fitted the picture perfectly.

Helen moved cautiously in her chair. She had spent most of Saturday riding with Matt, and was paying the price now. Her legs ached. Her back was stiff, and under the carefully applied make-up, she was sunburned. Despite all that, she felt better than at any time since she had walked into the *Australian Life* offices a year ago. The only frustration that lingered was that nothing had happened with Matt. Well, things had happened. They had ridden horses and laughed and talked about books and poetry and music. He had introduced her to Granny and helped her gain the nervous filly's confidence.

What he had not done was kiss her properly.

Helen didn't understand it. She hadn't done this in a long time, but it was supposed to be like riding a bicycle — once learned, never forgotten. Matt seemed attracted to her. She wondered if she was giving off the wrong signals. Maybe he somehow sensed she was damaged goods. No, she chided herself. Damn it. She wasn't damaged goods. One mistake all those years ago did not define who she was now. She was successful and attractive, and if Matt didn't see her that way, well, that was his problem!

'Helen?'

She looked up. Her assistant was standing in the open doorway, a slight frown on his face.

'Yes, Richard?'

'The editorial meeting — everyone is waiting . . . '

'I'll be right there.'

The pile of potential stories for the magazine's next issue was lying on Helen's desk. The folder with the big scoop about the gay actors was sitting to one side. It was the obvious cover story. Helen looked at it, troubled. Everyone had secrets, including her. How would she feel if the secret she had guarded for all these years was plastered over the front page of some magazine? She made a decision and dropped the folder back in her drawer.

For the first time since taking control of *Australian Life*, Helen had trouble concentrating during the meeting. The stories being touted for the next issue just didn't capture her imagination. They were nowhere near as good as the one locked in her drawer. She couldn't help wondering again what was making her so reluctant to use it. Was she going soft — or maybe developing a conscience? Were her growing feelings for Matt making a hard decision even harder? Or, now that the launch was over, was she simply losing interest in a magazine that she would probably never read if she wasn't working there? Whatever the reason, she wasn't going to run the story. Yet. In the meantime, she still had a magazine to fill.

'What follow-ups have we got for the farmer campaign?' she asked her team.

'I spoke to the canefarmer — Greg Anderson,' one of the writers replied. 'Molly went up to get some pictures. She has some good shots, and we could go with it — but I told him we would hold off.'

'Why?'

'Well, he intimated that maybe something was happening between him and this girl from Melbourne. This might be something. Our first engagement, maybe. It would be a better story if it was.'

Helen was surprised. 'That was fast. Okay. Molly can stay an extra couple of days and we'll see what happens. Any other responses?'

There was one story for the next magazine, but Helen wasn't satisfied with that. 'Make some more calls. I want to keep this going for at least a couple more weeks. What about that woman? The winegrower from the Hunter Valley. I definitely want a follow-up on that one. Someone call her today.'

Helen returned to her office feeling restless. She had compiled a magazine, but it wasn't what it could have been. If she was going to keep her sales figures up, she had to come up with some exciting new stories. The one that sat in her top drawer was just what she needed.

Richard appeared once more in her doorway. 'Helen, Matt Redmond is on the line.'

'I'll take it. Close the door, thanks.'

Richard did as he was instructed, but Helen could see the puzzlement in his expression. How much more confused would he be if he knew about the scoop she was hiding?

'Hello, Matt.'

'Hello.'

Just his voice was enough to bring it all back. The peaceful surroundings, the beautiful scenery, and most importantly, the man himself, with his open smiling eyes and his gentle strength.

'I was going to call you tonight,' she told him. 'I wanted to say thank you for the weekend. I had a wonderful time.'

'So did I.'

Helen knew he meant what he said. There was no artifice to Matt. She had already realised that, above anything else, she could trust him implicitly.

'I hope you don't mind me disturbing you at the office,' Matt continued, 'but it's the only number I have for you.'

'Of course I don't mind, but get a pen and

I'll give you my other numbers.'

'The reason I called,' said Matt, 'is that I am planning to come down later this week. I have some things that Ali wants. I was hoping I might sec you.'

Helen felt a small thrill in her chest. 'I'd love to see you. What day are you coming down?'

A few moments of silence followed. 'Matt?'

'You'vc got me,' he replied, chuckling. 'I can come down almost any day. I thought I'd see what your schedule was first, and make it a day when you are free.'

'Friday is my quietest day,' she said quickly before common sense could take over. 'Maybe I could cook you dinner this time. If you don't have to hurry back to feed the horses . . . '

Silence echoed down the phone, and for a heartbeat, Helen thought she had made a mistake.

'I'll be there,' Matt promised.

A quiet knock on the door forced Helen to end the call, after giving Matt her private numbers.

One of her reporters came in, looking less than happy.

'I called that woman in the Hunter Valley,' the woman said, smiling ruefully. 'I think it's a no-go. Apparently she did go out with someone, who turned out to be a bastard. She sounded pretty upset, so I let her be.'

'All right.'

After the reporter left, Helen reached for her files. Leigh Kenyon was the winegrower's name. She looked quite young and vulnerable in the photo. Helen hoped she was all right. When she devised the campaign, she had never meant anyone to get hurt. Maybe it was Matt's influence, but she was starting to suspect that for some people, her campaign wasn't quite the harmless bit of fun she had planned.

* * *

Rain was drumming on the glass patio doors. Simon stood inside his house, looking out towards his winery. The ground was already soaked. It was Monday. The start of a new week was usually a busy day at his cellar door, but the visitors' car park was almost empty. A single tour bus sat streaming with water as close to the buildings as it could park. He recognised the operator's logo painted on the side, and smiled. Those Japanese tourists had come a long way, and they weren't about to let a bit of rain stop them from sampling some wine.

Simon should be down at the winery too.

He had a million things to do, but he just didn't have the energy, which was most unlike him. The low grey skies perfectly matched his mood.

From behind came the sound of Tania packing. She had originally planned to stay with him for a week, but she was leaving today. Even the rain wasn't enough to discourage her from the long drive back to Sydney. Simon didn't have it in him to ask her to stay. He couldn't blame her for leaving. His behaviour at the Winegrowers' Dinner had been pretty bad. And nothing he had done since had been much to his credit either.

'I think I'd better get going.' Her voice cut into his thoughts. 'I want to go to the agency this afternoon.'

Tania's agent had called that morning with news of a job offer as part of the forthcoming Milan fashion shows. Tania had hopes that one job would lead to another, and she would be hired by other European designers.

'So you're going to accept the job?'

'I'd be a fool not to.'

Simon wasn't at all upset by the thought of Tania moving to Europe. They had been dating for just over a year, since meeting when Tania was modelling for a wine promotion. They had both kept the relationship fairly casual, always knowing it was never going to be permanent. He did care for her, but more as a friend than anything else.

'The rain is pretty heavy. Are you sure you'll be all right?'

'I'll be fine. Are you sure *you'll* be all right?'

Simon carried Tania's bags to the car, wondering just what she meant by that. As she left, Tania kissed him gently on the cheek.

'Bye, Simon. Take care of yourself — and sort things out with Leigh. She means more to you than you think.'

Simon stood by the door as she drove away, but his eyes didn't follow her car. He was looking across the grey rain-sodden valley to where Leigh Kenyon's vineyard lay hidden in the mist. He wondered how she was. After Saturday night, he suspected she was feeling even lower than he was.

How could things have gone so terribly wrong?

Like most of the men in the ballroom, Simon had spotted Leigh the moment she walked through the door. How could he not? He had always thought her attractive, but as she walked across the carpet, she was more beautiful than he could ever have imagined. It wasn't just the way she looked, although that dress was enough to drive a saint to drink. It wasn't just the way she walked, as if not touching the floor. Her smile made the chandeliers seem dim. She glowed with such brilliance and vitality that everything and everyone around her seemed to pale into nothingness. In those moments, she was every woman he had ever dreamed about — and the only woman in the world.

When Simon finally noticed the man at her side, conflicting emotions left him dazed. He was pleased that his idea had worked. Suggesting to Ian that he answer Leigh's magazine letter had seemed a brilliant idea at the time. Ian was a nice guy. He was in the same business. What Simon hadn't expected was that Leigh would . . . would what? He watched Leigh's face again as she turned to smile at her escort. Had she fallen in love with Ian? Was she sleeping with him? The mere thought made Simon feel slightly nauseous.

All that evening, Simon had been unable to take his eyes off her. At every moment, he knew exactly where she was and who she was talking to. Who she was smiling at. He heard her voice and her laugh clearly amid the music and conversation. He knew every time Ian Rudd touched her! And finally he lost it. An explosion of frustration and something very like jealousy had driven him to do something very, very stupid.

Now, when he closed his eyes, the Leigh he saw was not the shining beauty. He saw her face stricken with shock and hurt. And it was all his fault. Thank God she hadn't seen what followed. His knuckles still hurt. He would have to call Ian and apologise, before he found the police at his door. It wasn't like him to start a fight. But it wasn't like him to get drunk either, and yet that was exactly what he had done. Thankfully Tania had dragged him home before he embarrassed himself too much.

Tania. Simon felt bad about that too, but she seemed to understand. What had she said — about Leigh meaning more to him than he knew?

Simon examined a large drop of water as it dribbled slowly down the glass door, cutting across the reflection of a man who looked as bad as he felt. His wavy hair was unkempt and he hadn't shaved. The restlessness inside him was almost too much to bear. It wasn't just the rain, or the hangover from a long night drinking wine and staring at the wall.

His decision made, he turned away and reached for his car keys. He wasn't sure what sort of reception he would get; he just knew he needed to see Leigh. He had to apologise. He also had to find out just what the hell was going on . . . with both of them.

He didn't think to grab a jacket before he raced out the door, and spent some of the short drive to Leigh's place shaking water from his head. The downpour wasn't easing. If anything, it was getting heavier. He parked near Leigh's house and dashed for her door. Huddled under the awning over her patio, he knocked. And knocked again. He heard no sound from inside. Leigh's car was parked next to the house, and she would hardly be working in the vineyards in this weather.

He sprinted over to the wine sheds, not sure why he was bothering to run as he was already thoroughly soaked. He noticed a light shining through the partly open door of the old sales shed. He ducked through the doorway and shook himself like a dog.

The room was large and very dark with disuse. On this dull day, two smallish windows did little to shed light into the large open space cluttered with old tables, boxes and the detritus of failed dreams. One small bare bulb in the far corner of the room lit a table. Leigh sat at that table, surrounded by dust-covered boxes and papers and bottles. She looked very small in the vast empty shed. Before Simon could speak, she suddenly buried her face in her hands, and began to sob.

Simon closed his mouth without uttering a word. Leigh was crying! He had never thought to see her cry. She was the strongest, brightest woman he had ever met. She was a fighter, gutsy and determined. She didn't cry.

He thought back to that horrible weekend that had changed her life and his own. At the dinner, Leigh said she blamed him for her break-up with Jack Thorne. Simon didn't know why she felt that way. She wasn't the only one to lose a fiancé that night. He hadn't thought about it in a very long time, but he had never forgotten how it felt to be betrayed by someone you loved. He had been dreaming of a family. He'd even bought the ring. The night that Jack Thorne had shown his true colours, he'd ended Simon's dream as well as Leigh's. Simon wasn't ashamed to admit that he had shed a tear or two over his lost love. For weeks afterwards he had moved in a fog of hurt. But Leigh? Not her. Leigh just took control of her life and moved on. He never saw a tear in her eyes.

Not until now.

Simon was thankful for the rain on the roof. He didn't think he could stand to hear her sobbing.

Carefully he backed away, not wanting to intrude on her privacy. Slowly he walked to the car, oblivious to the rain, aware only of the terrible guilt that lay on his shoulders. He had hurt Leigh and made her cry. As he reached for the car door, he vowed that he would never again cause her even a moment of pain.

* * *

Leigh reached into the pocket of her jeans. Damn. She never had a hankie when she needed one. There was nothing for it but to wipe her eyes and nose on the sleeve of her sweatshirt. She thought she heard something, and glanced at the doorway. Nothing but the pouring rain. She must be imagining things. That was hardly surprising. She had not been exactly at her best these past couple of days. And now look at her, crying like some silly girl.

All because of a box of glasses.

She took another swipe across her nose with her other sleeve, and opened the box again. Carefully she lifted out two of the wine glasses.

They were tall and elegant, with long stems and gracefully curved sides. A logo of two wine glasses was stamped on the side, with red and yellow diamantés giving the impression of wine in the glasses. Above the logo were etched the words Bangala Wines.

Bangala. Leigh had found the name in a dictionary of aboriginal words. It meant a water vessel. The diamanté-studded glasses had been her idea as well. Something a little different and special for the tourist market. These samples had been delivered just a few days before all her plans had crumbled to nothing.

She was going to start crying again if she wasn't careful. She grabbed one of the glasses, to hurl it across the room in anger and frustration. Anger at Jack Thorne. And Ian Rudd. And Simon Bradford. And all men! She raised her arm, paused, then lowered the glass carefully and set it on the table.

Breaking an expensive wine glass wouldn't change anything.

Leigh twirled the glass in her hands. It had been a good idea. It still was. And it had been her idea. All the good ideas had been hers. Never Jack's. When he left her, he'd taken most of their money. But that was all. He hadn't taken any of the good ideas, because he'd never had any. He'd broken her heart, but surely she was over that by now. She must be, or she would never have had a fling with Ian Rudd.

Ian had called twice on Saturday, leaving apologies on her answering machine. She'd finally talked to him on Sunday. After accepting his apology, she said goodbye. She wasn't really that mad at him. After all, she had made the first move. She had picked his letter from the pile. She had invited him into her bed. But whatever magic they might have shared had been irretrievably destroyed at the Winegrowers' Dinner.

Destroyed by his connection with the odious Simon bloody Bradford!

Leigh set the glass down and shuffled aimlessly through some old papers. They were sample labels for bottles of Bangala shiraz and cabernet. Labels that had never been used. The rain was making her melancholy. That must be it. The rain and discovering this box of old dreams while clearing out some rubbish.

She had no reason to be sad, but she had every reason to be angry with Simon Bradford. He might be handsome and successful, but he really was the most appalling man. How dare he set her up like that! Hadn't he done enough already to ruin her life? Leigh felt the tears building again.

She stopped them.

What was she thinking? Her life wasn't ruined. Despite Jack Thorne, she still had the winery and was ready to start producing her own vintage. If nothing else, Ian Rudd had given her a very enjoyable interlude. She should simply say thank you to him for helping her to finally put Jack behind her. The scene at the dinner had been embarrassing — but she was as much to blame for that as Ian. She might have overreacted just a little. That was Simon Bradford's fault. In fact, she could blame Simon for just about everything if she wanted to. And she did want to. What right did he have to try to run her life? Just because his was perfect — with his successful business and his movie-star looks and his model girlfriend.

It was time she stopped wallowing in self-pity. Finding these glasses was just the spur she needed. She was ready to talk to the bank about a new loan. The glasses would add a nice touch to her pitch for expansion funding. In fact, in the back room she had a reasonable store of sample bottles she had been making over the past two years. She could attach one of these labels. A gift like that might help persuade the bank manager to give her the money she needed.

And as for Simon . . . Success would be her revenge. And she might even find a new man. That would really get under his skin.

Leigh got to her feet and lifted the cardboard box. She would start by washing the dust from the wine glasses.

* * *

Donna lay in bed listening to the silence. The sun had barely lifted over the horizon, but already the temperature was climbing. Above the bed, a ceiling fan turned slowly, but gave not even a hint of cooling breeze. Occasionally she would hear a faint sound, as if the house was sighing as the sun heated the corrugated-iron roof. Once she heard a dog bark. There was no traffic noise. No sound of human activity; only the distant cawing of the crows, which seemed to highlight just how far away she was from everything and everybody she knew and loved.

This trip to the outback was not going the way she had planned. In fact, it was nothing short of a disaster.

The morning after her traumatic journey to River Downs Station, Donna had slept late. Even when she woke, she was reluctant to leave the safety of her room. She was confused and just a little bit frightened. She didn't understand why Peter thought she had come to be a nanny for his children. She knew she needed to talk to him about it, but at the same time, she was a little afraid to face a man who would lie so badly to get what he wanted.

As it turned out, she needn't have worried.

Peter's sister Jenny had finally tapped gently on her bedroom door, bringing her a cup of tea in bed, and the news that Peter had taken his children away for the day, to give her a chance to rest. Donna needed an explanation more than she needed rest. Over several cups of strong dark tea, Jenny confessed.

At first Donna was angry. Jenny admitted that it was she, not Peter, who had sent the original letter and photograph to *Australian Life*. The tears shone in her eyes as she explained about Peter's continuing grief for his dead wife. Donna could see how much Jenny loved her brother, and she believed that she had sent that letter for the very best of reasons. She could forgive that, but it was harder to forgive the second set of lies. Jenny had lied to Donna, pretending those e-mails also came from Peter. That she had also lied to Peter made the whole situation impossible.

Despite everything, Donna found that she couldn't dislike Jenny. The pregnant woman obviously loved her brother and his children a great deal. Donna also suspected that Jenny's pregnancy wasn't proving an easy one. Reluctantly, she had agreed to say nothing to Peter, until Jenny could explain. That agreement was partly cowardice on Donna's part. She had very few clear images of Peter in her mind, mostly associated with her escape from the gully and the close encounter with the deadly snake. She was more than happy to let Jenny confess to this strong, hard man who was so at ease with a gun.

Jenny would explain everything, leaving one important question — would Donna stay at River Downs?

Two days later, nothing had been resolved. Peter still didn't know the truth. Before Jenny could tell him, he and Ken had flown to a neighbouring property to help transport an injured stockman to hospital. They were due back this morning, and Donna was determined that the truth would come out.

She hopped out of bed. The room she had been given was actually part of the shady veranda, walled off to form a bedroom with a small bathroom. Her space was long and narrow, but one whole wall was made up of windows looking out across the brown paddocks. The only sign of human settlement she could see was a single fence that vanished into the distant scrub. It was about as different from the view offered by her London flat as it was possible to get. Even the insect netting that covered the windows spoke of how far from home she was.

Donna was heading for the kitchen when she heard the sound of the Cessna. It made a low pass over the house, as if to tell those present that the men would be home soon. She put enough water in the kettle to make a big pot of tea. She had already learned that much about the family.

She was surprised that Jenny wasn't up. She wondered briefly if she should check that everything was all right. Jenny hadn't looked well the day before. Donna decided that the best thing she could do was let both Jenny and the twins sleep in. She could look after the men when they arrived. Then, when Jenny got up, they could all sit down and sort out this mess she had got herself into.

The tea was made and Donna was pulling bread out of the freezer when Peter and Ken walked in. Both men looked tired.

'Welcome back. Tea's made.' It seemed odd that she should be offering hospitality to the men who lived here.

'Jenny not up yet?' Ken asked.

Donna shook her head.

'I'll take her tea in bed.' Ken collected two mugs and vanished in the direction of the part of the house he shared with Jenny.

Donna took a seat at the big wooden table, uncertain what to say. The man sitting opposite her was a total stranger. Their only meeting had been brief and traumatic, involving a snake and a gun. On top of that, her very presence in the room was based on a lie that she couldn't correct without breaking her word to Jenny, the only person within a thousand kilometres to whom she had spoken more than a few sentences. She decided to play it safe.

'How is the injured man doing?'

'Not too bad,' Peter replied. 'By the time we got there on Saturday, it was getting dark — too dark to lift off again. It was a pretty long night for him. His leg was badly broken. We did the best we could, then flew him to Darwin at first light yesterday.'

'Is Darwin really the nearest hospital? It's a long way away.'

'Katherine is closer,' Peter said slowly, 'but Darwin is bigger. It's better for a serious injury.'

Donna could have kicked herself. Jenny had told her that Peter's wife had died because they couldn't get her to Darwin fast enough. She looked across the table to where he was sitting staring into his mug. The journey with the injured stockman must have brought back some terrible memories. His face showed signs of strain.

'Did you stay in Darwin last night?' Donna asked quickly to change the subject.

'No. We picked up some supplies while we were there, and flew back. We spent the night at Richmond.'

'Richmond?' Donna grinned. 'That's the name of a town not far from where I grew up in Yorkshire.'

'I imagine it's very different. My neighbour's property is a couple of hundred square kilometres of near desert. What's your Richmond like?'

'Green,' she said fondly. 'With a castle that's nearly a thousand years old. And a ruined abbey.'

Peter looked across the table, and as his eyes met hers, he smiled with her. It made him look younger.

'I'm sorry to have left like that,' he offered, 'when you'd only been here a couple of hours. That's how it is in the outback. If someone calls for help, you drop everything and go.'

'It's all right. I understand,' she said, liking the simple declaration.

'To be honest with you' — his smile faded as he spoke — 'I am worried that you'll find this place hard to cope with. It's so very different from England. You might not like it.'

This was her chance to confess. She almost did. Only her promise to Jenny held her back. But she knew that with each passing moment, the lie was getting worse.

'In my e-mails, I did say that I was from England,' she said.

'I think Jenny just forgot to tell me. I was very surprised when I heard your accent.'

'Jenny and the twins gave me a bit of a tour while you were gone,' Donna said. 'I think this place is amazing and quite beautiful.'

Peter looked at her thoughtfully for a few seconds, but before he could reply, Ken's return interrupted them.

'Jenny's not feeling too well,' he said.

'Nothing to do with the baby, I hope.' Peter's concern showed in his eyes.

'I'm sure she'll be fine,' Ken assured him. 'But I'd like to stay fairly close today.'

'No worries. In fact, I've got an idea.' Peter smiled across the table at Donna. 'If Ken stays here, he can keep an eye on Jenny and the kids, and I can give you another guided tour. If you are planning to be around for a while, you need to know how to work this place.'

The fine lines at the corners of his brown eyes spoke of many hours in the sun. And of laughter. They seemed to balance the lines that years of grief had drawn on his forehead.

'That would be nice,' she said.

They finished their tea and set off. They had taken only a few steps from the house when Peter suddenly stopped. 'You don't have a hat.'

'No, I don't.'

'Wait here.'

Peter walked back inside the house. There were some hats hanging in the laundry room. Quickly he searched for something that might fit the girl. He opened a cupboard, and found a lady's tan Akubra. It looked almost new. Peter frowned. He hadn't seen it before. He didn't think it was Jenny's. And surely all his mother's hats had long gone. Had this hat been Karen's? He couldn't recall his late wife ever wearing a tan Akubra.

He started to put the hat back, then stopped. Why shouldn't he give it to the nanny to wear? If he didn't remember it, his kids certainly wouldn't. It was only a hat, and the girl needed one. Donna needed one, he corrected himself.

On his way back, he stopped in the darkness of the veranda and looked across at Donna. She had crossed to the run where Chipper and her puppies were playing. As she leaned forward, the puppies were leaping up, trying to lick her fingers. From where he was standing, he could hear her laughing gaily. The sound seemed to wrap itself around his tired body and ease the tension from his shoulders.

The hat fitted perfectly. Peter positioned it carefully on Donna's wavy chestnut hair.

'It suits you,' he said.

'Thanks.' They resumed walking across the yard. Peter had to shorten his stride so she could keep up. She is quite tiny, he thought. The other evening, he had lifted her out of the gully as if she was a child. When she had cried against his chest, he had felt a surge of protectiveness.

'So, what am I getting to see on this tour?' Donna interrupted his thoughts.

'What did the twins show you?'

'The puppies featured highly. The ponies too. And a playhouse under the water tank.'

Peter smiled. 'I see. Well, I'd better show you some of the unimportant things — like the power generator and how the satellite phone works. And you might like to learn the easy route to the airstrip.'

Donna stopped. She looked up at him from under the brim of her new hat. 'I am really sorry about that. I realise how stupid I was to set out on foot. I will never try something like that again.'

Peter noticed that her face was still a bit red from too much sun the day she arrived. It wouldn't be long before she went as brown as he and the kids were. Or maybe she wouldn't, he thought. That fair English skin might just burn. She would have to be careful. Her fair skin and freckles were far too cute to destroy with sunburn.

Cute? He caught himself. Where had that come from?

'Nannies are pretty hard to come by,' he said quickly, dragging his mind back to the conversation. 'It took a long time to find you. I would hate to have to find a replacement this soon.' He smiled to show he was joking, but she didn't smile with him. Something in her face made him think he'd just touched a raw nerve, but he had no idea what it might be.

They carried on with the tour. Peter showed Donna the huge batteries charged by the solar power cells ranged on the roof of both the house and the sheds. He taught her how to start the back-up diesel generator, should it ever be needed. He made her drive the battered old utility to the airstrip and they returned with supplies from the plane loaded high in the back. Later the twins joined the tour, and once again puppies and ponies were included.

Peter was impressed at how quickly Donna took in everything he told her. There was no doubt that she was bright, and she seemed to have an affinity for the land. Not bad going for a Pommy, he thought.

When they returned to the house, Jenny still wasn't up. Donna set about making lunch. Peter was debating whether to knock on his sister's door when the phone rang.

He took the call in his office.

'I hope I didn't catch you at a bad time, Mr Nichols. I am calling from *Australian Life* magazine.'

'You're calling from Sydney to sell me a magazine subscription?'

'No,' the woman said. 'It's in relation to the Farmer Needs a Wife campaign. We had so many responses to your letter, I was wondering if you had replied to any. Or taken any of the queries further.'

'I'm sorry. I have no idea what you are talking about.'

Peter listened in growing horror as the woman explained.

'There's been some misunderstanding,' he said. 'I didn't take part in your campaign.'

'But we have your details, your letter . . . '

'You are mistaken.'

Peter hung up. He hated being rude, but he had to end the call because of his growing suspicion that the woman was speaking the truth. There was one way to find out.

Donna looked up as Peter walked back into the kitchen. His face told her everything. Somehow he had discovered the truth, and he wasn't taking it well.

She turned to the twins. 'I need some tomatoes for lunch. And some carrots for dinner tonight. Would you go and get them?'

With a cheerful yell, the twins set off to raid their aunt's carefully nurtured vegetable patch behind the house.

'I just got the strangest phone call,' Peter said as soon as they were gone. His voice was cold and hard.

Donna didn't answer.

'From some magazine called *Australian Life*.' He was watching her closely as he spoke. He must have seen something in her face. Some flash of guilt.

'You're not a nanny.' It wasn't a question.

'Peter,' Donna stepped forward to put her hand on his arm, 'I've been wanting to tell you, but — '

He shook her off. 'Tell me now.'

She did. She told him of Jenny's desire to find him a new wife. Their deal to say nothing until Jenny had explained; an explanation that had been delayed by circumstances and Jenny's poor health. As she spoke, Donna watched his face tighten with anger.

'You thought you would come here and replace my wife? Just like that?' His voice was quiet, controlled and very angry.

'No . . . I . . . I just . . . ' Donna stopped speaking and simply looked at him. She searched his face for some sign of forgiveness. There was none.

'I think it would be best if you were to leave,' he said coldly, before she had a chance to speak again.

'Peter . . . '

'I'll organise a seat for you on the next mail run to Darwin. If you want me to buy you a ticket back to the Gold Coast, I will. If you want to go somewhere else, that's your own business.'

'But . . . ' Donna wasn't sure what to say. She realised that she didn't want to leave. She had spent only two days with the twins, but she was already beginning to love them. The outback life was everything she had dreamed of back in her cold, damp flat in England. And as for Peter? This cold, angry man was the same person who had rescued her and forgiven her foolishness. He had been willing to teach her about his home and he had laughed with her. She had barely met him, and didn't know what her feelings for him might become, but she did know that she hadn't come all this way just to walk away from him.

'You deceived me,' Peter continued. 'I can't trust you. You have to leave.'

'She can't leave.' The voice from the doorway startled them both.

Ken and Jenny walked in, their hands clasped. Jenny immediately sat down, while

Ken took up a protective position behind her.

'Donna can't leave,' Jenny said again, 'because we are.'

'What do you mean?' Peter asked. 'You're not going for months yet.'

'No. We're leaving in the next few days,' Jenny said gently.

Donna moved to sit beside the woman who had become her friend. 'Are you all right?' she asked.

Jenny shrugged, a tear in her eye.

'We've decided to leave earlier than planned.' Ken spoke for both for them. 'Jenny is feeling the strain of the pregnancy, and I want . . . we want her to be closer to a doctor. A hospital. Not that anything is going to go wrong. But just in case.'

'Sis?' Peter's face creased with shock and concern.

'I'm all right, Peter.' Jenny smiled at him. 'Honestly. You knew we were going. We're just going a little earlier than planned. That's all.'

'The twins will really miss you,' Peter said. 'We all will.'

'You have Donna now,' Jenny said.

Donna looked across the room at Peter. His face was dark and troubled. He would let her stay because he had to, at least for now. But he didn't like it.

* * *

Molly was sitting at the kitchen table, working at her computer, when she heard the engine noise outside the house. Greg and Jasi were back. She glanced at the screen again. She had been using her computer to manipulate the photos of Greg she had taken in his workshop. She was also playing with some images of the jewellery he had made. She planned to give him those to use for his website or for advertising if he wished.

The photo on the screen was a shot of Greg working on his silver wing. He was bent over it, his face the very definition of intense concentration. The light in the shot was centred on his eyes, and on the glowing silver shape that was forming beneath his skilled hands. It was a powerful, compelling image.

The sound of the front door made her quickly close the software. When she looked up, Greg and Jasi were standing just inside the door. They had been to the beach, mostly at Jasi's urging. She had pouted prettily at Greg, complaining that the beach was so close but she had not yet had a chance to swim or work on her tan. Well, she'd tan in the outfit she was wearing. The blue shorts and tiny halter top left little to the imagination.

The way she was kissing Greg left little to the imagination either. Her arms were around his neck, her body pressed hard against him. Molly quickly looked away, but not before she got the impression that Greg was showing less enthusiasm for the embrace than might be expected.

Hoping they hadn't seen her, Molly tucked her laptop under her arm and left the room. It wasn't that she didn't like Jasi. The girl was nice, if not particularly bright. Molly just didn't think she was right for Greg. He needed someone who could understand and appreciate a creative mind. Someone who could help him in his artistic endeavours. Someone more like . . .

She tried to push the thought away, but it was too late. It had already formed. Someone more like herself. Not that she was interested. She wasn't interested in any sort of long-term relationship. Not with any man, but particularly not with a north Queensland canefarmer, no matter how attractive he was. She certainly wouldn't ever consider leaving Sydney. She loved the city and her career was blossoming there. If Greg was in Sydney, that might be a different matter. She sighed and reached for her mobile phone. It was time to call the airport and find a flight home.

When Molly returned to the kitchen, she

found Greg and Jasi there.

'How was the beach?' she asked.

'Wonderful,' Jasi gushed. 'I've started on my tan. Look!'

The girl spun slowly around to show off her slightly reddened skin. Molly had the feeling the action was directed more at Greg than at her. If it was, it wasn't really working. Greg barely lifted his eyes from the pile of paperwork on the table in front of him.

'Good for you.' Molly struggled to keep her voice casual. 'By the way, I'm flying back to Sydney tomorrow.'

That did get Greg's attention.

'I thought you were staying a few extra days,' he said quickly.

'I was, but something has come up.' She didn't feel happy lying to him, but it was the easiest way out. She had already stayed a day longer than agreed with *Australian Life*. The magazine would not be paying for that extra day, but Molly had decided to stay anyway. She told herself she was hoping to take some shots of the region for her own collection. In reality, she just didn't want to leave. But after seeing Greg and Jasi kissing in the doorway, she knew she had to go.

'There's something at work,' she added. 'I'm booked on a flight tomorrow afternoon.'

'Where are you going next?' Jasi asked.

'Somewhere exciting?'

'I really won't know until I get back and talk to a few people,' Molly answered automatically, her eyes on Greg.

'Well, I expect it must be interesting going to all those different places,' Jasi continued. 'Not for me, though. I'm a real home girl.'

Her words were obviously directed at Greg, yet he didn't seem to hear them. Molly's departure would be good news for Jasi, opening the way for further intimacy with the man she so wanted. Greg, however, had lapsed into silence, concentrating on the papers in front of him.

'I'll take you to the airport tomorrow,' he said at last.

'Thanks.'

An awkward silence settled on the room.

'I have to run some errands,' Greg said eventually, getting to his feet. 'I've got to go into town.'

'Oh, can I come too?' Jasi said. 'You could show me more of the town. Maybe we could stay and go out to dinner.'

'Sorry,' Greg answered quickly. 'I won't be going anywhere near the shops. Maybe another time.'

He ducked out of the room before Jasi could respond.

Molly saw Jasi's shoulders slump in

disappointment. She felt a twinge of sympathy.

'Well, once I've gone, you and Greg will have more time alone to get to know each other,' she said with a brightness she did not feel.

'That's true.' Jasi's smile returned. 'I think it's going really well with Greg. He kissed me just now.'

Molly just nodded in reply. The last thing she wanted was to encourage Jasi to share any confidences with her.

'You know, I gave up my job to come up here and be with him.'

The revelation surprised Molly. 'Really?'

'Yes. I worked in a shop. But all I've ever wanted was to get married and have babies. I know we only met a few days ago, but I think maybe Greg is the right man for me.'

Unable to really answer the girl, Molly mumbled something about packing, and escaped to the solitude of her room.

* * *

Greg's fingers tightened around the steering wheel as he steered the farm utility down the highway. The needle on the speedometer wound slowly higher and higher.

His meeting with his father had been even

more frustrating than normal. Robert Anderson had demanded to know why he had seen so little of Greg in the past week. It wasn't great love for his son that made him ask. Greg knew that his father suspected something was going on behind his back. In a way he was right, but it wasn't what he was thinking. While Greg had sat fingering the silver charm in his pocket, Robert had gone through the farm papers with even greater diligence than usual. He obviously thought that Greg might somehow be fiddling the books, or doing some harm to his precious farm. That his son was hiding the visit of a woman, or rather two women, would never occur to him.

Two women, Greg thought as he drove away from the hospital. That was the problem. Two of them. Tomorrow there would be only one. The wrong one.

He did not want Molly to leave.

Alone with his thoughts, Greg strove for total honesty. Jasi was pretty and sexy, and when she kissed him, he knew that she wanted him. That kiss in the doorway should have made him feel the same way — but it hadn't. It hadn't stirred any emotion in him, except regret that it wasn't Molly in his arms. He felt a wave of guilt. Jasi was a nice girl. She had come a very long way to be with him. She was willing to start a relationship

— but he wasn't. Jasi was sweet and pretty, but Greg found her a little bit irritating. She wasn't very clever, or interested in the world around her. She was a bit demanding and she had no real understanding of his creative drive. He suspected that he was being too hard on her. Subconsciously comparing her with Molly. Bright, creative, interesting Molly, who might not be as pretty as Jasi, but who had lovely green eyes and a genuine smile. She was self-sufficient and independent and free-spirited and just amazing. What was even more amazing was that she seemed to understand him.

The problem was that Molly would never stay buried on a cane farm. The very things that drew him to her were the things that were taking her away. Jasi, on the other hand, had made it very clear that she would be happy to settle on the farm with him. But he couldn't ask Jasi to stay, if it was Molly he really wanted. That wouldn't be fair to Jasi. To anyone.

A car overtook him, almost cutting him off as it ducked back in front of him. Greg glanced down at his speed and immediately eased back on the accelerator. Getting himself killed on the highway was not the solution to his problems.

A dark smudge in the distance drew his

eye. A cane fire. It was a bit early in the season for the burning to start. The thick dark grey smoke rising into the sky was a reminder that soon he would have to start his harvest. Jasi wouldn't like that. She liked him to spend all his time with her. He had hardly spent any time in his jewellery workshop since she arrived. Just that one session while Molly was taking photographs. When the harvest started, he'd have very little time for Jasi, and no time at all for his craft. The idea settled grimly around him, like the dark pall from the cane fire.

He glanced towards the smoke again. He wondered if Molly would like to photograph the fire. Burning cane was a spectacular sight, particularly at night. It was late afternoon now. The burn would last well into the night. She should get some good shots. Something to remember him by.

Molly jumped at the idea when he suggested it. Jasi was less pleased. She had already started preparing a farewell dinner for Molly, and couldn't leave it to look at a cane fire. Greg was secretly pleased, and hid his guilt by promising that he and Molly would be back in plenty of time for dinner.

As Greg and Molly drove back towards the fire, they talked about cane. Growing cane, burning it, harvesting and processing it.

Molly asked questions, and Greg answered them.

'Why do you do this?' That question was unexpected.

'What do you mean?' Greg asked, glancing at Molly as she sat next to him.

'Why do you stay here?' she said again. 'It's obvious from the way you talk that you really don't like being a canefarmer. You are a silversmith in your heart. A good one. So what are you doing on a cane farm?'

Without a word, Greg pulled over to the side of the road. He turned off the engine and dropped his forehead on to his hands, where they still gripped the steering wheel.

Molly said nothing. She waited until he was ready to speak.

'My father,' Greg said at last. 'That's what holds me here.' In a few quick sentences, he told Molly about his father's illness and the need to keep the farm working to pay his medical costs.

'He won't sell up,' he concluded. 'So what choice do I have?'

'You must love him a lot,' Molly said.

'No,' Greg replied in a toneless voice. 'That's it. I don't. He is a hard man. He was not a good father. Maybe it was grief after my mother died, but he had no right to take it out on me. I tried to make him love me. But he has no love to give anyone. Not even his son.'

Greg had never said the words out loud before. Not to himself, and certainly not to another person. He felt as if something tight inside him had finally snapped. He felt a soft touch on his arm. He lifted his head, and Molly's hand came down over his.

'I'm sorry,' she said.

Greg covered her hand with his own for a moment, then reached out and started the engine. They drove on for a few minutes in silence.

'Have you told Jasi?' Molly asked quietly.

'No.'

They said nothing more until Greg turned the vehicle down a farm lane. The smoke of the cane fire was thick and dark and directly in front of them.

'Wow,' said Molly.

'It's pretty impressive the first time you see it,' Greg agreed.

They got out of the car, Molly clutching one camera, with another hanging around her neck.

'Stay close to me,' Greg told her.

'Is it dangerous?' Molly felt a slight twinge of fear.

'Not really. But if the wind turns, and you are in the wrong place at the wrong time . . . '

Molly shuddered at the thought. 'All right.'

The cane was taller than she was. The thick stalks and broad dark leaves formed a seemingly impenetrable wall around them. Greg introduced her to the men who were supervising the burning. They carried small flaming torches, which they used to set the fires. A large patch of cane was already burning. The smoke rising swiftly into the air had a dark, sweet smell. Molly moved around, snapping shots of the men as they moved along a dirt firebreak, touching their torches to the dry leaves at the base of the cane. Each time they did so, a flash of flame leaped upwards with almost frightening speed. The fire caught quickly. The red and gold flames danced up the stalks, and within seconds Molly could feel the heat almost burning her skin. The crackling of burning leaves got louder and thicker until she could hear nothing but the roar of the fire.

Molly took her camera away from her eye. The wild heat of the fire was creating its own wind, which in turn was pushing the greedy flames deeper into the cane field. It was moving faster than a walking man. She felt a faint twist of fear, and looked around for Greg. He was standing right behind her.

'Is it always like this?' she asked.

He nodded.

Together they walked along the dirt firebreak, pausing as Molly took shot after shot. The sun was sinking quickly, the sunset and the fire blending to create a sky of extraordinary red and gold. The men working the fire line were now just dark silhouettes moving against the shimmering red glare. The fire seemed almost to have a life of its own, dancing before the rising wind of its own making.

The sun had vanished and it was fully dark when Greg tapped Molly on the shoulder.

'When you have enough here, there is one other place I want to take you.'

It took just a few minutes for them to drive out of the burning fields. Greg took a narrow dirt track that curved to the top of a steep hill. He parked the car in a small clearing with a view out across the blazing fields.

Molly got out and gazed at the vista below them. From this height, the cane fields were a patchwork of darkness and light. Greg watched her face as she looked out at the burning cane. Her eyes were lit by more than just the flickering orange light of the flames. She grabbed her cameras and started taking photographs, seemingly oblivious to Greg's presence.

He was content to sit on the bonnet of the car and watch her.

At last she lowered her camera and came to sit beside him.

'Wow,' she said.

'I know.'

They sat in silence for a few minutes, listening to the dull roar of the fire below them.

'Molly, I have something for you.'

Greg reached into the pocket of his jeans, for the charm that was always there. He took her hand and gently placed the silver disc on her palm. Molly held it up, smiling as the red glow of the flames glinted on the shining silver.

'No,' she said gently and handed it back. 'I can't take it. You need it to remind you of who you are, when you get trapped by all this.'

Greg didn't reply. He just slipped the charm back into his pocket.

'You have to leave,' Molly continued. 'You know that. For yourself. You have to leave.'

She turned to look at him. Greg returned the gaze of those lovely green eyes and nodded.

Then he leaned forward and kissed her.

Her face was covered in soot and sweat and her lips tasted of burning cane. It was the sweetest kiss he had ever known.

When at last they drew apart, they sat for a

few minutes, saying nothing, their fingers entwined as they watched the burning cane.

'It's getting late,' Greg said at last. 'We should go back.'

'I suppose we should,' Molly said gently. 'Jasi will be angry if we are too late.'

Greg took one long, slow breath, let go of Molly's hand and got back behind the wheel of the car.

⋆ ⋆ ⋆

As she waited in the queue at the cash register, Helen suddenly realised that this would be the first meal for two she had cooked in her flat. The thought caused her to frown. Was she that alone? Maybe she had been, and maybe, just maybe, she wasn't any more.

The person ahead of her in the queue moved away, and she started unloading her basket. She had seen this speciality food shop many times, but this was the first time she'd shopped here. The food was expensive, but interesting. She had smoked salmon for the entree and chicken breasts to follow. She'd make a tarragon cream sauce for the chicken. There would be no dessert. Dessert was one of Helen's few failings as a cook. She just couldn't do it. She could, however, assemble a fine cheese platter. She was sure Matt would be happy with that.

She handed over some cash, and left the shop. Her driver was waiting with the car. She quickly dropped her bags on the seat, telling him to wait while she visited the bottle shop. It was as she was leaving, laden with wine, that she recognised a face in the evening rush-hour crowd. The man met her gaze, then turned away, almost guiltily. Helen searched her mind for a name to put to the face. He was a photographer, she recalled, who specialised in candid celebrity shots. She had occasionally bought his pictures through an agency, but had never hired him directly herself. By the time she had remembered his name, he was gone, and she dismissed him from her mind.

Back in her flat, Helen dashed for the shower to freshen up. She emerged a few minutes later wearing a long full cotton skirt and a top edged with a touch of lace. It was a bit boho chic, but she was in the mood for something very different to her tailored work suits. Her hair was freshly brushed, and she wore little make-up. She felt younger and somehow lighter now that she had shed her editor persona. The buzzer by her door rang as she was chopping the herbs.

'Matt?' She spoke into the intercom.

'Hi.' His voice was distorted by the machine, but still recognisable.

Helen hit the button that would open the door on the ground floor, thankful that the security also gave her a chance to wash her hands and check her hair before she heard Matt's knock.

He was as tall as she remembered, and as brown and as handsome. Helen felt a little flutter in her chest. He had a small sports bag slung over one shoulder. Did that mean . . .

'Hello.' She smiled and stood on her toes to kiss his cheek.

As he bent to accept the greeting, Helen noticed that he was frowning.

'Is something wrong?' she asked.

'Not really.' Matt stepped inside and dropped the bag near the door. 'There was a man outside. He had a camera. I think he took my photo.'

'That's strange.' Helen opened the sliding glass doors that led on to the patio. Matt joined her and they looked over the railing to the building's entrance twelve floors below.

'From this height, it's hard to see anything,' Helen said.

'Really?' Matt indicated the bridge that dominated their view. 'I'd call that something.'

Helen chuckled, forgetting all about the

man with the camera. 'It is pretty impressive.'

'You can't see the opera house,' Matt said. 'I would have thought that was not negotiable for a place like this.'

'I did think about asking them to tear down the bridge pylon,' Helen said, joining in the joke. 'But then I thought — everyone has a view of the opera house. At least mine is different.'

They laughed as they went back into the flat.

'I have something for you.' Matt retrieved his bag and pulled out a large brown shoe box.

'Most men bring flowers. Or wine. You brought me shoes?' Helen took the box and opened it.

'Riding boots,' Matt offered. 'So that next time you come up to my place, you won't destroy another pair of your expensive shoes.'

Helen smiled ruefully. During her weekend at Willaring Downs, she had borrowed a pair of Ali's boots for riding, but they hadn't fitted very well. For the rest of the time, she had worn her own designer loafers that were now lying in her garbage, covered in mud and horse manure. She turned the boots over in her hands.

'How did you know my size?'

'I confess,' Matt said. 'I checked your shoe

size while you were at my place. Try them on.'

'Now?' Helen hesitated.

'Why not?'

Helen ducked into her bedroom for a pair of socks. The boots fitted perfectly.

'They're really comfortable,' she told Matt, putting one leg forward, lifting the skirt to expose her boot-clad leg. 'But I don't think they are quite the thing with this skirt.'

'Oh, I don't know,' Matt drawled in his best country-boy voice. 'On some people, riding boots and a skirt can be quite sexy.'

Helen's breath caught in her throat. She looked up into his dark eyes. 'Really?' she asked innocently.

'Oh, yes.'

Matt took one more step to close the distance between them and kissed her. It took a very long time.

* * *

Helen woke slowly. Through her closed eyelids she could sense the daylight streaming in through her bedroom window. She stretched and opened her eyes. The first thing she saw was a pair of brown leather riding boots, lying on the carpet near her bedroom door. Matt had dropped them there last night, after slowly and carefully removing each one. Matt did many things slowly and with much attention to detail, which accounted for the way she felt right now. Her body must be glowing, it felt that good.

The bed next to her was empty, but Helen could still feel Matt's warmth. She could still smell him on the pillows. He smelled of sunlight and open air, of all that was strong and good in the earth.

She found him in the kitchen, brewing coffee. He looked up as she crossed the room, and his smile wrapped her in a warmth she had never felt before.

She accepted the offered mug.

'I was wondering,' Matt said as he sipped his coffee, 'how you would feel about meeting up with Ali for brunch?'

'You don't have to rush back and feed the horses?' Helen asked.

'No. I've hired a jackaroo,' Matt said. 'If you'd rather not see Ali, I understand.'

'I'd like to meet her,' Helen said, 'but she'll know you spent the night here.'

'She's pretty smart,' Matt said. 'She'll figure it out soon anyway. Are you okay with that?'

Was she? Matt's love for his daughter was written all over his face. Helen could see something else in his eyes this morning. She wasn't ready to believe it was love for her, but it was something very like it.

'You ring her, while I have a shower,' she said.

'If I make it a quick call, can I come and wash your back?'

It was mid-morning by the time they left the flat. Riding down in the elevator, they held hands like teenagers. It felt good.

Helen saw them the moment she and Matt stepped into the foyer. Four men were loitering on the footpath outside the building. She stopped walking and let go of Matt's hand.

'Damn!'

'What is it?' Matt asked.

'Can you see those men outside? Is one of them the man who photographed you when you arrived last night?' Helen asked.

'The one in the blue shirt. Do you know him?'

'He's a paparazzo.' Helen led Matt towards the rear corner of the foyer, where they would be hard to spot from the street.

'Does he work for your magazine?' Matt asked, his face creased with confusion.

'No. He's freelance. I've run a couple of his pictures, but he'll sell to anyone.'

'What is he doing here?'

'He saw me shopping last night,' Helen explained. 'He must have followed me home on the chance of a shot. That's what he does.'

'A shot of what? Me?'

'Us. Together. There are papers that would pay for that.'

Matt shook his head in disbelief. 'Why? What business is it of theirs?'

'It comes with the job. I have a fairly high profile. It wouldn't be the first time I've been in the gossip columns, although never . . . not like this . . . ' Her voice trailed off.

'So, we'll go back inside the flat. Wait until he leaves.'

'He won't leave,' Helen said. 'He must have stayed here all night and he won't leave now until he gets what he's come for. And he's not alone any more. Word has gone round that he's waiting for something. The rest of the pack is gathering. It's a competition now. Whoever gets the best shot gets the most money.'

'We can just ignore them,' Matt said. 'Show them that we don't care.'

'That won't work,' Helen said. 'They'll follow us.'

'What? All the way to Ali's place?'

Helen nodded.

'If they go anywhere near my daughter . . . ' Matt's voice betrayed the shock he was feeling.

'I know.' Helen put her hand on his arm.

'This is a strange world you live in,' Matt said to her. 'I don't know why you stay.'

'There are times I ask myself the same question,' Helen said.

After a moment's silence, she took the decision she knew she had to make.

'Matt, I can handle this.' As she spoke, for the first time in her career Helen felt ashamed of her profession. 'But you have to leave. Preferably without them seeing you.'

'What do we do?'

'Where's your car?'

'Just around the corner. Parked on the side of the road.'

'Fine.' Helen was all business now. 'I'll distract them. Lead them away. You wait till it's clear, then get out of here as fast as you can.'

'And our plans?'

'Matt,' Helen said softly. 'They'll follow me all weekend now. We can't . . . '

Matt nodded.

Helen didn't know what else to say. In silence they returned to her flat, and Matt retrieved his bag. They held hands again in the elevator on the way back down to the foyer, but it was different this time, more for comfort than for the joy of being together.

'You'll go back home tonight?' Helen asked

as they stepped once more into the brightly lit foyer.

'Yes. I'll call you.' Matt squeezed her hand and smiled reassuringly. 'Are you sure it has to be like this?'

'Yes.'

'Take care.'

'I will.' Helen stood on her toes to kiss Matt briefly, then she turned towards the front door.

The glass slid open in front of her, and the small cluster of men on the street started moving.

'Who is he, Helen?'

'Where is he?'

Their questions were punctuated by the click of cameras.

'Who is who?' Helen asked, forcing a smile to her face as she moved quickly down the steps.

'You know who we mean,' one photographer said.

'Is he one of your farmers?' another shouted.

'Guys,' Helen set out to cross the road, 'I don't know what you're talking about.'

The photographers moved with her, dodging traffic as they went.

With a smile firmly fixed on her face, Helen made her way to the newspaper stand outside the station. The paper-seller had a slightly stunned look on his face.

'Good morning,' Helen said to him brightly.

'Ahh . . . good morning,' the man replied.

Helen took a few moments to flick through the newspapers and magazines on the stand. As she did so, she risked a glance across at her building. Matt had left the foyer. He was a few steps from safely vanishing around the corner.

'I'm just looking for some reading, for a quiet day at home,' Helen told the photographers, collecting two newspapers. She then placed a copy of *Australian Life* very prominently on top of her pile.

The photographers laughed.

Helen paid the paper-seller, who still looked faintly stunned.

'Bye,' she said to him and winked.

She kept the smile firmly in place as she made her way back to her building. Once safely inside the elevator, though, she sagged back against the wall, and the smile faded. She maintained her composure until she was back inside her flat. It seemed very empty. She threw the newspapers on the coffee table. Too angry and frustrated to read, she moved around the flat, pretending to tidy up.

When she saw the riding boots lying on the carpet near her bedroom door, she started to cry.

7

Simon sneezed loudly as he walked through the centre of Newcastle, ignoring the crowds of shoppers.

'Damn it,' he muttered under his breath. He was reaching for a handkerchief, when he sneezed again. He felt terrible. His nose was running, he was coughing and sneezing and his head felt like it was filled with wet concrete.

'Hi, Simon.' An acquaintance walked past smiling broadly. 'How are you?'

'Fine, thanks,' Simon muttered, not stopping to chat. He wasn't fine. He had the flu. He felt like death. That would teach him to go wandering around in the rain without a jacket. Nothing had gone right since the night of the Winegrowers' Dinner. Nothing at all.

He gave full rein to his self-pity, buried his face in his handkerchief and sneezed again.

When he looked up, Leigh was standing in front of him.

Simon stopped in his tracks, the handkerchief still clutched in his hand.

Leigh was very smartly dressed, in slacks and a light jacket. She had her hands full, with a leather satchel and a medium-sized cardboard box.

'Hi, Leigh, how are you?' Simon could have kicked himself for the inane greeting, but after their last meeting at the dinner, what was he supposed to say?

'Fine, thank you, Simon. You don't look so well.'

'I've got a bit of a cold,' Simon said. 'It's nothing serious.'

Leigh nodded, and for a few awkward seconds they stood there just looking at each other.

'Leigh, I want — '

'Simon, I think — '

They both spoke at the same time, then both stopped. Simon nodded to indicate that Leigh should speak first. She shifted the weight of the box in her arms.

'Can I help with that?' he immediately offered, reaching out as if to take the load.

'No, thank — ' Leigh stopped speaking as her eyes fell on his outstretched hand. She frowned, and Simon remembered the bruised knuckles, the result of his run-in with Ian.

'You really did hit him.' Leigh spoke softly, with a touch of disbelief in her voice.

'I shouldn't have. Leigh, I do apologise for — '

Leigh shook her head.

'Let's not go there, Simon. Okay? Not today. I've got other things on my mind. Let's just forget it.'

'But I — '

'Simon. I hope your cold gets better. I have to go. I have an appointment and I can't be late.'

She turned and walked away.

Simon stood rooted to the spot, his handkerchief still clutched in one hand. His head was spinning, and it wasn't because of his cold. During the past few days he had been trying to decide what he would say to Leigh next time he saw her. She had every right to an apology and an explanation. But it seemed she didn't want one. The Leigh walking away from him now was a very different woman from the one he had seen sobbing in the empty shed. With her smart suit and her head held high, she had an air of quiet determination. She looked happy. She looked contented. She looked just great.

Heads turned as he sneezed very loudly once more.

Sniffing a bit, he started walking again, wondering just what had worked such a change in Leigh. Had she been reconciled with Ian? Simon wanted her to be happy, but the thought that she was back with Ian was like a cold hard lump in the pit of his belly. It was almost like jealousy. But it couldn't be, because Leigh was nothing more than a neighbour who could have been a friend if circumstances had been different. Wasn't she?

Simon was so caught up in his thoughts that he walked right past his destination, and had to turn back.

The jeweller's shop was carefully lit to best display the expensive gems inside the glass cases. A well-groomed woman in black materialised at Simon's side almost immediately.

'Can I help you, sir?'

Simon reached into his pocket and put a black velvet box on the counter.

The saleswoman picked it up and looked at him. Simon nodded and she opened the box.

The brilliant cut diamond was the pale pink of delicate rose petals, set on a band of white gold. The woman turned the box so the light danced across the surface of the stone.

'This is lovely,' she said. 'The stone is from the Kimberley Ranges in Western Australia?'

'Yes,' Simon replied shortly. 'I wish to dispose of the ring.'

'Of course, sir. Please step this way.'

She led him to a small alcove, and left him seated there while she went to find the manager.

Simon sat looking at the ring, waiting for

the memories to come rushing back. He'd put such time and thought into it, buying a stone and then commissioning a jeweller to design the setting. He had planned to give it to the woman he loved on the night of the harvest celebration three years ago. He'd gone looking for her, the ring in his pocket, and found her with Jack Thorne. Simon sometimes wondered whether, had she known about the ring, would she still have chased Jack and his newly acquired money? Or would he now be married? And if he had married, would he be happy?

'I'm sorry to have kept you waiting, sir.' The jeweller was a man in his mid-forties, with eyes that seemed set in a permanent squint. 'My assistant tells me you have a ring you wish to sell.'

Simon handed over the ring. The jeweller placed a loupe over his eye and spent some minutes examining the ring and the diamond in great detail.

'This is a remarkable piece. Who was the maker?'

Simon told him, and also handed over the grading certificate for the stone.

'Are you certain you want to sell this? If nothing else, a piece this fine represents a worthwhile investment.'

'It was to have been an engagement ring,'

Simon said shortly. 'It has never been worn. I have no use for it.'

The jeweller tactfully said nothing, and returned to his examination of the ring.

Simon left the shop a short time later with assurances that the jeweller would be making him several thousand dollars richer in the near future. The money didn't matter that much to Simon. He'd found the ring by accident that morning, while looking for some old papers in his office. He remembered putting it in the back of a desk drawer the day after the party that had destroyed his need for it. He hadn't even looked at it since. The decision to sell had been a spur-of-the-moment thing. He had expected to feel something. Sorrow or regret. Maybe even a hint of pain. But he felt nothing. Maybe that meant he was ready to move on.

He smiled faintly as he got behind the wheel of his car, barely sniffing at all.

* * *

Leigh took a deep breath to compose herself as she walked down the street. Meeting Simon Bradford hadn't been the best start to her day. Ever since the Winegrowers' Dinner, she had been thinking about what she would say to him the next time they met. She wasn't really mad at him any more. Not for what happened with Ian. Her issues with Simon dated back to Jack Thorne. It was well past time she resolved those too. But not today. Today she had better things to do.

Leigh walked through the sliding glass doors of the bank, and presented herself at the reception area.

The loans manager was a smartly dressed man of about her own age, who raised an eyebrow as Leigh put her load on the carpet next to her chair.

'So, Miss Kenyon, let's talk about your application for a business loan.'

'Well,' Leigh took a deep breath, 'I have been selling off my grapes each year. But this season I want to start making my own vintage. Bottling it and selling it. To do that, I'm going to need some investment capital. I have all the figures . . . '

She started to reach for the leather satchel at her feet, but the loans officer held up his hand.

'I'm sure you do. And you can be sure I will go through them in great detail. What I would like to do now is just talk. I want to get a feeling for what you are trying to achieve.'

Leigh hid her surprise. He wasn't like any bank officer she'd dealt with before. He seemed nice. Interested. Not the least bit scary.

'I think there's plenty of scope now for a boutique winery,' she said. 'The tourist market is growing, and . . . '

Leigh talked for a long time, prompted by the occasional question from the man seated across the desk. At first she tried to maintain a cold professionalism, but she quickly gave up the attempt to hide her passion for her dream.

'And what makes you think you can make this work?' the loans manager asked at last. 'What are you going to do that the others are not doing?'

Leigh reached into the cardboard box. She placed two bottles on the desk. The label said Bangala Wines.

'I am a good wine maker,' she said with total confidence. 'I have been making a sample vat each year for the past three years. I think the wine I make is as good as any you'll get anywhere.'

'That's a good start,' the bank man said.

'And I've got ideas.' Leigh placed two of the diamanté-studded wine glasses on the desk. 'Things like this. They will appeal to the Japanese market. This is just a sample. I'll be looking for one new idea — a new gimmick or selling point — every year.'

The loans officer picked up one of the glasses, and turned it slowly in his hand.

'And I've got some ideas for expanding the vineyards too,' Leigh hurried on. 'I've talked to a couple of wine clubs in Sydney. People will actually pay to come up and plant vines. It will be like a holiday for them, and I get my expansion. I can give them a limited-edition first run on the vintage. I bet they'll happily pay a little extra for wine from their own vines.'

'All right.' The loans manager smiled. 'You've convinced me you can do it. Now, let's have a look at those figures and projections. If they are as promising as all this, I think we can do business.'

He began to hand back the wine and glasses, but Leigh shook her head.

'Please, keep the wine. And the glasses. They are just my way of proving to you that I am a good risk.'

'That's kind of you, Miss Kenyon,' the man replied with a smile, 'but I can't do that. It wouldn't look right.'

'Oh.' Leigh quickly returned the offending items to their box, and began laying her account books out on the desk.

When she finally emerged from the bank, Leigh's head was spinning. The loans manager had done what he had promised, and examined her account books and projections in the most minute detail. He had a very quick mind, and could manipulate figures in a flash. There were times when Leigh had felt quite left behind. But in the end, he seemed happy. She would have to wait for the official notification, but she had been told she should start preparing to move on her plans.

She could have kissed the loans manager when he said that. In fact, now she thought about it, he was rather good looking. Perhaps, when the paperwork was finished, she might invite him again to sample her wine. She laughed out loud at the thought.

A middle-aged couple walking towards her smiled when they heard her laugh. Leigh smiled back, then stopped in front of them.

'You don't know me, but I have something for you.'

She put the cardboard box down on the footpath and opened it.

'See this,' she said, pulling out a bottle of wine. 'As of today, this is the very first official bottle of Bangala Wine. My wine. I would like you to have it.'

Bowing slightly, she presented the wine to the gentleman, who accepted it with a broad smile.

'Well, thank you,' he said.

'Congratulations, my dear,' said his wife.

'Thank you. I would also like to give you . . . ' Leigh pulled the diamanté-studded glasses from the box, 'these.'

'Oh, my.' The woman turned the glasses in her hand. 'These are lovely. Are you sure you want to give them away?'

'I am very sure.'

'Then we shall use them to drink a toast to your success,' the woman said.

'Thank you. Enjoy the wine.'

Leigh picked up her almost empty box and walked on, leaving the bemused couple staring after her.

* * *

'Are you listening to me?'

Robert Anderson's querulous voice dragged Greg back to the reality of the hospital room with its bare walls and antiseptic smell.

'Sorry, Dad?'

'I asked if you had brought the latest issue of *Canegrower*.'

'Yes, I did.' Greg pulled the magazine from the bundle of papers already lying on the edge of his father's bed.

'All right.'

The old man flipped eagerly through the pages of the magazine, his hands shaking. He looked much worse than a few weeks ago. He had lost a lot of weight. His skin was pale, dry and cracked like ancient parchment. But still he clung to the illusion that one day he would be back at the helm of his cane farm. And still he found fault with everything his son tried to do.

Greg sat in silence, happy to be ignored by his father for a few minutes at least. Jasi wasn't here, of course. Greg still hadn't been able to tell her about his father. She thought he was attending to business at the sugar mill. He hated lying to her. Jasi was trying so hard to develop a relationship with him. She was always suggesting fun things for them to do together. Trips to the beach, or dinners. She had even hinted that she was ready to move out of the guest bedroom and into his. Greg knew she was disappointed that he hadn't taken the hint.

He couldn't sleep with Jasi, when the person he wanted was Molly.

He pulled himself out of his reverie. His father was still engrossed in the magazine, muttering under his breath as he read. Greg felt as if the walls were closing in. He started grabbing the papers from the bed.

'What are you doing?' Robert demanded. 'I haven't finished with those.'

'Fine. Keep them.' Greg dropped the

briefcase on the floor. 'I've got to go.'

He turned and almost ran from the room, ignoring his father's startled cries behind him. Once back at the car park, he leaned against the side of his ute, wishing that he smoked. Anything that might help him regain his lost equilibrium. At least out here he didn't feel as if he was going to be crushed. Another few minutes in that room and he would have suffocated.

He gazed up at the clear blue sky, and wondered where Molly was. He hadn't heard from her since she returned to Sydney. Not that he should expect to hear from her. That kiss on the night of the cane fire could never lead to anything. Not while he was trapped here and she was in Sydney. And certainly not while Jasi was with him. But it would have been nice to hear from her.

His restlessness increasing, Greg got behind the wheel of the ute. Automatically he turned the vehicle towards home. As he drove, wisps of smoke from the ongoing cane fires wafted across his view, reminding him that it was almost time he fired his own cane. Reminding him of Molly.

When he stopped outside his house, Greg's first instinct was to go to his workshop and lose himself in his work. He needed to feel the satisfaction and pleasure that came from moulding glowing metal into beautiful shapes.

But first he should go into the house to see Jasi. If he didn't, she would notice the car and come looking for him, and he didn't want to be disturbed once he started working. That thought caused such a wave of regret that his breath caught in his throat. This couldn't go on. Jasi deserved better from him. He had to forget about Molly so far away in Sydney, and give himself to the girl who was with him.

'Jasi,' he called as he walked through into the living room.

For a few moments there was no answer, then Jasi appeared in the hall wearing a short skirt and a light cotton vest. She had obviously just stepped out of the shower. She looked shining and fresh, still beaded with water. Her blond hair was wet, and the water trickling down her shoulders and on to her top rendered the white fabric almost transparent. Greg could see the dark shadow of her nipples.

'Hi, Greg,' she said, moving towards him, her lips parting in a welcoming smile.

She stood on her toes to kiss him gently. She smelled of flowers and soap. Greg reached for her, pulled her close and kissed her. Long and slow and hard. She was warm and welcoming. Her body melted against his.

The light fabric of her clothes hid nothing from him as his hands caressed her shoulders, her back, and slid down to pull her hips against him.

Her lips were as eager as his. Her arms went around his neck, pulling him even closer. Greg felt her quivering as his lips sought the soft flesh on her neck. Felt the pulse beating beneath the damp skin. He closed his eyes and gave himself up to his need. He slid his fingers under the fabric of her top, caressing the silky skin. It felt good. Her breath on his neck. Her hands in his hair. Everything would be all right if he could lose himself in her. Could love her. Could be with Molly.

Greg froze. His hands dropped to his sides and his rough breathing almost stopped.

'Greg?' Jasi's brow creased. 'What's wrong?'

Greg looked into those clear blue eyes, and realised what he had to do. Carefully he disentangled himself. He took Jasi by the hand and led her to the couch. He sat her down, but didn't sit next to her. Instead, he sat in an armchair opposite.

'Jasi,' he said slowly, 'we need to talk.'

The look on her face told him she knew what he was about to say.

'It's Molly, isn't it?' she asked quietly, tears already forming. 'You want Molly, not me.'

She was right. He did want Molly. He knew that now. But how could he tell Jasi that? She had come so far to be with him. And she had done nothing wrong. She just wasn't Molly. He couldn't lie to her, but he could try to soften the blow.

'That's not all of it,' he said. 'There's a lot I haven't told you. It's time I started being honest. Who do you think owns this place?'

Jasi looked puzzled. 'Well, you do. Don't you?'

'No.' Greg watched shock replace the hurt in her eyes. 'My father owns the farm and everything on it — including me.'

'I don't understand . . . '

Greg explained everything. His father's illness. His own decision to send a photo to *Australian Life*. He showed her the box of unopened letters still sitting in the small office, and told her that hers was the first he'd found that sounded even slightly promising.

'It's not you,' he told her. 'You're a really nice person and you've lived up to your part. It's my fault. I don't want the farm. This life. None of it.'

Jasi's eyes were still wet, but her crying had stopped.

'Jasi,' Greg said softly, 'in your heart, I don't think you want this either. You're not cut out to be a farmer's wife. You like the city life too much.'

She almost smiled then, and sniffed a little. 'Well, I do miss my friends. And the parties and clubs.'

'Well, maybe you should go home.'

She took it far better than he had expected. He rang the airport while she packed. He paid for her flight home. He felt it was the least he could do, and Jasi didn't argue. She was already looking forward to seeing her friends again, and talking about the job she thought she might get selling cosmetics at a department store. By late afternoon, it was as if she had never been there. Greg was alone in the house. He stood in the living room holding his silver charm in his hand. He had taken one step in the right direction, but it didn't feel good. His world seemed lonelier than ever before, and his mind was full of thoughts of Molly.

He found the piece of paper with the phone number and the name he was looking for.

'Greg,' the woman in Sydney answered cheerfully. 'I am glad you called. I would like to start writing that story very soon. I hope you have some news for me . . . '

'I'm afraid it's not good news.' He told the writer that she wouldn't be getting the story she had hoped for.

'I see.' The woman sounded disappointed.

Greg felt a little ashamed. He had deliberately misled her, just to keep Molly with him a few days longer. It hadn't worked out very well. 'Is Molly around?' He tried to keep the question offhand, as if it wasn't really important.

'Molly? No. She's a freelancer. She doesn't come in here often.'

'Oh.' He hadn't really expected her to be there, but he had hoped . . . he wasn't sure what he had hoped for. 'Well, if you see her, tell her I said 'hello',' he ended lamely.

'All right.'

The tone of the woman's voice as she hung up didn't leave him much hope that she would pass on his message. He couldn't blame her. He wasn't impressed with his behaviour either. He left the office, his feet turning instinctively towards the solace of his workshop.

* * *

In her Sydney flat, Molly was working when the phone rang. Her large desktop computer screen was filled with the images she had copied from her laptop. Images of the sugarcane fire. She had made a shortlist of a handful of photos that were particularly spectacular. Those she might find a market for.

She was also preparing the shots she'd taken of Greg and Jasi together. She was due to deliver them to *Australian Life*. She really wasn't enjoying the task. Every image of the two together was just wrong. It wasn't poor photography. Greg and Jasi made a handsome couple. They looked good together, but in her heart Molly knew it wasn't right.

She sighed and kept on with the job. This time tomorrow, they would be safely delivered. She could collect her payment and forget all about Greg.

For once, she welcomed the buzz of her mobile phone as it interrupted her work. It was Richard, Helen Woodley's assistant at *Australian Life*.

'I'll have the shots from the Townsville trip for you first thing in the morning,' Molly told him.

'That's actually why I was ringing,' Richard said. 'We don't need the shots. Sorry.'

'Oh.' Molly was stunned by the news. It was rare for a magazine to not use shots they had commissioned. But that wasn't what she was concerned about. 'Why?' She kept the question light.

'I'm not sure. I just got a message from the

writer to say the piece is cancelled.'

'Oh.'

'I think maybe they broke up. Do you want me to find out?'

'No. No. It's fine,' Molly said quickly. 'It doesn't matter. I just wondered. That's all.'

'Molly.' Richard's voice was hesitant. 'A few of us are going out for a drink tonight. I was wondering if you wanted to join us.'

It wasn't the first time Richard had asked her out. Molly's immediate reaction was to say no, as she had in the past. But she hesitated. This wasn't exactly a date. It almost counted as working, if the team from *Australian Life* was there. She might be able to pick up another assignment. And she might hear more about exactly what had gone wrong with the story about Greg and Jasi. She might even find out how Greg was doing.

'Where are you going?'

'The Lord Nelson.'

Molly had often been to the old stone pub in the historic Rocks area. A lot of media people drank there. The pub brewed its own beer, and it was pretty good. She was supposed to be going to her parents' place for dinner tonight, but she could easily cancel that. She'd tell her mother she had a date, which was almost the truth. That would work.

Her mother was always telling her she needed to date more.

'All right,' she said.

'Great.' Richard sounded too pleased. She would have to be careful later, not give him the wrong idea. 'We'll be there from about six. See you then.'

Molly dropped her phone back on the desk. The photo of Greg stared back at her from her computer. She smiled at him. She was glad he'd ended the relationship with Jasi. It wasn't right for him. She wondered what else he was doing. Would he find the courage to leave the farm? Maybe she could help a little.

She quickly found a selection of shots she'd taken of Greg's jewellery. She opened a new e-mail page and started typing.

I thought you might like to have these. Use them for your website, or for advertising if you want to.

Molly hesitated. Should she say something about Jasi? But what could she say? She was glad Greg wasn't with Jasi any longer. They were just not right for each other. She wondered who had called it off, and hoped Greg hadn't been hurt. In the end, she decided to say nothing.

I know a jeweller here in Sydney who would really like your designs. He might want to buy some of your stuff, or maybe get you to do some work for him. If you decide to get in touch with him, tell him I sent you.

She added the jeweller's name and contact details. She attached the photos and sat looking at the page. That was all she could do. Greg had to take it from here. She hesitated a moment over the keyboard, then ended the mail with just her name. She hit the send button quickly, before she could change her mind.

She started to close down her laptop, but stopped with one image still large on her screen. This one she would not sell. The shot showed Greg's face lit by the golden glow from the fire. He was looking towards something in the distance, totally unaware of the camera. The dramatic lighting served to make him look older and even more handsome than he actually was. It gave him a dark and brooding air. He could have been Heathcliff or Mr Rochester or even Mr Darcy; the flawed hero of a Victorian novel.

It was a great shot. Molly had no idea what to do with it, but she knew she would keep it.

* * *

Matt arrived at the restaurant five minutes early. He wasn't the only one.

She waved from the other side of the road, and Matt frowned. Her hair was covered with a scarf and she wore large sunglasses, despite the fact that the daylight was rapidly fading. She glanced from side to side, as if looking for someone, before darting across the road.

'Let's go inside quickly.' She took his arm and steered him through the door of the restaurant before he had a chance to speak.

As the door shut gently behind them, Matt dug his toes in. 'What's this all about?'

She removed the sunglasses and scarf and shook out her wavy auburn hair. 'Just dodging the paps. Now that my dad is a celeb, I have to be a bit careful.' She stood on her toes to kiss him on the cheek.

'Cut that out.' Matt hugged his daughter. 'It's good to see you.'

The waitress showed them to a table set for three.

'So, tell me all about it,' Ali said.

'Haven't we got this the wrong way around?' Matt asked. 'Surely I'm the one who is supposed to be asking you questions like that.'

'Oh, Dad. Don't be so old fashioned.' Ali laughed.

The waitress interrupted them, and as they ordered mineral water for him and a glass of wine for Ali, Matt marvelled that his little girl had grown into this beautiful young woman. Although their relationship had changed as Ali grew, they remained close, and for that Matt was very grateful. But he still didn't feel comfortable talking about his relationship with Helen. When he'd arrived for lunch alone the previous weekend, he had explained to Ali about the photographers at Helen's flat. That had distracted his daughter enough that she hadn't asked too many difficult questions. But he had a feeling he was going to have to answer those questions tonight, at least until Helen arrived. He wasn't sure what he was going to say.

Was he falling in love with Helen? That seemed far too simple a way to describe what was happening. He was drawn to her. He liked her. Was confused by her and attracted to her in ways that he couldn't begin to define. But falling in love? How could you fall in love with someone you had known for such a short time? Someone who kept so much of herself hidden? From the scar he had seen on her stomach to the choices she made, Helen kept her secrets. She might have told him about the exclusive story locked away in her desk, but she hadn't shared the secrets locked inside herself. Maybe one day . . .

'Come on, Dad, 'fess up.' Ali interrupted his thoughts.

'Confess what?'

'Helen. You know . . . your girlfriend.'

Matt didn't try to explain that 'girlfriend' was not a word that suited Helen at all. Instead, he decided to join Ali's mood.

'All right. Well, she has blond hair, and she's old enough not to tell me how old she is.'

'Dad!'

'I think she's close to forty,' he confessed, 'but she looks younger.'

'And . . . ' Ali teased.

'Well, she's the editor of some magazine.'

'Some magazine?' Ali was horrified. '*Australian Life* is not just some magazine. It's *the* magazine. It's really cool. Everyone at uni reads it.'

She reached for her large shoulder bag and dug around inside for a few seconds before emerging triumphant with a slightly battered magazine in her hand. She handed it to Matt, who flipped cautiously through the pages.

'Dad, you've never read the magazine, have you?'

'Well. No.'

'How can you date the editor and not read

even one issue? That's just so . . . ' Ali was lost for words.

She was right, of course. Matt knew he should at least look at the magazine that was so important to Helen. He just hadn't done it yet.

'Read that while I find the ladies'.'

Alone at the table, Matt flicked through the magazine. He imagined the fashion and beauty tips would go down well with the female readers. Much of the issue seemed to be given over to gossip about people he'd never heard of. Nor had he ever watched the television shows most of them seemed to star in. There was a story about a dairy farmer and the girl he had met through the Farmer Needs a Wife campaign. The piece hinted at a possible engagement. Matt hoped the pair knew what they were doing. He found it strange that his daughter had entered him in the campaign. She must have known it was not something he'd ever consider doing himself. Still, he thought as he looked up to watch Helen walk through the restaurant door, it had worked out pretty well.

She appeared to have come straight from work. She was wearing black slacks and a jacket, and her blond hair was clipped back behind her head. Even so, she attracted other eyes than his as she came into the room. She was a beautiful woman. Poised and confident. The image she presented to the world was very different from the woman he had taken to bed a few nights ago.

She had shed the poise with her clothes. Naked, she was equally beautiful, but she had been almost shy. Naïve perhaps. Matt suspected that few men had ever been allowed close enough to touch her, physically or emotionally. Yet despite the secrets she still kept, she had opened herself to him in many ways. She was a sensual and giving woman, with a great capacity for joy. Matt watched her walk across the room and realised that maybe, just maybe he was falling in love.

Helen was pleased to see that Matt was alone. She would have a few minutes with him before his daughter arrived. Ridiculous as it might seem, she was nervous. She had interviewed prime ministers and business tycoons, artists and killers, but she was scared of facing an eighteen-year-old girl.

But before Helen was halfway across the room, a girl who could only be Matt's daughter returned to his table. Matt said a few words, and the girl looked across the restaurant and smiled at Helen. Ali was quite lovely. Wavy auburn hair surrounding a heart-shaped face. The girl was wearing a short skirt and trendy jacket. Helen found herself wishing she had changed before she left the office. Well, it was too late now.

Matt rose to his feet as Helen reached his table, and kissed her on the cheek.

'Helen, this is Ali. Ali, this is Helen, although of course you two have already talked on the phone, conspiring against me.'

'Hi, Helen.' The girl smiled at her.

'It's good to meet you, Ali,' Helen said, meaning it. 'And one of these days, you must tell me how you talked your way past my assistant when you made that first phone call. Not many people can do that.'

'It's something I inherited from my dad,' Ali teased. 'It's called being stubborn.'

'Watch it, daughter,' Matt joked. 'I can always disinherit you — and turn Willaring Downs into a charity home for aged donkeys.'

'As if . . . '

Father and daughter were both laughing as they sat, and for a second Helen felt very much like an outsider. The feeling didn't last long as Ali turned the conversation to what Helen guessed was a favourite subject.

'Dad said you rode Granny when you were down at the farm the other week. What did you think of her? She's great, isn't she?'

'She is,' Helen agreed. 'She was very kind to me. It's a long, long time since I last rode a horse.'

'I think Granny could be a winner in the show ring, but Dad thinks she'll make a work horse . . . '

The conversation ranged freely as they ordered and ate their meals. Horses and Willaring Downs featured highly. As did Ali's studies at university.

'The vet school is really great,' was the verdict. 'It's hard work, but I do love it. And I love uni generally. The people. The social life.'

'Not too much of the social life,' Matt cut in, feigning parental disapproval.

'The social life is an important part of the whole experience,' Helen protested.

Ali cast a triumphant look at her smiling father, before the conversation turned in another direction.

Helen said little for the next few minutes. She listened to the ebb and flow of the talk around her, understanding for the first time what it must feel like to be part of a family. She thought she'd lost the chance of this a long time ago. Lost it through her own foolishness. She had accepted her fate, and turned all her energy instead to her career. Now it was almost as if she was being given a second chance. As if another path was opening up to her. Somewhere inside her was the hint of a desire to take that path, and choose a different life. The thought surprised her. It was unlike her to be so fanciful. Any moment now, her phone would ring and drag her back into the reality of her life.

It didn't.

Not until they were finishing dessert.

'I am so sorry,' Helen said as she pulled her phones from her bag.

'Two phones?' Matt raised an eyebrow.

'The work one is turned off,' Helen said defensively. 'But this is my private number. Only a very few people have this. I have to answer it.'

She took the phone, walked out on to the street and flipped it open.

'Richard, what is it?'

'I'm sorry to disturb you, Helen.' The voice at the other end of the phone sounded breathless. 'But there's someone trying to get in touch with you. I have just given them this number, and wanted to warn you.'

'This number?' Richard never did that without her permission. 'Who did you give it to?'

Richard told her.

Helen was stunned. The man was head of one of the world's biggest international media conglomerates. Why was he calling her?

'Helen, are you still there?'

'Yes, Richard. I'm still here.'

'I spoke to his PA when she called. He is

going to call you himself in just a few minutes.'

'Did she say what it was about?' Even as she asked the question, Helen knew what the answer would be. A man like that did not have to explain why he was calling. And he certainly would not explain to her assistant.

'All right. Thank you, Richard.'

Helen carefully closed her phone, and glanced back into the main room of the restaurant. Matt and Ali were sharing some joke, laughing quietly. Matt looked up and caught Helen's eye. She lifted the phone, to indicate she was waiting for another call. He nodded, and leaned forward to speak to his daughter again. Helen's phone rang. She allowed it to ring a second time while she took a deep breath, then answered.

'Ms Woodley?' She recognised the voice from interviews she'd seen on television.

'Yes.'

'I do hope you don't mind my calling at such a late hour.'

'Not at all,' Helen replied, wondering where in the world he was and what the time was there.

'I won't keep you. I will be in Sydney towards the end of next week. I was hoping we could meet. Over dinner, perhaps?'

'Yes, of course. It would be my pleasure.'

Helen was amazed that her voice sounded so calm.

'I shall look forward to it. Good night, Ms Woodley.'

'Good night.'

Helen stared at the silent phone. It must be a job offer. There could be no other reason why such a man would request a meeting with her. This was *the* job offer. The one she had dreamed about for longer than she could remember. The thing she had worked so hard for. This would be New York. The big time. She was surprised that her hands weren't shaking.

Gradually the muted sounds of the restaurant began to impose themselves once more on her consciousness. She looked quickly across at the table, where Matt and Ali were waiting for her. Matt looked up and caught her eye. Helen's gut twisted with actual physical pain.

She fixed a smile on her face, and walked slowly back to the table, preparing to lie to Matt for the first time.

* * *

The sharp crack of the rifle shot sent nearby crows flying into the air with raucous cries. The old paint tin remained stubbornly on top of the rock.

'You would probably have a better chance of hitting it if you kept your eyes open.' Peter was struggling to keep the smile from his face.

'They *were* open.' Donna was indignant.

'I meant when you pull the trigger,' Peter chortled. 'Try again.'

Donna glared at him. She flexed her stiff shoulders, then broke the rifle open to reload. She was careful to remember everything Peter had taught her. Always treat a rifle as if it's loaded, even when you know it's not. Keep the barrel pointed at the ground. Never point it at anyone or anything — unless you want to shoot them. Of course, in her case, she hadn't hit anything yet. But one of these days she might. She glanced over her shoulder to where Peter was standing, watching her. She saw the approval in his eyes and she liked the way that made her feel.

'Ready?'

Donna took position next to him, her eye fixed on the can. She raised the rifle to her shoulder and took careful aim.

This time, the can bounced high in the air.

'I did it!'

Donna spun to face Peter. He was grinning widely. She took half a step towards him, wanting to hug him in her pleasure. At the last moment she caught herself.

'Well done!' he said enthusiastically.

'Thank you.'

She removed the Akubra hat and wiped the sweat from her eyes. 'Can I have another go?'

'Sure. Give me a minute . . . and don't shoot me by mistake.'

He set out to retrieve the can.

Since Jenny and Ken's departure, Peter had spent a lot of time with Donna, teaching her the things she needed to know about living in the outback. At first the tension between them had been so thick it was an almost tangible thing. But it had quickly faded. Donna wondered how much of that was simply because there was no choice, or how much was because they actually got on together rather well. When Peter relaxed, he was easy company. The time they shared with the twins was a joy.

Donna wasn't sure where her stay at River Downs was leading. Officially she guessed she was some sort of employee, but no mention had ever been made of a wage. Not that there was anywhere within a hundred kilometres where she could spend it. She had decided just to let each day bring what it would. She could wait a few weeks, and maybe, just maybe . . .

Peter set the battered can back on the rock. Donna watched him walk across the dry brown earth, his long legs covering the distance in just a few strides. She liked to watch him move. He was a big, powerful man, yet he moved with an unconscious grace that, like so many other things, was very attractive. Donna sighed and forced her attention back on to the rifle.

After several more attempts to shoot the can, Peter called an end to the session.

'I hit it twice,' Donna said, a huge grin on her face. 'That's not too bad.'

'Not too bad at all,' Peter agreed. 'Now all you have to do is persuade the snakes to lie on a rock and not move.'

'I'll get there. Just you wait,' Donna promised him.

As they walked back to the house, Donna filled Peter in on the twins' latest scholastic efforts. He was always interested in what they were up to. No father could love his kids more. Almost on cue, Chris and Sara appeared on the veranda. They were carrying one of the big iceboxes used for storing food at the muster camps. They put it down at the top of the stairs, and waited.

'What are they up to?' Peter wondered.

The twins were laughing and whispering together.

'I don't know,' Donna said, 'but I think we're about to find out.'

As Donna and Peter reached the bottom of the stairs, the twins opened the esky. They reached inside and each pulled out something white and shiny.

'What the . . . ' Peter's words failed as he was spattered with something very cold and very wet. A second later, Donna was also hit.

'Snowballs!' The twins flung themselves down the stairs and danced around the two startled adults. 'We made snowballs. Were they good, Donna?'

'Snowballs?' Peter looked at Donna.

Donna was shaking with laughter,

'I was telling them about the snow back in Yorkshire,' she chuckled. 'And the snowball fights we had when I was a kid.'

'We made them out of the stuff in the freezer!' Chris said proudly.

'We scraped the ice off the sides,' Sara added, 'and turned it into snowballs.'

'You certainly did,' Peter told his daughter. 'The best snowballs ever seen in the Territory, I'll bet.'

'You mean the *only* snowballs ever seen in the Territory,' Chris insisted, proudly puffing out his chest.

Donna looked up at Peter. A few flakes of ice still clung to his cheek, startlingly white against his deep tan. Without thinking, she reached out to brush the flakes away. Her fingers gently stroked his cheek. She could feel the roughness of his stubble against the soft skin of her palm. As her hand dropped away, his eyes caught and held her so close to him that she could almost feel the warmth of his breath. Her smile faded just a little, her lips slightly parted and the whole world held its breath, as she waited for him to close those last few inches between them. For his lips to touch hers.

'Dad!'

Sara's voice called them back to reality. Donna almost cried out as Peter turned away to speak to his daughter.

'Can we go to England and see proper snow?'

'Maybe one day,' he told her absently. 'Now, I want that esky put back. It's almost time for lunch.'

'Yes, Dad.' The twins raced up the stairs.

Donna still couldn't move. Peter turned back to her, the strangest expression on his face. She waited for him to speak. Or to touch her. Or to . . .

Above them, the sudden roar of an aircraft engine split the silence. Donna looked up as the Cessna banked and dropped rapidly towards the airstrip. The mail plane was making its weekly run.

'I'd better go and meet him,' Peter said.

Donna nodded as he turned away. Of course he had to go and meet the mail plane. Bad things happened when he didn't. Last time, she had almost lost her life. If Peter hadn't walked away this time, she might have lost her heart.

* * *

Peter strode quickly to the machinery shed, fighting an almost overpowering desire to turn around. He knew that Donna was watching him walk away. He could simply retrace his steps. He could take her in his arms as he wanted to. He could kiss her.

He kept walking.

The roar of the motorbike engine couldn't drive away the sound of her voice. The hot, dry wind in his face as he sped towards the airstrip couldn't mask the scent of her hair. He gripped the handlebars of his bike as if to bend the metal. Standing there looking down at Donna, snowflakes glistening in her dark hair, he had felt like a schoolboy on his first date. What a sight she was, with her fair skin already starting to tan and sprinkled with freckles. A man could lose himself in her eyes. He almost had. He had wanted nothing more than to kiss her, but was too afraid to try.

He was going too fast as he turned on to

the airstrip. The bike slid in the soft red bulldust, and for a few seconds Peter fought to regain control. At the end of the strip, the pilot was standing by the plane, watching as Peter drew near.

'G'day,' he said as soon as the noise of the motorbike engine died.

Peter acknowledged the greeting and took the bag of mail being offered.

'I've got your supplies in back,' the pilot said, casting a questioning glance at the bike.

'Let's just put them next to the shed,' Peter said. 'I'll bring the ute down later for them.'

'Sure.'

The two men started unloading the boxes.

'How's Donna doing?'

The pilot's question took Peter completely by surprise, until he remembered that Donna had arrived on the mail plane.

'Ah, fine,' he said quickly.

'She seemed a good sort. Is she staying long?'

It was an innocent question, but Peter had no answer. He mumbled something, and changed the topic to the weather, the state of the roads and the forthcoming mustering season. The two men chatted for a few minutes, then, with a glance at the sun, the pilot was back behind his controls for the next leg of his run.

Peter should have taken the mail to the house. He should have fetched the ute, to take the supplies back to the homestead. There were many things he should have done, not the least of which was talk to Donna. Instead, he got back on the motorbike, and turned it towards the one place where he could always think.

The river wound its way slowly between the rocky outcrops on the edge of the desert. It did more than give River Downs its name. It was the lifeblood of the station. Even in the driest years some water remained in the deepest holes. Peter rode towards a low hillock beside a bend in the river. He left the bike at the bottom, and climbed to the top. From here, he had a beautiful view across the river flats to the homestead, and beyond to the red mountains in the distance. It had been one of his favourite spots since childhood. Karen had loved it too, and this was where she now rested.

Peter stood looking down at the block of red sandstone that marked the grave. He had hauled the rock here himself, then chiselled her name on the smooth face. Just her name. Karen. He needed and wanted nothing else.

Peter placed his hand gently on the stone, as he did whenever he came here. He closed his eyes and tried to recall his wife's face. Her deep brown eyes were easy. The twins had their mother's eyes. Karen's hair had been dark and wavy, and she had the best smile. That was what had drawn him to her in the first place. It was very important to Peter that he should still be able to remember his wife's smile.

The face he saw in his mind had a captivating smile. But it wasn't Karen.

Something had happened in those few moments by the stairs. As the snowballs disintegrated in the heat, and Donna wiped the flecks of ice from his face, something inside Peter had woken after a long sleep. It wasn't just physical desire, although that had hit him with the force of a cyclone. There was the hint of something more. Something he hadn't felt in a long, long time.

Peter opened his eyes and stared at the name carved in the rock.

'I'm sorry, Karen.'

He felt tears at the back of his eyes. Were they for Karen? Or for himself and the utter loneliness that had been his constant companion since she died?

He turned away from the gravestone to crouch in the dust and gaze towards the homestead, where Donna would be making lunch for the twins. Was she thinking about him and wondering where he was? When the snowballs flew, had something happened to her too?

He crouched there for a very long time.

When finally he rose to his feet, his decision was made. There was nothing he could do until the muster was over, but as soon as it was, Donna must return to her real home. He had brought one woman to this remote place, and she had died here. He would not let it happen again.

He walked down the hill, without looking back at the lonely stone.

8

'All right, everybody. Take a break while I check these.' Molly lowered the camera. 'If they look all right, we'll set for the next series.'

The models relaxed and started chatting. Molly walked to her laptop to download the shots she'd just taken. The fashion shoot was for a feature on high-end accessories. The room was littered with designer shoes and bags, with clothes to match. They were shooting in a tile factory. Each model was posed against a different display wall. The tiles ranged from simple sunburned terracotta to ornate hand-painted and glazed works of art. Molly was enjoying herself.

She walked to the table where her laptop was waiting, and started looking for the cable to connect the camera.

'Oh, very nice indeed.'

One of the male models was standing behind her, looking at her computer. The screensaver was running, cycling through some of her favourite images. It was currently showing the photo of Greg's face lit by the cane fires.

'I don't suppose he's gay, by any chance?' asked the model hopefully.

Molly thought back to the night she had taken the photo. A single kiss under a flame-lit sky.

'Sorry, Drew. Not a chance.'

The model sighed dramatically and walked away, leaving Molly looking at Greg's photo. Drew had good reason to sigh. The shot really was something else! Molly was faintly embarrassed that the model had seen something so personal. He probably didn't realise it *was* personal. He probably thought Greg was just another model, from some other shoot. He certainly was handsome enough for it. Molly closed the photo and turned her attention to loading today's shots. She had work to do, and besides, Greg hadn't even replied to her e-mail.

'Hi, Molly!'

She turned to greet the new arrival. 'Hi, Chatri.'

'I brought a good selection for you.'

Chatri placed a large carry-case on the table. He opened it to display a selection of fine jewellery. The small bright-eyed man had learned his trade in the gem factories of Thailand before emigrating and setting up his own business in Australia. He had left behind the conventional styles popular with the tourists and was developing a reputation as an innovative and interesting designer. He was also the jeweller she had told Greg to contact.

'There's some very nice stuff here, Chatri,' Molly said as she looked at the selection. 'This will work very well.'

Much as she wanted to ask, Molly would not. If Greg had contacted Chatri, the jeweller would say something. She had a job to do, and couldn't afford to be distracted.

The shoot lasted another couple of hours. Molly was tired by the time they were packing up. She checked her phone messages. There was one from Richard at *Australian Life*. It might be another job. It might also be a chance to find out something about Greg. Maybe. She hit the call button.

'There's a job next week,' Richard told her. 'An all-woman team is gearing up for some car rally. Helen wants to do a pre-race feature, then follow them during the race. They are in Western Australia. Can you go there for a few days?'

Molly mentally checked her diary. 'I think so. Sounds like fun.'

'Great. I wanted to find something for you, after the farmer thing fell through.'

'Thanks. Did you hear any more about that?' Molly kept her voice disinterested.

'No,' Richard said. 'We did well out of the campaign, but I think we've milked it for all it's worth. We're moving on now.'

Moving on. That was what she should be doing. Molly agreed to drop in to Richard's office the next day.

Most of the gear was packed away, and the models were leaving. Chatri came over to say goodbye.

'Oh, I got an e-mail from that man in Queensland,' he said as he turned to go. 'He sent me some photos of his work. It was good.'

'I thought so,' Molly said.

'I assume you took the photos?'

'Yes.'

'They were good too. Anyway, I told him if he comes here to contact me. I think we could work together.'

'Thanks, Chatri.' Molly kissed his cheek as he left.

She was pleased that Greg had made contact with Chatri. Pleased that the jeweller saw his potential. But why hadn't Greg contacted her? At least he could have e-mailed to say thank you. Chatri spoke as if he expected Greg to come to Sydney. Molly knew better. Greg was chained to his father and to a life he hated. She didn't know if he would ever find the strength and courage to break away.

* * *

When Greg arrived in the hospital room, his father was sitting up in bed, struggling with a shirt. The old man's face was flushed and his breathing seemed rough.

'It's about time you got here,' Robert Anderson snapped. 'It must be two hours since I called and got that infernal machine.'

It was just under an hour since his father had left his message, but Greg didn't bother to correct him. He'd found it when he took a break from his workshop, and had come as quickly as he could.

'What's going on?' he asked.

'I'm getting out of here.' Robert started pulling at the bedclothes. 'I'm not staying a day longer. But I need your help.'

Greg felt his mouth drop open with shock. Whatever he had expected when he heard his father's urgent message, it hadn't been this.

'Getting out? But I thought the doctor said — '

'Forget what he said.' Robert spat the words out. 'I'm going home and you're going to help me.'

Greg knew that something was wrong. He left without another word and went in search of his father's physician.

'I've told him he shouldn't even try to

leave,' the doctor said as they sat in the visitors' lounge. 'He is a very sick man. In fact, without help, I doubt he'd make it as far as the car park.'

'Then why is he so determined?'

'Greg, you know your father. It's not easy getting old, and for someone like Robert, illness is even harder to accept.'

'Realistically, could he go home?'

The doctor thought carefully for a few moments. 'Maybe. If he had round-the-clock nursing. And I mean round-the-clock.'

'I see.' Greg felt his heart sink. He knew what would come next. As a dutiful son, he would be expected to care for his father. To give up his dreams and nurse a bitter old man. He would have to do it, because to not do it would leave a burden of guilt too heavy for him to endure.

'I know what you're thinking,' the doctor cut in. 'And don't even contemplate taking that on yourself. It's too much for one person. You don't have the training for it. Or the facilities at home. To be brutally honest, no matter how much he hates it, your father is far better off staying here.'

Greg looked at the doctor, trying to hide the relief he felt. 'But if he really wants to go home . . . '

'It won't help him,' the doctor said gently.

'What he wants is to be young and strong again. You can't give him that. No one can. Don't waste your life trying.'

Greg thought about the doctor's words as he walked slowly back to his father's room. Robert was sitting on the edge of the bed. He had managed to pull on his shirt and was doing up the buttons slowly. Greg looked closely at his father's hands. They were shaking badly.

'Dad, I've talked to the doctor,' he said as gently as he could. 'He said you have to stay.'

'Of course he'd say that, you fool,' Robert answered. 'He's a vulture. They are all vultures.'

'Dad, he says you need more care than I can give you at home.'

'You're just not willing to help me,' the old man spat back. 'After everything I've done for you. What sort of a son would leave his father here?'

Greg didn't say a word. Instinctively his hand sought out the silver charm in the pocket of his jeans. He stood by helplessly, the charm clenched tightly between his fingers, as Robert continued to button his shirt.

'Get my trousers,' Robert ordered. 'They are hanging up in that wardrobe.'

'No, Dad. I won't.'

'What?'

'I won't get your trousers. You're not well enough to leave. The doctor says you're better off here, and I won't go against his advice.'

'Get them!' Robert almost screamed.

'If you were well enough to leave, you could get the trousers yourself,' Greg told him.

Robert glared at his son, then began to rise slowly from the bed. Greg caught his breath. Robert stood for a few seconds, then his legs began to buckle and he fell backwards on to the bed.

'Dad!' Greg lunged forward to help his father.

'Get away!' The old man slapped Greg's hand. The silver charm Greg had been holding spun through the air and fell to the lino floor with a dull thud. Greg watched his father pull himself back on to the bed, then went to retrieve the charm.

'What's that?' Robert asked in a shrill voice.

'Nothing,' Greg said, slipping the charm back into his pocket.

'It's more of that ridiculous art stuff, isn't it?' Robert demanded. 'That's why you want to leave me here. So you can ignore the farm and spend all your time in that workshop. And I bet you're robbing me to pay for it.

Aren't you? Well, I won't let you get away with it!'

Greg couldn't take it any more. He began moving towards the door.

'That's right. Run out on me. You're just like your mother. Worthless: the pair of you.'

Greg stopped. Robert never mentioned his wife. Anything Greg had wanted to know, he had always had to ask. And most of the time, the answers had been pretty abrupt.

'What do you mean, just like her?'

'She ran out on me too.'

Greg turned slowly around to face the man in the bed. Robert's lips were quivering, and spittle was running from one corner of his mouth.

'You told me she was killed in a car accident,' Greg said slowly.

'She was. Served her right, too. She stole my car and was running away. You weren't much more than a baby. She took you too. But she didn't get far.'

'The accident happened as she was leaving you.' Greg's voice came out as a whisper. 'So that's why you never kept any photos. Why you never talked about her.'

'She deserved it. She was no good.'

Greg barely heard the words. His mind was racing.

'I raised you,' Robert ranted. 'On my own.

I fed and clothed you. I deserve something in return for all that.'

'I bet there were times you wished I had died in that crash too,' Greg said quietly.

Robert didn't answer. He didn't have to.

Greg looked at the old man on the bed with something approaching horror. What sort of father could wish harm to his own child?

A thousand images flashed though Greg's mind — images of the boy who had worshipped his father. When he was small, he had aped Robert's words and mannerisms, trying to be like him. He had studied by torchlight in his bed, hoping that a good school report would earn a smile. As a teenager, he had worked around the farm until his hands bled, trying to earn just one word of praise. Even in his darkest moments, he had always believed that somewhere deep inside them both, a small flame of familial love still glowed, waiting only for circumstance to bring them back together.

That would never happen.

The realisation should have rocked him to the core. It should have left him hurt and grieving. It didn't. He felt as if a great weight had been lifted from his back. It wasn't his fault that his father didn't love him. He had done nothing wrong. He looked at Robert and saw only a bitter old man who did not want or deserve his love. In his heart, he felt nothing but pity.

Without another word, he turned on his heel and walked away, ignoring the angry voice calling for him to come back. He paused at the nurses' station.

'My father needs some help,' he said calmly. 'Could someone go to him, please.'

He walked down the long sterile corridor and out of the hospital.

* * *

Something was bothering Helen. Matt could tell just by looking at her.

They were riding along the side of the creek. Helen was once again mounted on Granny, while Matt rode a tall brown gelding. Both horses were young and new to the saddle, and with this in mind, Matt had led them on a gentle ride along the river flats. The horses were relaxed, walking with their heads extended, blowing gently through their nostrils.

Helen should be relaxed too, but she wasn't. She tried to hide it, but Matt could sense the tension in the set of her shoulders.

'Did you have a tough week?' he asked.

Helen didn't seem to hear him. Her eyes

were fixed on some distant point, but he knew she wasn't seeing the trees or the river.

'Helen?' He raised his voice a little.

'Sorry.' She was back with him. 'I was a million miles away.'

'That's all right,' he said. 'I asked if it had been a rough week at work. You seem tense.'

'It wasn't the best week. I lost a story I had been banking on for the next issue. The last one from the farmer campaign.'

'That's a shame,' he said. 'What have you done about the movie star story?'

'Nothing. The folder is still locked in my drawer.'

Matt watched Helen's face as she talked. He liked to watch her face, the way her lips moved and the tiny creases around her eyes when she smiled. Her face told him more than she might suspect, and today it told him that she was still keeping secrets. He wasn't going to pry. She would tell him when she was ready.

They made their way back to the stables and dismounted. Helen stretched her neck, rubbing the side of it. Matt stepped up behind her, and began to slowly massage her shoulders. Helen leaned back into his hands with a sigh.

'That feels good.'

'I'll tell you what,' Matt said softly. 'It'll be

almost dark by the time we're done here. You could have a nice relaxing bath, while I organise us some dinner.'

'That sounds good,' Helen said. 'I should have brought some bubble bath.'

'I've got some,' Matt said. 'I was a boy scout once, and you know the motto — be prepared.'

Helen chuckled slowly.

They took Granny and the brown gelding back to the stable block and began setting out the evening feeds. Then they set about bedding the horses down for the night. Helen worked alongside Matt, doing her share. By the time they were finished, it was just starting to get dark.

Back inside the house, Matt propelled Helen gently in the direction of the bathroom with its huge white enamel tub.

'There's bubble bath. Fresh towels. And some candles if you want them.'

'That sounds heavenly,' Helen said in a weary voice. 'Most men wouldn't have thought of all that.'

'As I may have told you once before, I'm not most men.'

Helen turned and looked up at him thoughtfully. 'No, you're not.'

She kissed him, for the first time since she had arrived. A long, slow kiss. Almost a sad kiss. Then she vanished into the bathroom.

Matt walked through to his bedroom, and began stripping off his sweat-stained work clothes. He thought about joining Helen in the bathtub. It was big enough for two. He could take a couple of glasses of wine and massage her shoulders until the tension went away. It was an inviting thought, but he pushed it aside. Right now Helen needed a bit of space. He walked through to his en suite shower, and set the temperature controls to cold.

He was in the middle of preparing dinner when Helen emerged from the bathroom. Her face was free of make-up and her blond hair was caught in a ponytail. She was wearing a pair of white cotton trousers and a pale blue shirt. The outfit, combined with her bare feet, contrived to make her look about eighteen. It was a very good look.

'So, what are you making?' she asked as she propped herself on a stool by the breakfast bench.

'For your dining pleasure tonight, we have lamb roasted with garlic and rosemary.'

'That's what smells so good. You keep this up and I'll get chubby.'

'Never,' Matt joked, pleased that Helen seemed more relaxed now.

Dinner passed pleasantly enough. The

lamb was good. So was the wine. They talked about books and poetry. About Ali's exploits at university. Matt let Helen steer the conversation. When she was ready, she would tell him whatever it was that was hovering at the edge of her mind.

They were just finishing coffee on the veranda when Matt became aware of the noises from the stables. Helen heard them too.

'What's that?' she asked.

'If it's what I think it is, you are in for a treat,' said Matt. 'Wait here.'

* * *

Helen watched Matt vanish in the direction of the stables. She liked watching him move. He was so big, yet so controlled and confident when he walked. It never failed to send her pulse up a notch, even when she was feeling tense, as she was right now. Matt had much to offer a woman. To offer her.

She took another sip of her coffee.

The same time the previous night, she had also been sipping coffee after dinner, with another man who had a lot to offer. His offer, though, had been strictly professional. A key role in a global media conglomerate. An office in New York. Power. Glamour. And more money than she was ever likely to be offered again. It was the job she had been working towards for her entire career.

So why hadn't she said yes?

She hadn't said no. They had agreed that she would take a few days to think about it and give him her answer next week. They both knew her answer was going to be yes. This offer really was too good to refuse, and if for some strange reason she did, there would never be another.

In the faint light from the stable block, Helen saw Matt returning. She had come here to tell him she was leaving. But somehow she just couldn't get the words out.

'Helen, get your boots and come with me.' He waited for her at the bottom of the steps.

Puzzled, she did as he asked, and they headed back towards the stables.

'What's this all about?' Helen asked.

'You'll see in a few minutes. But you'll have to be very, very quiet. We don't want to disturb her.'

'Disturb who?'

'Sshh!'

They slipped inside the huge old wooden shed that Matt used for storing hay and horse feed. One end of the building had been turned into a large stall. Inside, Helen could see a grey horse, moving restlessly. Matt led

Helen to a pile of hay bales. They climbed up and settled down on a thick rug he had laid there.

'That's Cassie,' he whispered close to Helen's ear. 'And sometime tonight she's going to foal.'

'Oh!' Helen bit off the exclamation before the noise could startle the mare. 'I thought they liked to be alone when they foaled,' she continued in a whisper.

'They do. But I want to keep an eye on her. She's already in labour, and if we're quiet she won't even notice we are here.'

'Isn't this the wrong time of year for foaling?' Helen asked.

'Yes. This wasn't planned.'

'What happened?' Helen asked.

'I'd taken her to a show. Some fool thought it would be a good laugh to open the stables and let the horses out during the night. She was in season. One of the other horses let loose was a stallion. And nature took its course. Which is a shame, because she's really too young to breed.'

'Did you think of . . . Well, could you have stopped the pregnancy?'

'Abort the foal? I suppose I could have done something. But that might have damaged Cassie. Made it impossible to breed her later. Besides, by the time I realised she was in foal, it was a bit late. I thought I should let the foal grow. Who knows what it might turn out to be.'

Helen fell silent. This conversation was just a little bit too close to home for her. Matt had seen the scar on her stomach. She had wanted to tell him, but it was hard to let go of a secret kept for so many years.

They made themselves comfortable and waited. In the stall, the grey mare moved restlessly, occasionally making low snorting noises as she sniffed at the thick bed of wood shavings under her feet. She lay down, and Matt tensed. But a few minutes later she got up again. When she lay down and rose a second time, Matt turned to Helen.

'I think there's something wrong.'

Carefully they made their way down to the stall. The mare watched them, her eyes rolling. As she moved, they could clearly see one tiny hoof visible under her tail.

'There should be two,' Matt said. 'One of its legs is bent and it's stuck.'

'What are you going to do? Call a vet?'

'No. I'm going to straighten the other leg. And I need your help.'

Before Helen could protest, Matt had slipped through the door into the stall, and was holding the mare's halter, stroking her face and crooning softly to her.

'Come in,' he called to Helen in the same soft voice.

She did as she was told, and moved to the mare's head.

'Take hold of the halter,' Matt continued. 'That's it. Now, I'm going to turn the foal. It's going to hurt, so hold her tight. She might try to fight you. Talk to her. Stroke her face. If you have to, twist her ear to give her something to think about.'

'But . . . ' Helen could feel the panic rising inside her.

'Keep your voice soft,' Matt said calmly. 'Okay, now if you've got her . . . '

Helen tightened her grip on the leather, and moved close to the grey mare's head.

'Okay, Cassie,' she said, trying to imitate Matt's soothing tones. 'This isn't going to be nice. But Matt is just trying to help you. So we need you to stand really still.'

'That's good. Keep talking to her.'

Helen was beginning to wonder whether it was the horse Matt was trying to calm, or her.

Cassie suddenly tensed and tried to leap forward. Helen tightened her grip and placed a restraining hand across the mare's nose.

'Hold on to her!' Matt's voice was taut with the effort of what he was doing.

Helen didn't look at him. She kept her attention on the grey, maintaining a constant stream of soothing talk, although she had no idea what she was saying. It took just a few minutes, but they seemed like very long minutes.

'Well done, both of you,' Matt said at last. 'Everything should be fine now. Helen, we'll just step away quietly and leave her to it.'

They backed out of the stall, closing the door behind them. Cassie seemed to forget about them immediately. Matt guided Helen to a water tap and basin near the corner of the stall.

'Just wait,' he said, as he washed his arm. He was drying himself on an old towel hanging near the tap when Cassie bent her knees and dropped heavily to the ground.

Helen strained herself to see over the wall. The mare was sweating and grunting, swishing her tail in pain. Then, suddenly, something dark and wet slid on to the soft floor. Immediately, the mare turned, nuzzling the new arrival and licking it with her long rough tongue. She nickered with a low throaty rumble as the foal lifted its head.

'Oh,' Helen gasped. 'It's beautiful!'

Matt stepped close to her and put an arm around her shoulder. 'It always is.'

In the stall, Cassie was struggling to stand. She began pushing the foal, urging it to its feet. The little one straightened one long leg, staggered and fell.

'Poor thing,' Helen whispered. 'It will never get all those long legs under control.'

But it did. The foal lurched to its feet and stood, shaking with effort.

'Well done, young man,' Matt murmured.

After a few seconds' frantic searching, the foal found his mother's udder. His head disappeared under her belly and his little tail wagged furiously to the accompaniment of loud sucking noises.

'He'll be just fine,' Matt said.

'Isn't that the most wonderful thing you've ever seen?' Helen asked in a hushed voice.

'Almost.'

Helen looked up at him.

'The most wonderful moment was when Ali was born,' Matt said in response to her unspoken question.

'Of course.' Helen felt the words as actual physical pain. 'I could never have children,' she whispered. 'And it was all my own stupid fault.'

Matt said nothing.

'I was a kid. Just out of university. He was a big fish in our little media pond. A one-night stand, but that was all it took.' Helen paused. She had never told a soul about this, but now she had started, she couldn't stop. 'I had an abortion. I had to. I was too young. He was married. I wanted a career. It was no big deal. Until something went wrong. I almost died. And by the time it was over, I was never going to be able to have children.'

'I'm so sorry.'

'That's why I never married. What man would want me after that?'

His voice was so soft she almost didn't hear it.

'I would.'

* * *

The night air was so charged it almost glowed. An electrical storm was building over River Downs, black clouds piling higher and higher over the parched red earth. The whole outback seemed to be holding its breath, waiting for the first bolt of lightning or roar of thunder.

Standing on the homestead steps, Donna felt as if she too was holding her breath. But the storm she was waiting for was a lot closer to earth. The twins were in bed and Peter was on the phone, so she had slipped out here. The air outside was hot and humid and heavy, but still far easier to breathe than the air inside the house when she and Peter were alone.

Her relationship with Peter had changed on

the day that the twins had tossed their snowballs, but not in a good way. During those few moments, as the ice melted in her hair, Donna had quite simply fallen in love. She had looked into Peter's eyes and realised he was everything she had ever wanted. Strong, but still gentle. Determined, but kind and loving. A sexy man and a loving father. She had fallen for him, and for a few brief seconds she had thought he felt the same way. But when he walked away to greet the mail plane, a different man had returned.

Since that day, Peter had been distant almost to the point of rudeness. He avoided being alone with her, and if by chance their hands touched, he would flinch away as if burned. Even the twins had noticed. At first Donna thought she could just ignore it. That he would get past whatever was causing the problem, and they could go back to the way things were . . . or rather, the way things almost were.

It hadn't happened, and now she was beginning to wonder if she should just leave. The thought made her want to cry out with the pain of knowing what she might have had, and had lost.

A flash of distant lightning caught her eye. She waited for the following thunder, but didn't hear anything. The storm was still a distance off, but it was rapidly moving closer. Propelled by a deep restlessness, Donna walked down the steps and across the station compound. Standing in the midst of the open space, she spread her arms wide to catch a slight caress of breeze. Wearing just light cotton shorts and top, she felt almost naked in the face of the storm. She closed her eyes, feeling the bare skin of her arms and legs tingle with the electricity around her. She raised her face, ready to welcome the first drops of rain.

Another flash of lightning lit the sky, and in the brief flare of light she saw Peter coming towards her.

'There's a storm coming,' he said abruptly. 'You should be inside.'

'I just want to feel the rain,' Donna said. 'I've been so hot all day. I thought it might cool me down.'

'There won't be any rain. This is the dry season. Electricity. Thunder and lightning, but no rain.'

Donna dropped her arms, feeling foolish. Once again she had proved her ignorance of the outback.

'Was that the mustering team on the phone?'

'Yes. They'll be here tomorrow.'

They had been expecting the contract mustering team for several days. The stockmen travelled between the cattle properties in the region, working as the seasons demanded. Peter needed them even more than ever now that Ken was gone.

'Are you sure you'll be all right here by yourself?' he asked. 'We'll be at the camp for — '

'I'll be fine,' Donna snapped back. 'I'm not an idiot. The kids will be okay.'

She spun around and began to walk swiftly away, feeling the tears pricking her eyes. She would not let him see her cry, even if she had to walk all the way back to Darwin!

With a few swift strides he was beside her.

'Donna . . . ' He reached out and caught her by the arm.

As he touched her, another bolt of lightning flashed. For one long second they were frozen in the light, then a loud crash of thunder shook the whole world.

Donna didn't know who made the first move. All she knew was that they were in each other's arms. Peter's kiss was as electric as the storm. Days of silent anger, indescribable loneliness, the desire for forgiveness and a whirlwind of pent-up passions exploded between them. Caught in the eye of the storm, Donna gave herself to the taste of Peter's lips, the feel of his strong, hard body pressed against hers and his hands on her flesh.

'Donna . . . ' He breathed the word against her lips, and she was lost.

The storm broke above them, unnoticed, until something hard and cold stung her face.

They stepped back from each other. Donna felt as if she was poised on the edge of a cliff. Would she fall or would she soar into the heavens?

A second hailstone hit her face. Another stung the bare flesh of her shoulder, causing her to flinch. The hail continued, even as the first drops of rain began to fall.

Peter reached out and grabbed her hand. He almost dragged her at a run back towards the house, and they sprinted up the stairs to the shelter of the veranda.

Panting slightly, and not just from the run, Donna turned to Peter.

'I thought you said there would be no rain.'

Peter leaned down, and with the tip of his tongue tasted the water drops on the soft skin at the base of her neck.

'I was wrong,' he said, and pulled her to him.

* * *

The morning after a storm, the sky is always clear and bright. Lying in her bed, looking out the window, Donna wished the same rule applied to people. Peter was no longer with her. He had slipped away while she slept. Only the pleasurable glow of her body and the fear in her heart told her that he had ever been there.

She glanced across at the bedside clock. It was after seven o'clock, and already she could hear the sounds of activity outside. She raised herself up on one elbow, as a thumping mechanical beat grew louder and louder. The house almost shook as a helicopter passed low over it, making for the airstrip. The contract mustering team had arrived.

Donna dressed quickly. By the time she stepped outside, the homestead was awash with movement. She looked around for Peter, but saw only a confusion of men and horses, motorcycles and trucks.

'Morning, miss.' A rangy, sun-browned man tipped his hat at her. 'I don't suppose there's any chance of a quick cuppa before we set out, is there? The boys have been travelling most of the night.'

'A cuppa? Yes. I suppose. How many of you are there?'

'An even dozen, miss.'

'Oh . . . all right. I'll see what I can do.'

'Thanks a lot.'

The man wandered off again. With still no sign of Peter, Donna decided there wasn't much she could do, except make the tea. She was filling the kettle in the kitchen when Peter came in.

She froze as he walked over to the sink, reached out and turned off the tap.

'That will never do for the whole crew,' he said gently, taking the kettle from her hand. He opened the door of the huge pantry and rummaged around inside for a few moments, before emerging with what appeared to be two large tin cans with wire handles.

'Just boil these billies. The boys will take it themselves from there.'

'Billies?'

'Billy cans.' Peter avoided her eyes as he filled the cans with water and placed them on the gas burners, taking more time than was strictly necessary to set them down and check that their lids were tight.

'Peter?' Donna was beginning to panic. She and Peter needed to talk, before they were overwhelmed by the new arrivals.

He turned slowly and finally met her gaze. 'I — '

Before he could say another word, the kitchen erupted with noise as the twins burst in.

'Dad, can I ride in the helicopter?'

'Dad, can I come this year? Please!'

Peter shrugged helplessly. 'No, you cannot

come this year,' he told his son. 'And Sara, you might be able to have a ride in the helicopter when the mustering is finished.'

'Me too,' Chris chimed in.

'I said you *might* be able to,' Peter insisted. 'There's work to be done first.'

'Yeah!' the twins cheered.

Peter turned back to the stove. He lifted the lids off both billy cans, and tossed a handful of tea leaves into each one.

'Now, we are going to show Donna how to make billy tea,' he told the twins. 'Come on. Outside. The boys are waiting.'

Chris and Sara took Donna's hands to lead her outside. She had no choice but to go with them. Peter emerged a few seconds later. He was wearing his leather work gloves, and one billy can hung from each hand.

'Smoko!' he called loudly.

Donna could hardly believe her eyes, as Peter began to spin the billies at arm's length. The cans full of boiling water sailed high above his head, held tightly in his grasp. He brought them back down with not a drop of the precious liquid spilled.

'That's how you make billy tea,' the twins enthused loudly.

The stockmen were gathering, enamelled tin mugs at the ready, adding their voices to the clamour.

Donna felt like putting her hands over her ears to block out the noise. She wanted to scream at everyone to shut up and go away. She needed to talk to Peter.

The stockmen quickly downed the scalding black liquid. The same rangy man she had spoken to earlier thanked her for the tea.

'We're ready to go now, boss,' he told Peter.

'Then let's move out.'

One by one the stockmen tipped their hats to Donna and moved away.

At last she was alone with Peter. But not for long.

'I know it's a madhouse, but it's always like this at the start of the muster. I'll try to get back in a day or two,' he told her. 'Don't worry, though. You may not see me for a week or so.'

He hesitated for a few seconds, his eyes meeting and holding hers for the first time that morning. He took a long deep breath, then paused as if searching for the right words.

'I'm sorry,' he said at last, then turned and strode purposefully away.

Donna was left wondering just what he was sorry for.

* * *

Peter whistled his dog and swung his leg over his motorcycle. He barely waited for the dog to jump on behind him before he kicked the engine into life to lead the way to the mustering camp. The roar of the engine did nothing to drown out the demons in his head.

What had he been thinking?

He had fought so hard to deny his feelings for Donna, only to lose control at the worst possible moment. He could blame the storm. He could blame Donna. But the fault was his and his alone. It should never have happened, but how good it had felt to hold her in his arms! The taste of her lips. The scent of her skin. Even now, he wanted nothing more than to turn the bike around and go back to her.

He twisted the accelerator of the motorcycle savagely, and the machine leaped forward. Behind, he felt his dog scrabbling for purchase on the seat. He slowed down again.

Last night he had lost his wife for the second time. Since her death, he had clung tightly to his every memory of Karen. Each day he had taken a few minutes to recall her face and the sound of her voice. As the years passed, it had been getting harder and harder, until it seemed the only memories he had left were those in the photographs he kept.

Now, when he closed his eyes, he saw only Donna. When his thoughts turned to home, he saw Donna laughing in the kitchen. Donna with his children. Donna in his arms. Donna in his bed.

He had no idea what to do. He desperately wanted her to stay. To share more than his bed. He wanted to share his life with her. But could he ask her to give up her own world for his? Could he ask her to face the same life that had killed Karen? Did he have the strength to make her leave?

He told himself that the hard work of the mustering camp would help clear his head. Help him make the right choice.

It didn't. For the next three days he worked from dawn till dusk, chasing wild cattle on horseback and on his motorbike. Despite being bone-achingly weary each night, he sat late by the campfire and thought of Donna. As he lay in his swag, staring up at the stars, his heart and his mind and his body longed for her.

Rising from afternoon smoko on the third day, Peter was thinking of Donna as he untied his horse from the side of the truck, and prepared to mount. He put one foot in the stirrup and swung carelessly into the saddle. Barely had the seat of his moleskins touched the leather when the horse, a big half-wild brute, dropped its head and started to buck. Peter gripped its sides with his legs, as if he would squeeze the life out of it. He grabbed the pommel of the saddle with one hand, and dragged on the reins with the other. Stiff-legged, the horse bucked and propped its way across the camp to a rousing chorus of cheers from the stockmen. Peter hung on for grim life as the beast reared, dropped to all fours and bucked again.

It was too much. Peter carved an ungraceful arc through the air, and hit the ground with a solid thump.

He lay staring up at the sky, listening to the laughter of the men. Slowly he raised his bruised body from the ground. His former mount was trotting wildly around the camp, one of the stockmen in pursuit. The rest were too busy teasing him.

He picked up his hat, dusted it off and set it back on his head. He should have paid more attention to the horse. This early in the muster, they were still fresh and full of oats. The spotter's helicopter frightened them. So did the motorcycles and almost everything else they took a dislike to. If his mind had been on the job, he wouldn't now be nursing a bruised backside that would only get worse with several hours' riding still in front of him.

'Hey, boss.' The helicopter pilot was still chuckling. 'I think I'll head back to the strip this afternoon. I want to do some work on the hydraulics.'

'Okay.' When it came to the maintenance and safety of the helicopter, the pilot's word was law. As a pilot himself, Peter understood this.

'I'll be back before dark. Want to come along for the ride?'

How he wanted to go. He could see Donna. Maybe they could talk. Sort something out. But then Peter realised that that just wouldn't happen. He'd only have about an hour before they had to come back. The twins would be all over him. There would be things he had to do. No.

'You go ahead,' he said. 'I've got a horse to talk to.'

The pilot chuckled, and about the same time as Peter took back the reins of his errant horse, the chopper blades began to turn. Before he mounted, Peter made a decision. Tomorrow he would go back to the homestead. He would see Donna. He would tell her . . . well, he would tell her something.

About an hour later, Peter was chasing a young heifer though the scrub, sweat pouring from both him and his horse, when he spotted a stockman racing towards him at full gallop. He reined back and waited for the man to catch him.

'It's Jim, on the radio. There's a fire back at the homestead.'

The man had barely finished speaking before Peter turned his horse's head towards the camp, and the radio that was their only communication with the outside world. He used his stock whip to urge the tiring animal to greater speed. He thundered into camp, and flung himself off his horse.

'What's going on?' he asked the assembled stockmen.

'Jim called,' one of them said, handing over the radio handset.

'Jim, this is Peter. What's going on?'

The set crackled. It was at the very limit of its reach and the voice at the other end was hard to understand.

'Jim. Say again,' Peter almost yelled into the set.

' . . . storm last night . . . ' The pilot's voice was very faint. ' . . . bushfire . . . the house . . . get here . . . '

Peter stared at the handset in horror. Bushfire!

'Is everyone all right? The twins? Donna?' He should never have left them.

' . . . all right. But we need . . . to fight the fire. Get everyone here. Fast.'

Peter turned to the stockmen, but they were already moving. Horses were turned loose, and the men were climbing into the truck. It would take an hour or more to get to the homestead.

'Jim. Come and get me.' The chopper would be much faster.

' . . . needed here. Just come.'

Peter didn't even sign off. He ran to the motorcycle and kicked it into life. With a roar he was away, knowing the stockmen would follow at the best speed their old truck could manage. He didn't wait for them. He had to get back. To Chris and Sara. To Donna.

Please God, he prayed as he weaved at dangerous speeds through the scrub, don't let it happen again.

* * *

Leigh stood in the doorway and looked at the empty room. All the rubbish was gone. She had replaced the burned-out lightbulbs, and cleaned the layers of grime away from the windows. The doors were wide open to let the sunlight stream in. Later today, the painter would be coming by to give her a quote. The tables and chairs she had ordered would be delivered next week. The long wooden bar at the end of the room was gleaming. It wouldn't be long until her cellar door would be open for business.

Smiling with satisfaction, she walked through into the kitchen. It too was gleaming. The new fridges were humming quietly, and behind the cupboard doors, stacks of plates and bowls awaited her first customers. Leigh had been busy since the bank approved her loan. She had worked long, hard days — cleaning, dealing with contractors and suppliers. They had been followed by long, hard nights working the columns in her accounting books and sending e-mails to her contacts.

But every minute had been worth it. Her plans were starting to come together. She would be opening for business far earlier than she had hoped. Everything was great! Well, almost everything. There was still Simon Bradford.

She hadn't seen or heard from Simon since that brief encounter in Newcastle. She had half expected him to come by with another attempt at an apology. He hadn't. It appeared the next move was hers.

The first thing she had to do was tell him that she would no longer be selling her crop to his winery. She could do that in a letter. She had tried. Several times. But somehow she just couldn't get it right. The words sounded too stiff and formal. There were issues she had to resolve with Simon that had nothing to do with grapes and wine.

Leigh carried a box of glasses through to the bar, and started unpacking them on to the shelves. Many wineries did their tastings in disposable plastic cups. Not her. Bangala Wines would be tasted as they were meant to be drunk — in a glass. The wines themselves were stored in a large windowless room beside the bar. She walked in and looked around the stacks of boxes with some satisfaction. There wasn't a lot of wine, just the test vintages she had made every year, but it would be enough to keep her cellar door open until the next vintage was ready. Then there would be no stopping her.

All she had to do now was tell Simon he couldn't have her grapes. If she did it in person, instead of a letter, she might also be able to get past the memory of the night he had helped Jack Thorne break her heart.

Leigh wandered back into the kitchen and opened one of the fridges. It was lightly stocked with food samples. As a one-woman operation, she would have to prepare the food for her customers, as well as look after the wine-tastings. She was planning a simple menu, with open sandwiches and cheese platters, Italian-style antipasto plates and maybe some fancy breads. Coffee and tea, of course. She pulled some of the food samples out of the fridge. It was well past lunchtime, and she was feeling a bit hungry. She could try one of her planned recipes.

She was taste-testing a hummus and roasted pepper sandwich when she heard the approaching car. Snatching another quick bite, she walked to the door, then stopped in surprise. It looked like Simon Bradford's car. What was he doing here? She wasn't ready to face him yet.

But the man getting out of the car was not Simon. Where Simon was tall with gold-streaked hair and blue eyes, this man was shorter and darker. Simon moved in such a way as to make a girl's heart jump. This man was stocky and looked fit, but he would never set her pulse racing. Simon was young and strong, whereas this man's hair was flecked with grey.

'Hello. You must be Leigh Kenyon.'

Leigh dragged her errant thoughts back under control. What was she doing, thinking about the way Simon Bradford moved? 'Yes. I'm Leigh,' she said hurriedly.

'Mark Wallace. You asked me to come and quote for painting your tasting room?'

'Of course.' Leigh felt a little foolish. Simon wasn't the only person in the world to drive a white Toyota. 'Come through.'

They had been discussing colours and

types of paint for a while when Leigh noticed Mark casting a quick glance at the remnants of her lunch.

'Have you eaten?' she asked.

'Well, I haven't actually,' he said with a grin. 'I didn't want to be late for our meeting.'

He might not be Simon Bradford, but he had a nice smile. 'Let me make you something,' she offered.

'I don't want to impose,' he said.

'It's no imposition,' she replied. 'I'm trying to decide what will be on the menu. You can tell me what you think. In fact,' she added as an afterthought, 'I'll just open a bottle. We have to see if the food complements the wine.'

She opened a bottle of her own cabernet, but Mark had only a small taste.

'I have to drive,' he said, munching his way through a second sandwich.

He left just on five o'clock, promising to send a final quote in the mail within a couple of days. Leigh walked back to the bar with a feeling of intense satisfaction. The painting was going to cost less than she had expected. And Mark had made some very complimentary remarks about her plans, and about the food. Feeling quite pleased with herself, she poured another glass of wine. It was rather good, she thought as she cleared away the sandwich plates.

She opened another box and found more of the diamanté-studded glasses that dated from the days of Jack Thorne. She twirled one in her hand, then realised she had never drunk from one of them. Well, she thought as she poured herself a generous measure, I shall drink a toast to the day Jack left.

She looked at the bottle. There was just a small amount left in the bottom. It would be stupid to put that much away. She might as well drink the last of it. She had earned her little celebration. She had survived Jack Thorne. In fact, she had done much better than survive.

She emptied the last few drops from the bottle and stood up. She walked to the door, and raised the glass in the direction of the Bradford Winery.

'Take that, Simon bloody Bradford,' she said, and drained the glass.

She took the empty glass back to the bar, still thinking about Simon. She had never said anything to him about that night. Well, if she was moving on, it was time to get that off her chest as well. She left the glass on the bar and walked out into the early evening.

Her car keys were in the house, but she hesitated. She had drunk a couple of glasses of wine. More like three or four glasses. She probably shouldn't drive. But it was a long way to walk, and she felt just a little unsteady. She would take the farm ute. If she drove through the vineyard to the back fence, she would be close enough to walk to Simon's place. And she wouldn't have to worry about being on the road when she was . . . well . . . not entirely sober.

Satisfied with her solution, Leigh climbed behind the wheel of the ute. She started the engine and very carefully set off along the track between the vines.

It wasn't far, and she never got the vehicle over second gear. In her mind she was rehearsing just what she would say to Simon. She would tell him how he had wrecked her dreams. All men were pigs, it seemed, and Simon bloody Bradford was no exception! As her indignation grew, her foot pushed down harder on the accelerator. The ute was moving faster, bumping over the uneven ground, but she didn't care. She had her eyes fixed on the buildings still visible ahead in the fading light. Simon Bradford was there, and he was about to get an earful!

The ute bounced past the last row of vines, then suddenly a fence post appeared in front of her. Leigh slammed her foot down on the brake, but the ute slid sideways, fishtailed across the track and smashed into a post with a grinding of metal, and a shattering of glass. Leigh was thrown forward and her head hit the steering wheel. From somewhere, a piecing horn started to sound. It stopped only when she slumped back into her seat.

* * *

The sound of the car horn carried to Simon, where he sat working in his study. Puzzled, he walked to the glass doors that overlooked the winery. All was quiet there, as it should be now the workers had left for the day. Then he spotted something near his fence. A crashed vehicle. His breath caught in his throat as he recognised it. He threw open the door and started to run.

The horn stopped sounding before he was halfway to the ute. By the time he got there, Leigh was fumbling with the door handle. Simon beat her to it, pulling the door open and reaching to help her.

'Leigh, what happened? Are you all right?'

'Let go. I'm fine.' She tried to push his hands away as she stumbled out of the car.

'Are you hurt?' he asked again, still holding her by the shoulders.

'Let go of me.' Leigh shook him off and staggered a few steps away from him.

Simon watched in growing amazement. 'You're drunk,' he said.

'So what?' she said belligerently. 'That's not your concern. If I want to drink, I will.'

Simon wasn't sure whether to laugh or call a doctor. 'At least come up to the house, so I can take a look at you. Make sure you're all right.'

'I'm all right. I'm better than all right,' Leigh insisted, but she allowed him to take her arm and lead her away from the car. 'I wasn't for a long time. And that was all your fault.'

'Was it?' Simon said gently, as he guided her up the steps and into his house.

'Of course it was. You. And your party. And the stripper.'

'The stripper?' That caught his attention. What was she talking about? Maybe the bump on her head was more serious than it looked.

'Yes. The stripper. Jack told me all about it. How you hired a stripper for that party. He screwed her. I could smell her on him when he got home. The bastard.'

Simon lowered Leigh gently on to the couch. He tilted her head back to have a better look at the bruise starting to form.

'You need some ice,' he said. 'Don't move.'

He darted into the kitchen and opened his

freezer, his mind racing. What was she talking about. A stripper? There was no stripper the night of that party. The woman Jack Thorne had seduced that night was Simon's girlfriend. The girl for whom he had bought a diamond ring. The girl he wanted to marry.

He decided it was useless to try to make sense of what Leigh was saying. She was drunk and shaken from the accident. He wrapped some crushed ice in a tea towel and took it back to her. She winced as he laid it gently on her forehead.

'Hold that,' he told her.

'It was all your fault.' She kept talking as if the flood that had started could not now be held back. 'Jack told me everything. How you hired a stripper for the party. He was celebrating because of our lottery win. I was home with a cold and you gave her to him. That was generous of you, Simon. But you ruined my life.' There were tears in her eyes now. Simon was beginning to feel really concerned.

'Stay here,' he told her again. 'I'm calling the doctor.'

The doctor was reassuring. Leigh hadn't been knocked unconscious. She was showing no signs of nausea or memory loss, and her confusion was probably due as much to the alcohol as the bump on the head. The doctor told Simon to keep her well clear of any more booze, and let her sleep it off. He did suggest, however, that she shouldn't be left alone. Someone should keep an eye on her just in case the bump was more serious than it seemed. If she showed any symptoms of concussion, Simon should take her to the hospital.

When Simon returned to the living room, Leigh had dropped the ice pack and was curled up on the couch, almost asleep.

'Come on, Leigh,' he said. 'I think we should put you to bed.'

'All right,' she murmured softly.

It was the easiest thing in the world just to pick her up. She slid her arms around his neck and laid her head against his chest. Simon liked the way that felt. He decided she would be better off in his bed. The room had an en suite bathroom, should she need it during the night.

'You didn't really ruin my life,' Leigh said in a slow, sleepy voice, her mouth close to his ear. 'I'm better off without Jack. He was a prick. I know that now. You're almost as bad. Why do I always fall for the bastards?'

She kissed him on the lips.

Gently he laid her on the bed. She was almost asleep. She sighed softly and rolled on to her side, her eyes closing almost immediately. Her breathing was low and slow, but strong and even. He thought she would be all right.

Careful not to disturb her, he sat on the edge of the bed and thought about what she had been saying. It appeared Jack Thorne had been a bigger liar than anyone had realised. At last he understood Leigh's attitude. All this time, she had blamed Simon for the events of that night. Blamed him for the break-up of her engagement without knowing that Thorne had also destroyed Simon's hopes. Tomorrow he would tell her the truth. Maybe then things would be different between them.

He sat for a while just watching her sleep. She looked so young and vulnerable, with a shadow of a bruise already darkening her forehead. He wanted to lie next to her and take her in his arms. He wanted to soothe the hurt away. He wanted . . .

He forced himself to his feet. He had no right to sit here and watch her sleep. No right to think what he was thinking. Tomorrow that might change. Tonight he would be her friend. He'd sleep in the spare room, leaving the door open so he could hear her if she woke. If she needed him, he would be there.

9

The phone rang twice, then Matt found himself talking to Helen's voicemail. He left a brief message and hung up. The things he wanted to say were not for voicemail. In fact, the things he wanted to say weren't for a phone call. He would drive down to Sydney in the morning to talk to Helen.

His mind made up, he left the house and wandered back to the stables. He stood for a while watching Cassie and her foal. She might have been too young to be a mother, but Cassie was doing a fine job with her colt. He was strong and healthy. Matt had let them through into this small safe paddock earlier today. The youngster was enjoying stretching his legs but he never strayed far from his mother. It was still too soon for that.

Matt wondered if it was too soon for Helen. They had known each other such a short time. Their lives were so very different. He truly believed they could have a future together — but he had a hard time seeing what it might be. She was a city-dweller, with a career to pursue. He was a horseman, only at home on the land. But despite all that, he believed they were good for each other. He had become certain of it the night Cassie's colt was born. He suspected he was the first and only person Helen had ever told about her abortion.

It was a great pity that Helen had never had children. She would have been a very good mother. After just one dinner, she and Ali were showing signs of becoming good friends. Matt wasn't one to dwell on things that could not be changed. The mistakes of Helen's past were just that — the past. They had simply helped to make her the woman she was today. The woman that Matt wanted to share his life with.

But there was still something keeping them apart. Some other secret that Helen had yet to share with him. He had sensed it during her visit last weekend. He had become even more certain of it during their brief phone conversations since. He was determined to find out what it was.

His mind made up, Matt busied himself around the stables. He wasn't surprised when the loud jangling of the phone interrupted him. He knew before he answered that it would be Helen.

'I'm sorry I missed your call,' she told him. 'It's just hell here today.'

'That's okay,' he said. 'I understand if

you're too busy to talk.'

'Hang on a moment.'

Down the line, Matt could hear Helen talking to someone, then she was back.

'That was my assistant, Richard. I've told him to shut the door. I have a few minutes.'

'What's all the fuss about?' Matt asked.

'Well, one of our competitors has broken a big story. About two male movie stars and their relationship.'

'Ah. I see.' Matt knew she was talking about the story she had hidden for so long.

'Yes. Everyone is now scrabbling to catch up. Us included.'

'You won't tell them . . . ' Matt didn't like to put the question into words. He didn't know what the implications might be for Helen.

'No.' She paused, as if considering the need to defend herself. Finally she spoke again. 'It doesn't really matter any more.'

Matt could sense from her voice that she was feeling very uncomfortable. 'I can understand that it's difficult to talk about — '

'No. That's not it,' Helen interrupted him. 'Matt, there is something I should have told you during the weekend.'

Now that it was coming, Matt was suddenly a little afraid of what she might say.

'Yes?'

'I . . . I have been offered another job.'

Matt waited for the rest of it.

'It's a great job. Based in New York,' she hurried on. 'I told them they'd have their answer today.'

Matt felt as if someone had knocked his feet out from under him. 'You're going to take it?'

'It's what I've wanted all my life.' Her voice quivered slightly.

'Well, congratulations.' Matt took refuge in convention, because he couldn't voice the pain he was feeling. 'I'm sure you'll do a great job.'

'Thank you.'

Neither of them said anything for a long, long time, and Matt knew he wouldn't be driving to Sydney the next day.

'I have to go.' Helen broke the silence. 'There's someone at the door.'

Helen hung up and closed her eyes. There was no one at the door, but she couldn't have stayed on the phone one minute longer. Even down the phone line, Matt's hurt was almost a tangible thing. She felt it because it was reflected in her own heart. It was going to be very hard to say goodbye.

The noise outside her office caught her attention. It wasn't going to be hard to say goodbye to *Australian Life*. The job here was only ever supposed to be a stepping stone.

That was why she had been so desperate for the farmer campaign to be a success. It had drawn her to the attention of the people who mattered most in her industry.

Helen unlocked her desk drawer and pulled out the unpublished scoop. If anyone ever saw those photographs, her career would be in tatters. She wouldn't do the same thing next time. Couldn't do it. In the cut-throat world of the New York media, she would have to publish, and damn the consequences. She wouldn't be able to hesitate there. She sat for a while staring at the folder, then took the contents to the shredder that sat in the corner of her office. Whatever happened to the two actors and their families, at least she had a clear conscience. Her memories of this job would be of the success of the farmer campaign, not of damaging the two men's reputations. Slowly she fed the papers through the shredder, watching the thin ribbons of paper fall into the tangled pile in the plastic bin.

Her memories of this job would also be memories of Matt.

* * *

A bushfire is a terrifying thing. It consumes everything in its path. With a driving wind, the flames move faster than a running horse. They can leap to the treetops and pass above a person, only to fall back to the ground, trapping them. The fire will suck the very air from its victim's lungs. It leaves nothing behind but black devastation and pain.

Peter had seen what a bushfire could do, and as he raced towards home, his fear painted pictures that pushed him to even greater speeds.

Each time he topped a small rise, he could see the pall of black smoke ahead. It was growing larger by the minute until it seemed to almost fill the sky. He pushed his motorbike and himself to the limit, careless of his own safety in his desperate need to get to Donna and the twins.

As he drew near the homestead, the smell of smoke grew stronger. He could feel ash blowing against his face, and the occasional flare of pain as a glowing cinder touched him. The paddock beside him was a charred and smoking waste. The fire's passage had been blocked by the gravel road, or else the wind had changed direction. Ahead of him, it was moving parallel to the road. Moving, as he was, towards the homestead. Peter gunned the bike to top speed, racing the flames.

He skidded to a stop in the home yard and looked around. None of the buildings had been touched, but it wouldn't be long before the flames reached them.

'Donna!' he called. 'Chris! Sara!'

There was no answer. On the verge of panic, he spun around, looking for some sign of them. Then he heard the sound of the diesel generator and the water pump at the far side of the house. He ran towards the sound. The twins. They were standing in the shelter of the huge water tank. In their hands they held the wide hose that was normally used to pump water from the underground bore into the tank. Now water was pouring from the tank, and the twins were directing the stream on to the veranda and roof of the house.

'Dad,' they cried in unison as they saw him. They dropped the hose and flung themselves at him. Peter dropped to his knees and wrapped his arms around his children.

'Thank God you're all right,' he said.

'Donna told us to stay here and spray as much water on the house as we could,' Chris told him. 'The house isn't going to burn down, is it, Dad?'

'I don't know, son,' Peter said. 'But we're going to do everything we can to save it. Where's Donna?'

'She's over near the machinery sheds,' Chris said. 'With the pilot. They're working on the other bore.'

Peter felt a wave of relief.

'Dad, I'm scared!' Peter could barely hear his daughter's voice, muffled against his shirt.

'It's all right to be scared,' he told her gently. 'But you're going to be all right. The rest of the mustering team are right behind me. They'll help us fight the fire.'

Sara nodded, and Peter hugged her tightly.

'Now, Chris,' he said to his son. 'I have to go and see Donna. I want you and your sister to stay here. Keep using the hose. But do not leave the water tank. Do you understand?'

If things took a turn for the worse, they were safest near the tank. There were no trees near them, and the grass was cut short and sparse. If they kept spraying water about, they should be fine.

'Yes, Dad,' Chris said.

'All right. I'm relying on you to look after Sara.'

'I will.'

It took every ounce of Peter's strength to leave the twins, but he had to find Donna. The wind was increasing, and smoke was blowing across the home yard, stinging his eyes and burning his lungs. He coughed as he sprinted towards the machinery sheds. There was another bore there, and a pump to bring the water to the surface under pressure. He hoped he would find Donna there.

When he reached the pump, he saw Jim, the pilot. He was carrying several smoking chaff bags. He held them under the water pouring from the pump until they were dripping wet, then moved away.

'Jim!' Peter called.

The pilot turned.

'The wind is starting to change direction,' the pilot gasped. 'We're trying to hold it at the fence line.'

'Donna?' Peter yelled over the roaring of the flames.

The pilot pointed.

Peter looked up and saw her. She was silhouetted against the fire. In her hands she clutched dripping sacks, which she was using to beat back the flames. She wasn't the only thing he saw. A dark shape was running through the burning grass, its coat already smouldering. Before he could shout a warning, the huge wild boar had crashed through the fence and into Donna. Peter heard her scream as she was flung to the ground.

'Donna! No!'

Peter started to run. He had no gun. If the boar turned on her, he would be unable to stop it. But driven by the pain and fear, the beast just kept going.

In a few seconds, Peter and Jim were at Donna's side. Blood was already welling through her shirt. Her eyes were wide with pain, and she grabbed Peter's arm like a lifeline.

Peter ripped open her shirt. The boar's tusk had torn a large gash in her side.

'Peter . . . ' Donna's voice was little more than a whisper, barely audible against the roaring of the bushfire.

'It's all right. I'm here.'

He didn't know if she heard him. Her eyelids slowly closed, and she passed out.

'I've got to get her to hospital,' Peter told the pilot as he tore off his shirt. He pressed it against the wound, then took the shirt Jim offered as well. Jim was an old bush hand and understood exactly what was needed.

'Get the twins,' Peter said abruptly. 'They're by the water tanks. There's a first-aid kit in the house. They'll show you where it is.'

Peter gathered the unconscious Donna up in his arms and began to run for the machinery shed. He carefully laid her against some grain sacks near the ute. Moments later, Jim and the twins appeared, moving at a run across the compound. As soon as the children saw Donna, their faces went ashen. Sara stared to cry.

'It's going to be all right,' Peter told the frightened girl. 'We're going to take her to the hospital. In the plane. But first I have to put a bandage on the wound. You and Chris get in the car while I do that.'

Peter caught the pilot's eye, and Jim took the twins to the ute. Once they were out of sight, Peter pulled the blood-soaked shirts off Donna's side. The wound was still bleeding heavily. He bit back a moment of fear, and took a large dressing from the first-aid kit. He packed the wound and strapped it tightly. In a small tin at the very bottom of the kit, he found a needle and a bottle of clear liquid. Under normal circumstances, such strong painkillers would have to be administered by a doctor. But after his wife's death, Peter had decided that normal rules did not apply at River Downs and had taken steps to prepare for any emergency. Carefully he slipped the needle under Donna's skin.

He didn't have time for anything more. He lifted Donna into the ute with the children, then got behind the wheel. The fire was still burning, but the road to the airstrip was untouched. So too were the aircraft parked there. His small Cessna was always kept fuelled and ready to fly. He carried Donna inside, and placed her gently in a seat. Then he strapped the twins in, and handed them a bottle of water and some pills.

'Now, if Donna comes round,' he told Sara, 'that cut is going to hurt a lot. So I want you to hold on to these. If she wakes up, you have to make her swallow them. Can you do that?'

'Yes, Daddy,' Sara said in a small, scared voice.

Peter hugged her briefly, praying that Donna would remain unconscious. Then he strapped himself into the pilot's seat and reached for the ignition switch. The small plane's single propeller started to turn. He took a long deep breath and forced all thoughts of Donna out of his mind. All his attention had to be on flying the aircraft.

He taxied the little Cessna to the far end of the airstrip, revved the engine and sent the plane hurtling into the smoke-filled air. He banked, seeing the broad front of the bushfire moving slowly, destroying everything in its path. Somewhere down there, the mustering team would be fighting to save his home. He wished them luck and turned the plane's nose north-east towards Katherine.

He thumbed on the radio.

'Bravo Tango India calling Tindal. I am inbound with a medical emergency on board. Requesting assistance.'

'Bravo Tango India, this is Tindal. What is your ETA?'

'Tindal, my ETA is sixty minutes.'

'Roger. Sixty minutes. Do you require an ambulance?'

'That's affirmative, Tindal. I have one person with an injury to her side. She's unconscious and losing blood.' Peter had to struggle to keep his voice calm.

'Roger, Tango India. I'll get back to you shortly. Tindal out.'

Peter turned in his seat to look back at the twins and Donna. Donna was still unconscious, her head lolling against the seat. Sara was beside her, holding her hand tightly.

'Did you hear that?' Peter said. 'They will have an ambulance waiting for Donna. Everything is going to be all right.'

He forced a smile to his lips, then turned back to his aircraft, his eyes automatically scanning the instrument panel as he silently hoped that he wasn't wrong.

* * *

Donna did not want to wake up. Waking up meant fighting the flames again. They were so hot, and the flying cinders burned her skin. Waking up meant dealing with the pain that had haunted her sleep. Waking up meant facing the beast with fire in its wild eyes and great stained tusks.

She moved her head. No . . . no. She would not wake up.

Then she felt a hand touch her cheek, a cool, soft touch. She opened her eyes and looked up into the smiling face of a young aboriginal woman.

'Well, you're back with us at last.' The girl spoke softly.

'What . . . where . . . ?'

'You're in Katherine hospital,' the nurse said. 'And you are going to be fine.'

'In the hospital?'

'Don't worry if it's all a bit foggy. You're still on pain medication.' The nurse helped Donna to raise her head and sip from a glass of cool sweet water.

'Your family brought you in,' the nurse said. 'They've been here with you all night.'

'My family?' Donna was confused. Her family was back in England. What was the girl talking about?

The nurse nodded towards the next bed. Carefully, Donna turned to look. Sara and Chris were tucked up there, sound asleep. When last she had seen them, they had been covered in soot, but now they were clean-faced and someone had given them hospital pyjamas. They looked so beautiful just lying there. Donna felt her heart clench at the thought of the danger they had faced

. . . was it yesterday? Alone at the homestead when the lightning struck and started the fire. Peter not there to help . . .

'Peter?' The word was a whisper.

The nurse pointed at an armchair near the foot of the two beds. Peter was slumped in the chair, also deeply asleep. Though showing signs of a perfunctory wash, his face was still stained with soot. He was wearing a hospital shirt over torn and filthy moleskins.

'He's been there all night,' the nurse said. 'Shall I wake him?'

Donna shook her head. 'Leave him.'

The nurse smiled. 'If you need anything, there's a call button right there. Okay?'

Donna nodded and the girl left.

Carefully, and wincing at the pain in her side, Donna raised herself a little against the pillows. A thick dressing covered her right side, and there was a drip in her arm. Despite everything, she didn't feel too bad. Maybe it was the drugs, or maybe it was the sight of Peter and the twins.

Her family, the nurse had called them. How she wished they were!

In the chair near the foot of her bed, Peter stirred. His eyes fluttered, then shot open.

'Hi,' Donna said.

In one swift movement, Peter was out of

the chair and at her side. 'You're awake! How do you feel?'

'Not too bad,' Donna told him. 'I think it's the drugs.'

'God! I was so worried about you.'

'I don't remember much,' Donna said. 'The fire. The helicopter came, and the pilot . . . '

'Jim.'

'Yes. Jim. He was helping beat back the flames. There was something in the bush. Running at me . . . '

'It was a wild boar.' Peter sat on the edge of the bed. 'Running from the fire. It trampled you, and slashed your side with its tusk. The doctor says you have a cracked rib too.'

Donna winced at the remembered pain. 'There I go again,' she said bitterly, 'always in the wrong place at the wrong time.'

'No. Not always,' Peter said. He took a deep breath before continuing. 'In the plane . . . flying here with you unconscious in the back. Then last night sitting here. I had a lot of time to think.'

Donna said nothing; she just waited for him to go on.

'My wife . . . Karen . . . is gone. What wasn't gone was my guilt. It was my fault she died.'

'No . . . '

'Oh, not directly. She was thrown off a horse and hit a tree. Her back was broken and she died before we could get help. It was a freak accident. But all these years I've felt guilty because I was the one who brought her to River Downs.'

'Would she have blamed you?' Donna asked gently.

'No. Not for an instant. But I couldn't get past the guilt. Then when you came, and I started to feel . . . Well, that only made it worse.'

He took Donna's hand in his, almost absently stroking it as he talked.

'I remember loving her. I still do love her, I guess, deep inside. But it's you I look for when I come home at the end of the day. It's you I think of when I lie awake at night. I love you, and that terrifies me.'

Donna's breath caught in her throat. 'Why?'

'What if the same thing happens again?' The words were filled with all the fear of the past day. 'When I got the call about the fire, when I saw the boar hit you, I was afraid that I was going to lose you too. That would have been too much to bear.'

'You're not going to lose me, Peter,' Donna said. 'When I was hurt, I looked up and saw you there. I knew you'd look after me.'

'I will always look after you. That is, if you'll come back. I will understand if what has happened has made you — '

Donna put a finger across his lips to stop him talking.

'Just you try and get rid of me,' she said. 'I don't ever want to be anywhere else.'

Peter reached for her. He pulled her into his arms and kissed her. Ignoring the pain in her side, Donna put her arms around him and returned his kiss. When they parted, she eased herself back against the pillows, wincing as she did.

'Do you need the doctor?' Peter asked anxiously. 'Or more painkillers?'

'I think I am going to want more drugs.' Donna smiled ruefully.

'I'll get the doctor.' Peter began to rise.

'No. Not for a minute. Let's wake the twins first. Tell them that everything is going to be all right.'

'That can wait another minute too,' Peter said, and kissed her again.

* * *

Leigh had the mother and father of all hangovers. She lay in bed not daring to open her eyes. If this was how she felt after drinking her own wine, she should give up the winery right now. No one was going to drink something that left them feeling this bad.

She raised a hand to brush her hair away from her eyes.

'Ouch!'

That was no hangover. Tentatively she ran her fingertips over her forehead, and found a lump there the size of the Sydney Opera House.

Carefully she opened her eyes. The walls and ceiling didn't look familiar, but right now she didn't care. Her main concern was sitting up without her head falling off. It took a couple of agonising minutes, and when the room stopped spinning, she realised that it really *wasn't* familiar. She had no idea where she was.

She decided not to worry about that just yet. She had spotted the door to a bathroom, and her first priority was getting her legs to take her that far. The bathroom was as unfamiliar as the bedroom, but Leigh still didn't care. She splashed some cold water over her face, and drank some. Then she took a good look at her forehead. The lump wasn't quite the size of the opera house, but it was the most peculiar shades of purple and blue.

She drank some more water, and returned to the bedroom to try to figure out just what had happened last night.

She remembered opening the wine to offer the painter a glass. She remembered using one of the diamanté-studded glasses. She thought she remembered an empty bottle. But after that it all got a bit hazy. It might help if she knew where she was. Not feeling well enough — or brave enough — to leave the sanctuary of the bedroom, she walked to the window, parted the curtains and looked outside.

'Oh no!'

She recognised the buildings clustered on the far side of a neatly mown lawn. Simon Bradford's winery was just outside the window . . . and that must mean she was inside Simon's house! She took a better look at the room around her. There were no cushions on the bed. A plain blue robe hung behind the door. Thinking back to the bathroom, there was no sign of make-up. Or perfume. Or any other feminine clutter. This was a man's room. This was Simon's room. She had spent the night in Simon Bradford's bed!

Leigh buried her head in her hands, wincing as she inadvertently touched the bump on her forehead. She had to figure out what had happened. She took a quick inventory. She was still fully clothed, apart from the shoes lying next to the bed. That was a good sign. Perhaps if she sat still for a few minutes, it would all come back to her.

Yesterday afternoon, after the painter left, she had drunk the rest of the wine. Then . . . she had decided to drive somewhere. Here, obviously. She must have been drunk. Had she taken a car on the road? That was unlike her.

Then it all came flooding back. Driving through the vineyard. Hitting the post. At least that explained the bump on her head, and the headache that was threatening to split her skull. She had a vague recollection of Simon bringing her to the house. But not much else.

Taking great care not to move too quickly, Leigh went back to the window. The winery seemed deserted. If Simon's employees weren't here yet, they soon would be. She had to get out of here. She slipped her feet into her shoes and walked carefully to the door. She opened it just a crack and listened. There was no other sound in the house. She wondered where Simon had slept. If she was lucky, he would still be asleep. Carefully she tiptoed to the front door. Quiet as the proverbial mouse, she opened the door and slipped outside.

She shivered as she stepped out into the

chilly early-morning air, but it might have been the hangover that made her hunch her shoulders like an old woman as she tiptoed across the lawn towards the road. She almost stumbled when she saw her ute. The vehicle had slid at an angle into one of the thick strainer posts of her fence. The front lights were smashed. The bonnet and grille were dented. The driver's door was hanging open. She had no idea if it was damaged or had just been left like that.

Leigh dropped down on to the grassy slope on the side of the road. It really didn't matter how badly damaged the ute was, she wouldn't be driving home. Her head hurt, and she wasn't stupid enough to drive when she felt this bad. At least, this morning she wasn't that stupid. Last night, it seemed, had been a different matter, and look how that had ended.

More of her foggy memories of the night before were coming back. She remembered talking about Jack Thorne, although she had no idea what she had said about her former fiancé. She also had a vague memory of Simon's arms around her. No. That wasn't right. Simon had been carrying her. And she had . . .

'Good morning. You're up earlier than I expected.' Simon dropped to the grass next to her.

Leigh almost yelped. She hadn't heard him approach, and now she had lost her chance to slip away without facing him.

'You look like this might help.' He passed her a mug of steaming coffee.

'Thanks.' Leigh clutched it like a drowning woman might grab a life raft. She took several deep sips of the strong black liquid. It did help a bit, but nothing was really going to make the next few minutes any easier.

'I was going to bring it to you in the bedroom, then I noticed you had decided to get some fresh air.' Simon sipped his own coffee, seemingly oblivious to Leigh's tension. 'How are you feeling?'

'I've been better,' Leigh replied.

'How much do you remember about yesterday?'

'Enough.' She really did not want to relive yesterday's embarrassments with Simon. He would probably take great pleasure in watching her squirm.

'I'm just asking to check if you have concussion,' he explained cheerfully. 'The doctor said that if you couldn't remember yesterday, I should bring you in for a checkup.'

'Oh.' Leigh thought for a few seconds. 'I remember getting into the car. I sort of remember the accident. I definitely remember you taking me to the house. You gave me an ice pack.' That memory had just returned to her.

'That's good. Do you remember what you told me?'

With a sinking feeling, Leigh realised that she did.

Simon turned towards her, his eyes searching her face. 'I think you do. I want you to tell me again.'

There was no way Leigh was going to do that.

'Look,' she said abruptly. 'I appreciate your concern. I do remember everything. I don't have concussion. Tell the doctor he doesn't have to worry about me.'

'This isn't for the doctor — this is for me. I want you to tell me again what you told me last night. You're sober now, so hopefully it will make more sense this time.'

'There's nothing to tell. It's an old story, and you know most of it.'

'Tell me anyway.'

Leigh was too tired and her head was hurting too much for her to argue. She had apparently come here last night to have this conversation. She might as well do it now. The morning could hardly get any worse than it was.

'Three years ago,' she said abruptly, 'not

long after we bought the winery, Jack and I won the lotto. Not millions, but a good amount. Enough to do everything we wanted with the place, and still put a fair bit aside for the future. Our future. That was a joke.'

It was like letting go of a hot coal that had been blistering her hand for years.

'You were having a party, I can't remember what the reason was. I had a cold, so Jack came up here alone. When he got home . . . ' Her voice broke. The pain was gone, but not the memory of it. 'When he got home, I could tell he'd been with someone else.'

'And he told you . . . ' Simon prompted when she didn't go on.

'He told me that you had hired a stripper for the party. A prostitute. He said you had given her to him. As a present.'

'And you believed him?'

'Of course I believed him. I was engaged to him. I had to believe him . . . but then I wasn't engaged any more.'

'You broke it off?'

'He said she meant nothing to him — but what he did meant everything to me. And I guess I couldn't trust him any more. If he did it once, he might do it again. Even if I hadn't thrown him out, I think he would have gone anyway. The lotto ticket was in his name. He took all the money and left. I got to keep the winery and all the debts.'

Leigh put the empty coffee mug on the ground and looked up. A gentle smile was touching the corners of Simon's mouth.

'That's why I came up here last night,' she said slowly. 'To say thank you, Simon bloody Bradford, for ruining my life.'

Simon started to laugh. He knew he shouldn't, but he couldn't help himself. He finally understood everything. He understood Leigh and, even more importantly, he understood himself. Now all he had to do was make Leigh understand.

Leigh wasn't impressed by his laughter. She made as if to rise, wincing at the pain in her head. He took her hand and gently pulled her back to the grass beside him.

'Leigh, I'm sorry. I'm not laughing at you. I'm laughing at us. All this time . . . '

She was confused. He could see it in her eyes. With difficulty, he forced his voice to be calm.

'She wasn't a stripper. She was my girlfriend. Almost my fiancée.'

'What?'

'She was my girlfriend. At the party that night, I was going to ask her to marry me. I even had the ring.'

Simon felt nothing but relief as he spoke. It was well past time that he told Leigh the truth. She wasn't trying to leave any more, but he kept hold of her hand, just because he liked the way it felt.

'I went looking for her and saw her with Jack.' He wasn't going to describe how he found them. They had sought privacy in the back seat of someone's car — and they were so busy with each other, they hadn't even noticed him.

'I guess it was the money,' he added. 'He'd been bragging about it all night.'

He saw a flash of anger in Leigh's eyes, but it wasn't directed at him. 'He screwed both of us that night, didn't he?'

Simon nodded.

'All this time,' Leigh said slowly, 'I've been blaming you. I should have known better. You're not that sort of guy. Jack was. He was a bastard. I guess he always was. I just didn't see it.'

'I don't know,' Simon said. 'I sometimes think he did both of us a favour.'

They sat in silence for a few minutes, each lost in their own thoughts. Simon still held Leigh's hand, and was absurdly pleased that she didn't take it away.

'I'm sorry about Ian Rudd,' he said after a while. 'I just thought . . . Well, as they say, it seemed like a good idea at the time. I never meant for you to get hurt.'

'I know you didn't,' Leigh said. 'It doesn't matter. In some ways I think it helped me. At last I think I'm over what happened that night.'

'So, we are all right now?' Simon asked.

Leigh smiled. Simon watched the corners of her mouth lift. He saw the tiny crinkles form around her lovely eyes.

'Yes,' she said. 'I think we're all right.'

He took a deep breath. Once before he had thought about a future. He had planned that night to the finest detail. It hadn't worked out. He hadn't planned this morning, but maybe . . .

'I don't suppose that there is any chance we could be better than just all right?'

Leigh looked up into his face. Her eyes held his for a long, long time.

'Better in what way?'

'Last night. You kissed me.'

'I did.' It wasn't a question. He could see in her eyes that she remembered.

'Yes. Don't you remember?' he joked.

'Not really,' Leigh teased him. 'How was it?'

'It was . . . nice.'

'Nice!' Leigh looked at him aghast. 'Nice?'

'Well, in your defence, you were drunk. And concussed. Under the circumstances, I thought nice was a pretty good effort.'

She seemed to consider this for a while.

'I don't suppose I could try again, could I?' she asked.

Simon smiled. The day was golden.

'If you like,' he said.

It was better than nice.

* * *

'What'll it be, mate?' the taxi-driver asked. 'The bridge or the tunnel?'

'Oh, the bridge, please,' Greg replied.

'Bridge it is.'

Greg looked out the window at the cityscape rolling past. He could see the high-rise buildings of the city centre, and glimpses of the tall spire that was Centrepoint Tower. The harbour was somewhere ahead of him. He had seen it from the window of the plane as they'd come in to land. It was bigger and bluer than he had imagined. In fact everything about Sydney was bigger and better than he had imagined. He loved it already.

'First time, eh, mate?'

'Sorry?' Greg pulled his attention back to the taxi-driver.

'First time in Sydney?'

'Yeah. I guess it shows.'

'It does a bit.' The driver gave a

good-natured chuckle. 'How long are you here for?'

Greg wished he knew the answer to that question. He was here for a day, or for ever. He didn't know. A lot depended on what happened at the end of this taxi ride.

The confrontation with his father had decided him. There would not be one more harvest. There would not be one day more than necessary. The future was his; all he had to do was take it. But now that he saw the magnitude of what he was trying to do, he suddenly wondered if he had the strength. What chance did he have of forging a life for himself in this city when even the taxi-driver recognised him as a hick? He pulled the silver charm out of the pocket of his jeans. His fingers sought the comfort of its familiar lines. It helped to stop his hands from shaking with tension. Whatever happened, he was done with the cane farm. He would create a new life for himself.

The taxi had skirted the edge of the city and was now on the approaches to the bridge. Greg's heart lifted as the vehicle followed the road between the great stone pylons and on to the bridge itself. He didn't care how much of a hick he looked. He strained his neck to gaze at the great iron arc soaring above him. It was a stupendous sight.

The crossing was far too short. Greg had read that it was possible to walk over the metal arch. He would do that one day — but not today. Today, there were more important things to do.

The taxi pulled up in front of a small brick building in a narrow tree-lined street. Greg paid the driver and walked up to the front of the building. A metal security grille covered the main door. Next to the buzzer, a small engraved brass plaque told Greg he was in the right place. He pressed the buzzer.

'Yes?'

'Greg Anderson. I have an appointment with . . . ' He paused. For the life of him, he could not even begin to pronounce the man's name.

'Come in.'

The latch on the security grille clicked, followed by the lock on the glass door behind it. Greg walked through into a well-appointed reception room. A small Asian man entered from a side door.

'Greg. Pleased to meet you. I'm Chatri.'

Greg took his hand. 'Thank you for agreeing to see me.'

'Not at all. A recommendation from Molly carries a lot of weight with me. And I did like those pictures you sent.'

Greg mumbled his thanks, and tried not to

think about Molly. It was like trying to stop breathing. Since he had walked out his front door, several hours and more than two thousand kilometres ago, she had never been far from his thoughts. Just to know that he was in the same city as her was driving him a little crazy. He was desperate to see her, but he couldn't telephone her yet. He needed to find his own answers before he had the right to ask anything of her.

'So.' Chatri broke into his thoughts. 'Come through to the workshop. I am anxious to see what you've brought me.'

Greg picked up the rucksack he'd nursed all the way from Queensland. In it were samples of his work, including the wing brooch that Molly had watched him make. It was now finished, and he thought it was his best piece. There were a couple of rings, and some other items that he hoped might convince Chatri that he had some skill. He wished that they were presented in velvet boxes, rather than wrapped in T-shirts and clean socks for protection during the journey.

Chatri showed him through to a bright, open workroom, well equipped with the tools of the jeweller's art. Greg suddenly realised that Chatri wouldn't care what his pieces were wrapped in. All that mattered to the artist was the quality of the work.

When Greg walked back out through the metal security door an hour later, his rucksack was noticeably lighter. His pieces were all locked away in the big safe in Chatri's workshop. The man had liked his work, and immediately offered to display and sell the pieces in his exclusive boutique. And if that wasn't enough, he'd also suggested that they work together. The details still had to be finalised, but as soon as Greg could relocate permanently to Sydney, the job was waiting for him. It was an opportunity he had hardly dared dream might happen. He would never have to plant or harvest another stalk of cane.

Now he could talk to Molly.

Her e-mail to him had included both a home and mobile phone number. He tried her mobile, but the recorded message suggested it was switched off or out of range. On her home number, he got her voicemail. He smiled as he listened to her voice. He didn't leave a message. The phone book listed her home number at a block of flats in nearby Waverton. The taxi took only a few minutes to get there. The buzzer for the top-floor flat had her name written next to it. There was no answer, but he had expected none. It didn't matter. He could wait.

He walked down the road to get some

coffee and a sandwich. When he returned, someone was just leaving the flats. Smiling innocently, Greg slipped through the open security door and took the elevator to the top floor. He settled himself reasonably comfortably on the carpet and took the lid off the coffee. It was mid-afternoon. Molly would be home later. When she finished work. He would wait for her.

* * *

Molly hated taking the red-eye. Her delayed flight had left Perth at one in the morning Perth time, and arrived at Kingsford Smith airport at seven o'clock in the morning Sydney time. She had barely slept on the flight and she was tired and cranky. Even this early the traffic from the airport was heavy, and as her taxi slipped into the harbour tunnel, she wanted nothing more than to get home to have a shower and a few hours' sleep. She had an assignment that evening, shooting at the opera house, and she wanted to be in good shape for that.

She paid the taxi outside her block of flats, and retrieved her small suitcase from the boot. She turned towards her front door and suddenly stopped. A dishevelled man was sitting in the early-morning sun on her top step, a cup of coffee in one hand and a croissant in the other.

'Greg?'

He looked up, and his handsome face broke into a smile that almost broke her heart.

'Molly!' Greg leaped to his feet and raced down the steps in two great strides. For a moment he looked like he was going to hug her, then he stopped and just stood grinning at her.

'What are you doing here?' Molly asked.

'Waiting for you,' he said. 'I thought I was going to miss you.'

'Miss me?' Molly was feeling a bit confused. 'When did you get to Sydney? How long are you here for? What — '

Before she could go any further, the blaring of a car horn behind her cut her short.

Greg waved at a taxi that had just pulled up.

'Molly, that's my cab. I've got a plane to catch. Please, come to the airport with me.'

'The airport? I've just come from there.' Molly was having trouble keeping up. 'What's going on, Greg?'

'I've been waiting for you since yesterday. I have to fly back to Townsville now, but we need to talk.' He took both her hands in his. 'Please come to the airport with me.'

Molly looked at Greg's rumpled clothing

and unshaven face. 'Did you sleep here last night?'

'Well, not on the steps. I got inside and slept in the hallway outside your flat.'

'What? You're lucky someone didn't see you and call the police.'

'I guess. I didn't think of that.' The taxi's horn sounded again. 'Molly, please come to the airport with me.'

His dark eyes were pleading with her, and Molly gave in. If he had spent the night sleeping at her door, it was the least she could do.

'All right. Just give me two minutes. I'm not lugging all this gear back to the airport.'

She reached for her key.

'I'll hold the taxi,' Greg said, his grin growing wider by the minute.

Molly dashed into her flat and dropped her suitcase and camera bag. She was back at the front door a minute later, carrying only cash and her keys.

The taxi-driver looked annoyed at the delay. Greg looked as if he would never stop smiling. They bundled into the back of the taxi, which drove off into the traffic.

'All right,' Molly said. 'Now, tell me what is going on.'

'It's good to see you, Molly. You look wonderful.'

She knew she didn't look wonderful. Her eyes were puffy from lack of sleep. She hadn't bathed in over twenty-four hours. Her clothes must be a mess. But as she looked into Greg's eyes, she realised that to him, she did look wonderful. Much as he did to her, even with his unshaven chin and rumpled clothes. She wanted to kiss him. She almost did. But she needed to know what was going on.

'It's good to see you too,' she said gently. 'But please tell me what's happening.'

'There's so much to tell you,' Greg said. 'Jasi went back to Melbourne.'

'I know,' Molly replied. '*Australian Life* told me not to bother with the photos.'

Greg's face fell. 'I didn't think about that. Did you lose money because of me? I'm sorry. I will pay you back.'

'No. It's fine,' Molly assured him. 'They still paid me for my time.' The money was the least of her concerns. 'How did Jasi take it?'

'I think deep down she was relieved. It wasn't quite the rural idyll she had imagined. I think she was very pleased to go home to Melbourne.'

'I'm glad she wasn't too upset. She was a nice girl.'

'Maybe I should have been insulted that she didn't want to stay with me.' Greg grinned cheekily. 'But I was glad to see her go. It was lonely up there, though. Then I got your e-mail suggesting I get in touch with Chatri. So I did.'

'Yes, he told me. Is that why you came to Sydney?' she asked.

'Part of the reason.' Greg grinned at her. 'I saw him yesterday. He's great, Molly. He liked my stuff, and . . . ' He paused dramatically.

'And what?' she almost screamed in frustration.

'He's offered me a job in his workshop.'

The words had barely started to sink in when the taxi stopped. Molly looked out the window. She was back at the same terminal she had flown into such a short time before. Slowly she got out of the car and walked with Greg to the check-in counter. She watched as he dealt with the formalities. He was a different person to the one who had left her at Townsville airport a couple of weeks ago. He was brimming over with energy and confidence. He almost glowed with enthusiasm. He was still talking about the job with Chatri as they made their way to the boarding gate. Once there, Molly pulled him into a seat.

'Greg, this is all good news. But what about your father? You told me you couldn't leave the farm. Couldn't leave him. What's changed?'

She saw a shadow cloud his eyes.

'He lied to me, Molly. All these years. He lied about how my mother died.'

She reached out to take his hand. He gripped hers tightly and she realised then that whatever had passed between him and his father, the rift was final.

'She was leaving him,' Greg said. 'Taking me with her. That's when the accident happened.'

'Oh Greg. I am so sorry.'

'Molly,' Greg turned to her, the hurt showing deep in his eyes, 'there were times he wished I had died with her.'

There was nothing she could say. She simply put her arms around him. He buried his face in her hair and she held him for a very long time.

The boarding announcement was an unwelcome interruption.

'I have to go,' Greg said.

'Why are you going back?' she had to ask.

'He is my father,' he replied in a voice devoid of all emotion, 'and I have to see him cared for. I'm going to hire a manager for the farm. Then I'm coming back here — where I can live my own life.'

A second boarding call sounded loudly. Behind them, passengers were filing on to the air bridge. Molly didn't know what to say. She said nothing. She stood on her toes and kissed Greg gently. He turned to go, then hesitated. He took her hand again and pressed something into it.

'Look after this for me. Until I come back.' He smiled again, that heartbreakingly handsome smile that caused her heart to flutter wildly.

As he walked away, Molly looked at the silver charm in her hand. It was still warm from his touch. She closed her fingers around it, and placed it against her heart as Greg vanished through the doorway.

* * *

The view from her flat was truly wonderful. Helen stood breathing in the crisp autumn air and wondered if her new-found appreciation of the view was because she would soon be leaving it behind. An apartment in New York would have an equally spectacular but very different view. In the Big Apple, she would be looking at towers of concrete and glass. Instead of the 'harbour glimpses' so favoured by Sydney real-estate advertisements, she would no doubt be offered 'Central Park glimpses' or possibly 'Hudson River glimpses'.

And he sees the vision splendid of the sunlit plains extended,
And at night the wondrous glory of the everlasting stars.

Helen couldn't get the stupid poem out of her mind. Perhaps it was because of Matt. Leaving him was even harder than she had thought. He would stay in her mind like Clancy, while she took another path. How had Banjo Paterson described life in the city? She searched her memory.

And the hurrying people daunt me, and their pallid faces haunt me
As they shoulder one another in their rush and nervous haste.

It wasn't a bad description, and Paterson had written that in Sydney a hundred years ago. Helen wondered what he might think if he saw New York today. He would probably be even more eager to change places with Clancy, leave the office behind and become a drover.

She shrugged at her own fancy. Her mind wandered strange paths now there was no work to occupy her thoughts. *Australian Life* was behind her now, and much as she was looking forward to the future, she was feeling restless. There was so much she should be doing if she was going to move to New York. There was her visa to deal with. Packing. A flight. Her new employer would provide a hotel for as long as it took to find a flat . . . an apartment, she corrected herself. In the city that never sleeps, people live in apartments.

It will be wonderful, she told herself. It's a dream come true. Matt had told her not to let go of her dreams. But was she holding on to the right one?

The restlessness was getting worse. Helen grabbed her wallet and keys. After leaving the flat, she walked across the road. The newspaper-seller smiled at her as she approached.

'Morning,' he said.

'Good morning.'

'The usual?' He offered her a copy of *Australian Life*.

'Not today,' she said, trying not to smile at the shock on his face.

She ran her eyes over the display. There weren't any New York papers, but she hadn't expected any. The *International Herald Tribune* would do. She took a copy. The glossy colour photograph on the cover of another magazine caught her eye. She pulled it off the rack and offered money to the paper-seller, whose look of confusion deepened as he glanced at the magazine she had chosen.

Helen returned to her flat and threw her purchases on the table. She looked at the magazine, with its photograph of a mare and a foal and its headline offering advice on rearing premature foals. What was she thinking? She had already made her decision. It was the right decision for her. It was the only decision.

She walked through into her bedroom. She could start thinking about the move. That would give her a firm purpose. Keep her mind fixed on the future. She would start in the bedroom. Decide what to take and what to leave behind. She opened the sliding doors of her built-in wardrobe. The shoe rack was well stocked with designer classics. And it also held a pair of brown elastic-sided riding boots. They were almost new, with just a few scuff marks to show they had ever been worn.

Helen picked up the boots. She turned them round in her hands, and a feeling that had been lurking in the back of her mind suddenly flared with absolute certainty.

She looked at her watch and did a quick international time zone calculation. She took the boots with her as she went to make the call. She wore them when she left the flat an hour later, a rucksack slung over her shoulder and a magazine in her hand.

The drive seemed longer today than in the past, but Helen didn't mind. With every kilometre she travelled, she felt more certain that this time she had got it right.

The white oil-drum mailbox by the side of the road was the most welcome sight she had ever seen. She turned off the highway on to the long tree-lined drive towards the house with the wide veranda where she had sipped wine with Matt. It felt like coming home. She parked the car and walked towards the stables.

'Matt!' she called.

The only answer came from one of the horses.

He must be out riding. He would be back. She spotted a familiar grey horse in a small paddock and wandered over to lean on the fence. Cassie was moving around, picking at the green grass. Not far away, her colt was investigating the water trough. He touched the surface with the tip of his nose, then snorted loudly. He started backwards as drops of water splashed his face. With a toss of his head, he skittered away from the water trough, trotting back to the comfort of his dam. His head vanished underneath her, and his tail began to wag furiously as he drank.

Helen was still laughing when she heard hoof beats behind her.

She turned around. Matt was riding Granny from the direction of the river. He hadn't noticed Helen, or her car. She watched him approach, marvelling at the warm glow that pervaded her whole body. Granny saw her first. The filly flung her head up and stopped in her tracks. Matt followed his horse's gaze, and he too saw Helen. The smile that spread across his face was all the welcome she needed.

He urged Granny forward, until they arrived at the fence where Helen still waited. He swung down off the horse, took Helen in his arms and kissed her for a very long time. When they finally parted, there was nothing that needed to be said.

'The colt looks good,' Helen said, turning to lean on the gate.

'He's a battler,' Matt said, as he moved to stand very close to her. 'All he needed was a bit of tender care.'

'Has he got a name yet?'

'No.' Matt dropped his arm casually around her shoulders. 'Why don't you name him?'

Helen looked up at him in surprise. 'I thought Ali named all the foals.'

'Not this one.'

‘All right. I’ll have to think about it.’

‘You do that,’ Matt said.

‘How about something from the Paterson poems? Clancy, maybe?’

‘He could do worse.’

‘Maybe. Can you give me a bit longer to think about it?’ Helen said.

Matt smiled down at her. ‘Take all the time you need.’

For a long time they stood looking at each other. Helen reached out to touch Matt’s brown cheek and nodded. They turned away from the fence and the foal who was half hidden under his mother’s belly as he happily suckled. Matt draped Granny’s reins over his shoulder, and the three of them walked back to the stables together.

Other titles published by
The House of Ulverscroft:

WHAT'S LOVE GOT TO DO WITH IT?

Lucy Broadbent

Beautiful and broke, British nanny Bella Spires is in LA with one goal: marry a rich man so she can start living the good life. And with gorgeous (loaded) husband Jamie Shawe soon at her side, maybe she's played the game and won. But in La-La land, nothing's ever done and dusted, and Bella's new world is soon showing cracks. Will she ever realise that love, not money, is what she *really* needs?